A Continuing War:

At Home and at Sea

1803-1804

by

John G. Cragg

A Continuing war: At Home and At Sea – 1803-1804

Book 2 of the series The Napoleonic Wars: At Home and at Sea

Copyright © 2017 by John G. Cragg

Dedicated to

My most encouraging and
helpful critic

Olga Browzin Cragg

Special Thanks to

Eric Bush

Joan Lundell

Dawn McDougall

Table of Contents

Chapter I   1
Chapter II   15
Chapter III   29
Chapter IV   41
Chapter V   53
Chapter VI   69
Chapter VII   89
Chapter VIII   111
Chapter IX   133
Chapter X   147
Chapter XI   165
Chapter XII   177
Chapter XIII   189
Chapter XIV   201
Chapter XV   221
Chapter XVI   235
Chapter XVII   249
Chapter XVIII   267
Chapter XIX   285

Author's Note   297

Glossary   299

Preface

This is a work of fiction that follows on from the first volume in this series, *A New War: at Home and at Sea, 1803*. It is available at Amazon.com and other Amazon sites by searching for my name or the title. This tale takes place in 1803 and 1804. A great many things have changed in the two centuries since then, including items and phrases that may be unfamiliar to many readers. To help those who are curious, a glossary is provided at the end of the book. Items that appear in the glossary are flagged on their first appearance in the text by a * as in, for example, taffrail*

Chapter I

The coach rumbled along the coast road from Brighton to Portsmouth. It swayed alarmingly, especially when the road was open on both sides where it could be buffeted by the full north-east gale and be lashed by rain. Inside the coach, Captain Sir Richard Giles sat on the right-hand side, staring out at the bleak countryside and idly comparing the uses of the land here with what he hoped for on his own estate. In the opposite corner sat his wife, Lady Daphne Giles, staring at the bushes, brush and hedgerows that usually prevented her from seeing the English Channel. When the sea could be seen, it was laced with whitecaps that speckled the water, even though the waves were being blown away from the land. Neither traveler seemed able to take the first step in talking about the separation that would soon be upon them nor to spend the time that they still had recalling the joyous times that had marked the start of their life together.

Across from the married pair sat Elsie, Daphne's maid. This trip was the first time she had been away from Dipton, and it was the only time she had ridden in a coach. She was a bit scared by the way the coach swayed in the gusts. She couldn't help thinking of stories of how coaches could turn over. She was very thankful that Miss Moorhouse – no, Lady Giles – she must get used to calling her by her new name – that Lady Giles had let her ride inside. She knew from other lady's maids that most mistresses would have had her riding on the box with the coachman. That was typical of Lady Giles; she always thought of others, no matter what their status.

She hoped that Lady Giles had not made a mistake in marrying Captain Giles. – It was odd how he liked to be called simply Captain Giles rather than Sir Richard and then had insisted that Miss Moorhouse's new name was to be 'Lady Giles' and not 'Mrs. Giles'.

Elsie knew that it would not have mattered to Miss Moorhouse what name she assumed. She had hardly known him when he asked her to marry him. Of course, that often seemed to be the way with the gentry, but this had not been a marriage formed as a business alliance. Lady Giles had known the Captain only for a day before he had had to leave Dipton for some ship, and then he had only returned for a few more days – with a broken head to make matters worse – before he proposed to Miss Moorhouse and she had accepted him. And they had been together for less than a week in terms of the number of days in which they had actually seen each other, before she married him. There had been letters between them, and Elsie was still surprised how often Miss Moorhouse had reread the ones she received. Even so, Lady Giles hardly knew the Captain when she married him.

They had certainly made up for lost time in Brighton. They took long walks in which Elsie knew that they talked constantly. And they had been together every afternoon in the room they shared. But now, they weren't talking. Elsie wondered if Miss Moorhouse should have waited until she knew Captain Giles better.

Of course, Elsie thought, she had known Mr. Carstairs, Captain Giles cox'un, for even less time than Miss Moorhouse and Captain Giles had known each other, and she and Mr. Carstairs hadn't exchanged any letters. Nevertheless, Elsie was sure that she would marry him in a flash if he asked her. Of course, they were different from Miss Moorhouse and Captain Giles, though Elsie couldn't have said how, exactly.

Mr. Carstairs wasn't even with them on this journey since he had gone ahead to make arrangements for a late luncheon in Chichester and for an inn in Portsmouth. She could daydream about him. She knew that he wanted to have a pub when his days at sea were over. Tom, the landlord of the Dipton Arms, was complaining about how heavy his work was, and how hard it was on his back, and how he would like to sell up. The Dipton Arms would be ideal for Mr. Carstairs, and, of course, he would need a wife.

Elsie's daydream was interrupted by Daphne's jerking to attention and turning to her husband. "Is that the sort of ship you will have?" she asked the Captain.

Giles turned from looking at rain-soaked haystacks to glance out the left-hand windows. The Channel was visible in this stretch, and there was a frigate beating* to windward.

"Yes, my love, though mine will be bigger, and that ship is English built while mine is French."

"Isn't it too rough out there for the ship?"

"No. It's only just blowing a gale. We don't seek harbor for this sort of wind. You have to remember that we can't usually go into port when a storm comes. I wonder how much wind those haystacks can take." Giles nodded towards the haystacks near a barn on his side of the coach. This led to a discussion between Giles and Daphne about how to make haystacks, what was the best land for growing hay, whether and how hay should be part of a crop rotation, where in their own holdings hay should be grown, and, finally, what livestock they should raise and how many of them to keep over the winter. Elsie was delighted to see them diverted from brooding about their imminent separation. They had discussed many of these items in Brighton, she knew, and, usually, neither of them had a tendency to return to old topics without much new to add to them, but this conversation was for diversion from grimmer thoughts, not exchanging information and making plans.

The arrival in Chichester, where luncheon would be served at the posting inn, presented Elsie with a good change of activity as she ate in the common parlor, but she noted that Giles and Daphne had reverted to their glum silence by the time they were on the road again. However, before long, Daphne made some observations about how the cottages seemed to be different from those around Dipton, and a lively discussion ensued about regional differences even in common items, the difference in climate in different places, and then how the appropriate agricultural practices differed so one could not just follow a treatise based on one area in planning improvements in another. Hedging got particular attention until the coach arrived in the outskirts of Portsmouth when they started to talk loosely about the fate of the many seamen who had settled there when their time in the navy was over.

Arrival at the inn was met with a bustle of activity, as Carstairs directed Giles and Daphne to a private dining room while he arranged for the luggage they would need immediately to be taken to their room before he sent the rest of Captain Giles's things to the quay to be transferred to *Impetuous*, Giles's frigate. Lady Giles had whispered to Elsie that, after she had arranged her things in the room, Elsie was free to go for the evening, but Lady Giles would need her help first thing in the morning. Elsie kept a straight face even as she thought of the implications of Lady Giles's not needing any help to undress. Her mistress would have a difficult time getting out of her clothes without help, so she must be expecting Captain Giles to assist. The Captain must be what Elsie's mother would term a "randy rascal."

Elsie was not at a loose end for long after she had finished her duties. Carstairs was waiting for her – it was strange how everyone called him 'Carstairs' while surely below stairs Mr. Carstairs would be more appropriate – and whisked her off to a private dining room. There was laid on a meal of pea soup, excellent roast beef, and a quince blancmange. There was a large jug of ale from which Carstairs happily refilled her beaker whenever needed. The conversation began with news on what had transpired since Carstairs had had to leave to arrange for their stops and went on to various matters about people living in Dipton, both masters and servants. But just as Elsie was beginning to doubt the wisdom of consuming so much ale with a man she hardly knew, the conversation took a quite different term.

"Look, Miss Elsie," said Carstairs – his calling her 'Miss Elsie' was one of the things about him which appealed to Elsie – "I don't want to be a sailor all my life. I has a good berth now with Captain Giles, though he does produce more action than most captains. But I would like to have a wife and maybe children, and the sailor's life is not all that good for family life. Captain Giles gets us more prize money than most other captains, and I has a good stake set aside – I'm not one to spend it all in the tavern when we gets ashore."

Carstairs broke off at that point and lapsed into silence, staring at a point somewhat above Elsie's left shoulder. She realized that she might never find out what else he might be thinking if she didn't intervene.

"Yes. Mr. Carstairs. You were saying that you were thinking of coming ashore. Where did you have in mind to live?"

"Why, Dipton, of course. That's where Captain Giles will be and others who I now know. Yes, I thinks I told you that I want to have a pub, or an inn or something, to manage and provide me with a living. I has set aside just about enough money. And I hears that Tom Arbuckle at the Dipton Arms may be thinking of selling, and I might just have enough to buy it. So what do you think of the idea?"

'It is a grand place. But how can you manage it if you are at sea? And Tom won't wait very long. His back is hurting more and more, and there are some strenuous bits to being the landlord of a pub that he says are getting beyond him."

"I suppose. I would need someone to manage it while I was away at sea."

"And who might that be?"

"Oh, Miss Elsie, I have gone about this all wrong. But it is not something a man gets any practice at. Miss Elsie, I wants to marry you. Oh, how I wants to marry you! But I knows you cannot stay with Lady Giles if you are married, and certainly not if there are children on the way. And I can't just quit Captain Giles now, and as long as I am a sailor, I knows that I would have to be able to look after you, even if I was killed. So that is where the Dipton Arms comes in. You could manage it while I was away."

"So, Mr. George Carstairs, you only want to marry me so that you can get someone to manage your public house."

"No. No. It's not like that. I wants to marry you, no matter what. And if you don't want to run the pub, I'll just have to find someone else. But I wants to marry you in any case. Please, Miss Elsie, will you marry me?

"Well, I don't know. Don't they say that a sailor has a girl in every port? How many other wives do you have?"

"I'm not like that. I don't spend my money on women. I don't have any other girl at all. Never had. You are the only one who interests me. I've dreamed about you ever since that first day at Dipton Manor when you was trying to find out all about Captain Giles."

It was Elsie's turn to be flustered. "I wasn't doing that," she blustered, but her deep blush gave away just how accurate had been Carstairs's appraisal of their meeting.

"Doesn't matter. When I told Captain Giles, he laughed and said that Miss Moorhouse was quite capable of getting all the information about him that she wanted. But that isn't the subject here. Will you, please, marry me?"

"Yes, Mr. Carstairs. Yes, I will!"

Carstairs's response was to take Elsie in his arms, and a lengthy period of kissing and hugging ensued, but when Carstairs tried to slip his hand into Elsie's bodice. She roughly shoved him back even though she was panting quite loudly. "None of that, Mr. Carstairs, not until we are married. I won't risk becoming with child, not until we are married, and if we go any farther down that lane, I don't know if we could stop. I'm a good girl, and I need my position with Lady Giles."

Somewhat to Elsie's surprise and disappointment, this was enough to get Carstairs to withdraw to the other side of the table. He poured them more ale, and they continued talking until they realized that it was getting late and that they had to rise early in the morning, well before those they served.

Dawn revealed that the weather had little improved. Daphne found herself wrapped in a large boat cloak and almost carried into Captain Giles's boat.

Carstairs had already seated Elsie in the sternsheets*, having gotten permission from the Captain to have her visit with her mistress. After they had shoved off, the boat pitched and rocked rather alarmingly in the short, choppy waves of the anchorage, and Daphne was amazed at how easily the boat's crew seemed to adjust to the gyrations of the craft, keeping a steady pace, with the oars dipping gracefully into the water to be pulled smoothly through the water, even though the boat was rocking and bouncing.

Daphne had no way of recognizing which of the many ships tugging at their anchors was her husband's. They were of different sizes, but several looked to her eyes as being identical, and their names were too far away to be read. However, Carstairs and the midshipman who nominally was in charge of the boat – Mr. Stewart, whose name, luckily, Captain Giles had mentioned, since Daphne recognized the face from their wedding but couldn't recall his name – seemed to have no problem selecting the proper one toward which to head. It was confirmed when a hail from the ship produced a bellow from Mr. Stewart of '*Impetuous*,' which would have been more impressive if his voice hadn't broken on the fourth syllable.

When they came to the side of *Impetuous*, Daphne was alarmed about how her husband would safely board the large ship, but the operation seemed to give him no problems as he scaled the side of the ship as if he were climbing a ladder on land. It surprised her that this was accompanied by the most unmelodic of whistles whose origin she could not see. Just as she was wondering how she could possibly emulate Captain Giles transfer to the ship in her petticoats and with the boat's arbitrary rocking, the problem was resolved by the ship lowering into the boat a contraption that looked like a cross between a chair and a swing seat. Mr. Stewart and Carstairs helped her into it, and then she was pulled up until she was above the deck of the ship, whereupon they swung her across the side of the ship and lowered her to the deck in a flounce of petticoats. Giles was on hand to help her out of the chair, and he then presented her to the officers, even though they had all been introduced to her at their wedding a few days before. Daphne was glad for Giles's naming them since some names had slipped her memory.

At the end of the line was a young midshipman in what was obviously a new uniform. "You must be Mr. Dunsmuir. I see your father got you kitted out. Welcome aboard," said Giles. Daphne recalled that, in Brighton, they had encountered an older naval captain who had introduced himself to Giles while she and her husband were out walking. Giles had spent some time talking with him, at the end of which the captain had asked, very shyly, if Giles might have a berth for a midshipman or a servant. It developed that the older captain was trying to secure a place for his son. Giles had agreed at once to take the boy, provided he could get to Portsmouth with his gear before *Impetuous* had to sail. Daphne was still too inexperienced with naval ways to realize how very rare it was for a captain to grant such a request to any but a very close friend when there was no hope of getting any favor in exchange.

With the introductions made, Giles called for the ship's company to be gathered so that he could read* himself in. As he pronounced the words that gave him command of the ship and effectively the power of life and death over those who sailed in her, Daphne was astonished to realize how great a responsibility the orders placed on her husband. She also noticed that the officers and crew were actually paying little attention to the words; they had all heard them before, and, when sailing with Captain Giles, they had no reason to fear the highly arbitrary authority he had been given.

When the ceremony ended, Giles ordered that the hands be dismissed to go about their duties and took Daphne on a tour of the ship. She was amazed at how neat everything was and how little space there really was for all that had to be kept on hand and for all the men who were aboard. They completed their somewhat abbreviated tour in the Captain's cabin. While, by the ship's cramped style, it might be considered a huge space, Daphne was conscious that it was smaller than any of the rooms Giles or she herself would regularly use in Dipton Hall. Also, how plain were the furnishings. That wouldn't do! She couldn't do anything about the space, but she would make it a priority to get Edwards to supply furnishings more suitable for her Captain.

They didn't linger long over the refreshments that had been laid on. Daphne knew that Giles was impatient to start the business of getting to know the ship better, as well as to get her underway as soon as possible, and Daphne herself had a lengthy trip to make to return to Dipton. She was surprised and delighted that when the time came for her to use the special chair to get into the boat, Giles came as well. She had presumed that he would simply see her safely into the boat before turning to his many duties on a new command, but she found that he had no desire to part from her any sooner than was absolutely necessary. He seemed more relaxed than on their trip out to his frigate and spent the naming the ships as they came into sight and pointing out the landmarks on the shore.

All too soon, they arrived at the quay, and Giles made sure that Daphne was safely transferred from the boat to the jetty and then joined her on the walk up to where the carriage awaited. Somehow, he maneuvered them behind the carriage, where he took her in his arms for a final embrace before handing her into the carriage. Daphne noted that he then spent some time talking to their coachman while Carstairs appeared to be taking a passionate farewell from Elsie. But soon, Elsie joined Daphne in the coach, the coachman started the horses, and they were off.

To divert herself from the despondent thoughts that arose from the parting with Giles, with no knowledge of when she would next see him, Daphne decided to tease Elsie.

"You seem to have made a real admirer of Carstairs, Elsie," she remarked.

"I suppose so," was the response. "My Lady, he has asked me to marry him."

"You don't say. And what did you tell him?"

"I accepted him. Of course, we can't get married until he has settled how and where we would live. I told him that you wouldn't want a married lady's maid, so we would have to first have a place."

"I don't see that, Elsie. You could certainly be with him when he and Captain Giles are not at sea, though I can see why you would want a home of your own."

This observation totally flummoxed Elsie, who was expecting strong objections from Daphne about how taking up with Carstairs would be most disruptive for Daphne. Finding that her mistress was quite amenable to the suggestion that Elsie could get married and still work for her until Carstairs was settled ashore, she shared all her excitement and dreams. Before long, the two women were planning and speculating on when the marriage could occur and how the couple could combine their positions with their desires until Carstairs was ready to leave the sea. Daphne insisted that Elsie should be married from Dipton Hall and at Captain Giles's and Daphne's expense and that they would happily provide the wedding breakfast. The plan to buy the Dipton Arms met with Daphne's full approval, and she was sure that Carstairs would have no trouble acquiring the inn since the Dipton Arms was owned by Captain Giles and was only leased to Tom.

Their excited talk took them all the way to the inn where they were to spend the night, Daphne discovering that Captain Giles had worked out the best way for her to return to Dipton and had provided a purse to the coachman to purchase what was needed. Daphne was embarrassed to realize that she had not thought how her return to Dipton would be effected or how she would pay for it. That was not at all like her! She prided herself in always being in control of the practical matters of everyday life and, even if her husband were making the arrangements, she would want to know what they were. But she rejoiced in realizing that she had a husband who looked out for her needs, even when he must have matters on hand that most would think more pressing.

Chapter II

Giles watched the coach pull away and only turned to go back to his ship when it had disappeared around a corner. He immediately saw a familiar figure coming towards him.

"Mr. Hughes!" Giles greeted the man, "Well met. Have you heard that I lost *Patroclus*?"

"Oh, aye. And there are some who blame it on me for her having the too heavy bow chasers which I recommended."

"I don't think that is fair, Mr. Hughes. We were hard aground at the time and in a duel with a French third-rate. It is true that *Patroclus* split apart at the bow, so we had to abandon her, but we did a great deal of damage to the French ship and her crew. That helped when we had to board her."

"I heard about that capture, Captain Giles – and about your other exploits. In fact, that is why I am in Portsmouth. The Ordinance Board wanted me to assess the armament of recently captured French vessels and recommend how it might be improved and of some recaptured British frigates, where the issue was whether they had been adequately armed. I was surprised and pleased to learn that you had been responsible for us acquiring almost all of them, and not just the *Quatorze de Juillet*. There are, in fact, one or two things arising from my assignment about which I would like to consult you."

"Oh? There is not much time, Mr. Hughes. We have to sail at the turn of the tide."

"One of the ships that I should have examined is *Impetuous*, but I couldn't get to her before she had been moved to Spithead. I would like to see her. My next assignment is at Chatham, where I hear you are bound. Do you suppose I could trouble you to take me with you?"

"I would be delighted. I would also like to have your opinion on *Impetuous*. I have only just taken command of her, and anything that you can suggest that would make her more formidable would be greatly appreciated. Do you have your dunnage? If you do, we can go out to *Impetuous* now. My barge is just at the quay here."

They continued their conversation as they were rowed out to *Impetuous*. Hughes was particularly interested in the details of *Patroclus*'s various battles and how the bow chasers had performed. He especially wished to hear about her end.

"I don't suppose that you had a chance to examine just where and how she split apart at the bow, Captain Giles."

Giles laughed. "No, we were too busy gathering material to burn her and get ourselves away before the next broadside came our way to examine the damage to the bow."

They pulled up to the ladder at *Impetuous*'s entry port, and Giles preceded Mr. Humphries aboard. When the whistles of the pipes announcing his boarding had died away, Giles addressed his first lieutenant.

"Mr. Milton, I apologize for not discussing the state of the ship with you in more detail earlier. We must do it now. But first, let me introduce Mr. Hughes of the Ordinance Board. I have offered him passage to Chatham with us. He has agreed to look over our guns and make any suggestions that might improve their effectiveness. I know that you know your business, but it never hurts to have another opinion. Could you find him a place in the wardroom*? Then I would like to see you in my cabin."

Giles had hardly begun to look at all the paperwork that had already accumulated relative to his new command when the marine sentry announced, "The First Lieutenant, sir."

Giles looked up to see the stocky figure of James Milton enter the cabin. He was a fairly slight figure, standing possibly five foot nine, and weighing ten stone. His hair was dark, and his eyes were a nondescript brown. His face in repose was glum. He appeared to be in his late twenties.

"Mr. Milton. I am delighted to have you as my first lieutenant. I much appreciated your initiative in requesting permission to go after *Aristeia* and in taking her."

"Thank you, sir. I am still not sure that we should not have turned around to come to your aid."

"And disobeyed my orders? The thought does you credit, but you must remember that *Perseus* had already stopped and was in a position to take off my people from *Patroclus,* Only my guess as to how much damage we had done the French seventy-four warranted my taking the two crews to board her. No, you made the right decision. Tell me, how do your prospects for prize money from that venture look to be?"

"Mr. Edwards's representative in Portsmouth – we are all using Mr. Edwards having learned that he is the prize agent used by Captain Bush and yourself – tells us that we five, the three lieutenants and Captain Bush and yourself will be dividing up the captain's share of the money for the two French ships. We – the lieutenants – will not be getting anything for the ships we released. Apparently, we are treated as having been supernumeraries until the vessels were retaken and we took command."

"I'm sorry about that."

"Don't be. We didn't expect to get any prize money. At best, we hoped to get some sort of appointments, and we got more than we could possibly expect and better positions."

"Have you prepared the watch* and station bills?"

"Yes, sir. They should be on your table. Sir, I did have the help of Mr. Brooks and Mr. Miller. They were very helpful. I must say, sir, that it is a pleasure to work with a crew who are all experienced and who are volunteers."

"They weren't all volunteers originally. Some came via the press* and the prisons. But they were volunteers on *Patroclus,* and some of those from the press are among our best men."

"So, Mr. Milton, what have you discovered about *Impetuous* so far?"

"Not very much, to tell the truth, sir. We sailed her here in a very light breeze that could tell us little about her capabilities. She was responsive in the light wind, and we had to tack* a few times, and she did not miss stays*. I was helped greatly by the master, Mr. Brooks, I must say. Probably because of her draft, *Impetuous* is not stiff, sir, not at all stiff. But I cannot really say I know her, not on the basis of that little voyage. I hope to learn a great deal more after we sail."

"That reminds me, we need to sail with the turn of the tide. Are we ready?"

"Yes, sir. But might I suggest that we wait for half an hour beyond that in view of this gale that has been blowing for some time?"

"Make it so, Mr. Milton."

Giles turned away, clearly ending the interview. He was turning so as not to show his First Lieutenant that he had just passed a little test. Giles had expected Milton simply to agree with him, at which point Giles would have had to point out to the First Lieutenant that the turn of the tide according to the standard calculations was, in fact, not the appropriate time. It took daring on Milton's part to contradict his captain, even in the most mild and polite way, and Giles was glad to see that Milton both knew his trade and would stand up for what he thought was correct.

Mr. Brooks, the Master, was on deck when Milton appeared.

"Did the Captain say when we would be getting underway, Mr. Milton?"

"He said that we should weigh the anchor at the turn of the tide. But I suggested that it would be better to wait another half hour."

"Did you now? And what did he say."

"He agreed. His words were, 'Make it so.' Did I do right to suggest the change, Mr. Brooks? Do you think he will hold it against me?"

Mr. Brooks laughed, "No, Mr. Milton, you did quite right. He would have been disappointed if you had not corrected him. I should tell you that he asked me when the tide turned when he came aboard and indicated that we would have to adjust for the storm surge before sailing. He would have been disappointed had you simply agreed with him. And been less willing to rely on your judgment."

"So he doesn't mind having his judgment questioned?"

"No, unless it is an urgent matter when he will not brook argument. But otherwise, he is open to suggestion. If he doesn't agree, he will say why and you will find he is usually right. That is one way we all learn from him."

"That is not at all like my previous captain, I have to confess."

"No doubt. And you won't have learned as much as you will from Captain Giles, and your ship was probably not handled as well as she could have been. Now, I have work before we can get underway, and you must have too."

Milton looked about himself with increasing trepidation. Getting the ship underway in a gale, even if it might be described as just a half-gale, in the crowded anchorage of Spithead, with wind against tide when the tide had turned, was an invitation to disaster. He would be commanding a new ship for the first time in any sort of difficult situation, especially when he was only starting to know the strengths and weaknesses of the various crew members. He imagined that Giles would turn the maneuver over to him; certainly, his past captain, Captain Tomlinson, would have done so. If anything went wrong, Captain Tomlinson would have tried to shift the blame to his lieutenant.

Giles appeared on deck a few minutes before they were to raise the anchor. He looked around to see the readiness of the ship and then turned to Mr. Brooks.

"You have the courses specified to get us out of here, Mr. Brooks?"

"As near as may be, since we will be beating into the wind."

"Quite. Mr. Milton, it appears that all is ready."

"Aye, aye, sir." Now he would be severely tested. While he had often taken *Prometheus,* his last ship, to sea, it had never been in a situation quite as tricky as this one. Milton could almost see his hope of advancement, indeed even his present berth, going by the board.

"I hope you won't mind if I take her out, Mr. Milton. I want to see just how responsive she is and I may need to issue orders in a hurry."

"Of course not, sir." Milton hoped that his relief was not evident.

"Very good. I've got her. Mr. Stewart, you may raise the anchor."

Clank by clank, the capstan turned, the nippers did their task, and *Impetuous* was hauled to windward. She showed an alarming tendency to yaw, which Giles met by commanding, "Set the driver."

Soon the shout came that the anchor was up and down, followed by the information that it was aweigh.

"Larboard* your helm," came next as *Impetuous* started to gather sternway. Milton realized that Giles was clipping off most orders to get them issued more quickly, knowing he had a crew and petty officers who would know exactly what he wanted. The jib was raised and sheeted* home, the mainsail set, double-reefed, together with the foresail, also reefed. The sails filled, and *Impetuous* checked her sternway to surge ahead.

"Pinch up to clear that next bowsprit," Giles ordered the helmsmen. They did indeed clear it but only by twenty yards. Milton realized that the slight resentment he felt, illogically, at Giles's taking over to get *Impetuous* underway, was quite unwarranted; while neither Giles nor he knew the capabilities and foibles of the ship, Giles was fully aware of the capabilities of his crew and how quickly they would respond to orders. Milton would not have dared to pinch up as Giles did, and would have been faced with executing far more complicated maneuvers. He realized that Captain Tomlinson, under whom he had served most recently, would not have known what his men were capable of or how to get them to respond as precisely as Giles had. Milton vowed to himself that he would become just as familiar with the crew as his captain was.

These thoughts were interrupted by Giles saying to Mr. Brooks, "I think we should tack now. It will not be too serious if we miss stays."

"I think you are right, sir."

As Giles issued the order, "Stand by to come about," Milton reflected on the oddity of a captain asking a master's opinion on ship handling. Giles before long tacked again and then once more. On that tack, they were able to clear the Foreland on the Isle of Wight comfortably. Milton expected the Captain to relinquish his control at that point as the master told the helmsman the course to steer, but that was not Giles's way.

"Mr. Milton, Mr. Brooks and I will be trying different sail combinations to see how she performs. Perhaps you could observe to see if any awkwardness develops in the assignments of the crew."

"Ah, Mr. Kirkpatrick," Giles addressed the second lieutenant who had just appeared on the quarterdeck. "We shall be exercising the guns before long. Make sure that all is in readiness for doing so. Tell me when you are ready. We will start with mock practice without powder or shot. Larboard side first."

Giles started shouting orders to alter the sails that were set and how much they were reefed. Mr. Brooks beside him seemed to be keeping meticulous notes and frequently logged their speed. After a few minutes, Giles broke off to go to the quarterdeck rail and call to Mr. Kirkpatrick, "You can start the drill when you are ready, Mr. Kirkpatrick. Three times each per gun."

Giles and Mr. Brooks continued their methodical study of the sails and their effects in various combinations. Milton had never seen or heard of such a procedure, but he realized that the two officers were finding out as quickly as possible the various strengths and weaknesses of their ship. He was still straining to note and remember the effects of each change when some loud voices drifted up from the gun deck—actually, one loud voice, that of Mr. Kirkpatrick.

Giles stopped what he was doing. "The ship is yours, Mr. Milton," he said as he hurried towards the quarterdeck ladder. On the gun deck, he found that Mr. Hughes and Mr. Kirkpatrick were standing just about nose to nose with Kirkpatrick berating the man from the Ordinance Board.

"What is the trouble, Mr. Kirkpatrick?" Giles asked in a mild tone.

"This man was trying to interfere with the exercise of this gun."

"Yes? Mr. Hughes?"

"I was suggesting to Mr. Kirkpatrick that he examine the gun carriage before using it, sir. Some of these French gun carriages were made with wet wood and have a tendency to split when in action."

"Did you examine the carriages before the drill, Mr. Kirkpatrick?"

"No, sir. I didn't think it would be necessary."

"It appears that it is. Do so now, and ask Mr. Hughes to assist you."

Kirkpatrick ran a rather cursory eye over the carriage and pronounced it sound. He was about to order the resumption of the exercise when Giles forestalled him by asking, "Do you agree, Mr. Hughes?"

"No sir," was the answer. "If you check, here on the left side, you can just see a crack that weakens the structure. There is a corresponding one on the other side. I am not sure what will happen if we fire the gun."

"Let's find out. Mr. Abbott, get down to your magazine and issue a cartridge. In fact, I want to test all the guns with powder and shot, so you can expect more need for powder."

Activity had halted for a moment as everyone waited for the cartridge of gun powder to arrive. Giles soon put an end to this idleness. "Mr. Kirkpatrick, carry on with the exercise until we are able to fire this cannon. Be sure to check each cannon and carriage before running them in and out."

When the gun was finally loaded and run out, Giles told the gun crew to get out of the way of any mishap and had the gun captain fire the cannon. The gun boomed and jumped back on its carriage until brought to a halt. Giles and Mr. Hughes sprang at the gun to assess any damage. The crack on the left side had widened, and the right side was showing signs of coming apart.

"As I feared," said Mr. Hughes. "A couple of more rounds and the carriage would fall apart, and one could only guess what would happen to the gun."

"Mr. Evans," said Giles, "What do you think can be done about this? Can you repair it?"

The carpenter carefully examined the carriage and even slid an awl into the crack to evaluate how serious the damage was. "It won't take more than one or two more discharges before the carriage breaks in two, sir," he reported.

"Can you fix it?"

"We could put a couple of braces on each side to take some of the strain. It might work. But what we really need are new carriages for the guns, sir."

"Go ahead and try it. When you finish, have the gun fired a couple of times, so we know whether the repair is satisfactory. In the meantime, Mr. Kirkpatrick, continue to examine the guns, carefully if you please, and practice mock-firing them."

Giles returned to the quarterdeck, where Mr. Brooks was continuing his evaluation of sail combinations. But before long, they felt that they had learned all they could that day. The drill of mock-firing the guns was also soon completed, with several more carriages appearing to be defective. Giles ordered that all the carriages be reinforced before being used and then be tested with powder and shot. The ship settled into its normal routines, except for the noise of the carpenter and his mates working on the gun carriages and the boom of their work being tested as each one was completed. That work continued, as the wind steadily eased, until nightfall.

28

Chapter III

Daphne and Elsie resumed their journey at nine in the morning. Daphne had slept soundly and long, and even Elsie, who had helped her mistress get ready for bed and had had to be on hand for her waking, was well-rested. The weather was gloomy without actually raining much, and they both were lost in recollections of recent events. Neither had had any real idea of what a warship was like. When they were not remembering the happy moments that they had enjoyed recently, each one was brooding on the conditions her man would be enduring.

Daphne shook off the mood after they had stopped to rest the horses at an inn where Daphne had some coffee while Elsie had some tea with the coachman. Last night had been one of the very few occasions when Daphne had dined by herself since she had come out*, and it had brought home the change in her circumstances. She was now the mistress of Dipton Hall, and she would have to assert her authority, making it clear that it was her home first and foremost. Only secondly was it the refuge that had been provided for Lady Marianne Crocker and her two daughters. Daphne realized that Lady Marianne was now her half-sister-in-law, but Dipton Hall was her house. Daphne wondered if they should call each other by their first names, or should she be called Lady Giles while Marianne was Lady Marianne. Daphne would be happier to use first names, and she realized with a shock that it was now up to her, as the woman with the higher status, to ensure that this was their practice. The two girls were now her half-nieces-in-law, and she really should take some responsibility for their futures, dim as their prospects might seem. It would take some real effort on her part both to enforce her control of the house and to live on amicable terms with its other inhabitants.

Daphne almost wished that the Dower Cottage had not been let to Captain Bush, though she regretted the thought almost as soon as it was formed. She liked Captain Bush and his mother. He was now a close friend of her father, and he was unquestionably a close friend of her husband. But maybe the hope of finding other accommodation for Lady Marianne might not be impossible. It was a pity that the Earl of Camshire had totally washed his hands of his daughter and of her daughters.

Daphne's mind turned to more interesting topics as she reviewed what she would have to do about the estates. Some drainage should be done in the coming winter. Plans had already been made but needed to be executed. It was amusing to think that her initial contacts with Richard had involved drainage. In tandem with that work, some field boundaries might be changed and new hedges planted. Decisions had to be made on what livestock to keep over the winter and what would be the best crops to plant in the spring. It was really exciting to be in charge of not only Dipton Hall's holdings but also those of Dipton Manor since she presumed that her father would want her to keep managing them, just as she had before she married. Of course, she hoped that her father would not feel too lonely with her gone. She would dine with him frequently, and he at Dipton Hall, but it would not be the same. She was also looking forward to having people come to visit her, especially those who had always looked down on her as the daughter of a man who was only the first generation of his family away from trade. Now, as the wife of the son of an earl, a son who had a title in his own right which he had earned by his own merits, she could expect rather different reactions to her, and she would not be above letting people know that she thought their change in attitude was hypocritical, though, of course, only in the nicest ways. In the past, she had pretended to ignore their slighting her, but she had been hurt by them and would be glad to get her just due and put them in their places. That might be a nasty thought, but she wasn't going to give it up on that ground.

Elsie was also ruminating about how her life would be changed. Of course, she would still be a lady's maid, but being a lady's maid to a woman who now was titled 'Lady' and the Mistress of her own House was a big step up in the servants' hierarchy. She would have her work cut out for her. Lady Giles's clothes and other possessions would all have to be moved from Dipton Manor to Dipton Hall and properly arranged there. That would be Elsie's job – not the physical moving, of course, but making sure that everything was properly packed and finding the appropriate places for them would be her task. She might get some resistance to this from Mrs. Haycock, the housekeeper at Dipton Manor, who had set her on her way to her present position, but Elsie wouldn't take any objections from Mrs. Wilson, even if she had been the housekeeper at an Earl's London house before coming to Dipton Hall. Elsie did wonder if she could ask Mrs. Haycock for the help of some of the maids at Dipton Manor in gathering Lady Giles's things together. With only Mr. Moorhouse in residence, the maids would not be overly busy surely. They had all managed very well when both Captain Bush and his family and Colonel and Mrs. Craig had been staying at Dipton Manor, and the only change to that staff would be her own following Lady Giles to Dipton Hall.

These thoughts absorbed the travelers in the coach until it turned into the drive leading to Dipton Hall. Daphne was startled by the turn before recalling that, of course, this was now the way to her own home. After taking luncheon at her new residence, she would have to see her father without delay since he wouldn't be at Dipton Hall to greet her.

Looking out of the coach window, Daphne was already thinking about whether all was in order or whether some attention to the grounds was needed. It would be different – and easier – to be managing the gardens at Dipton Hall as her own rather than as the volunteer who had been managing them until Captain Giles could find someone suitable. Yes, the challenges were now more than intellectual puzzles, and the rewards of her efforts would be her own – and, of course, Richard's.

Daphne alighted from the carriage with the aid of a footman to find that Steves had lined up the full complement of servants to welcome her. He had calculated when Lady Giles could be expected and had warned the staff to be ready. Since Lady Marianne had shown little interest in when Lady Giles would be arriving, he had only informed her when the carriage was seen in the drive that someone was arriving, without troubling her with his own inferences about who that person might be. He took his own delight that the arrival was marked by the presentation of the servants without the attendance of the upstairs occupants of the Hall. Daphne had been taught by her father that taking account of the servants and saying a few words with them paid off many times in getting more thoughtful service, so she made a point of going along the parade of servants and making a friendly remark to each of them. Steves was methodically introducing them to her formally, even though she knew most of them from the many times she had been at the Hall before her marriage. Elsie, for her part, told two of the footmen, as soon as they had been presented, to take the luggage to Lady Giles's dressing room so that she could lay out a suitable ensemble for luncheon.

On entering the house, Steves did step ahead of Daphne to open the drawing-room door and announce, "Lady Giles has arrived." Daphne sailed into the room to greet a startled Lady Marianne and her two daughters. They exchanged pleasantries before Daphne declared that she had to change after her trip and that Steves should serve luncheon when she was ready. With this, she swept out of the drawing-room to ascend the stairs.

Luckily, Lady Marianne and her daughters were left sitting in the drawing-room and did not notice Daphne's slight confusion on reaching the top of the stairs in not being fully aware of which room was hers. Daphne had, of course, been all over Dipton Hall when Mr. Edwards's workers were readying it after Captain Giles had purchased the estate, but she didn't remember the details. Her own accommodations when she was married were something that she had neglected in her planning. Luckily, Steves and Mrs. Wilson had attended to the selection and preparation of her quarters, and Elsie had had an eye out to direct her mistress to the appropriate place. Elsie, herself, was gratified to find that Steves and Mrs. Wilson must have connived with Tisdale and Mrs. Haycock at Dipton Manor to have all of Daphne's possessions moved to Dipton Hall. All Elsie would need to do was to arrange them in a convenient way. She had already laid out a day gown into which Daphne could change from her traveling garments.

Daphne did not waste time in changing, though she was tempted to keep her new relations waiting for her just to show who was now in charge. However, she realized that the sooner lunch was over, the sooner she could engage in activities that she regarded as pressing due to her having been away. Lunch itself was a stilted affair, for Lady Marianne and her daughters were little interested in what had occurred on Daphne's short honeymoon or in Captain Giles's frigate. Animation only arose when Lydia Crocker, the younger of Daphne's nieces-in-law, started reminiscing about the ball held at Dipton Hall in the not very distant past. Her sister and even her mother joined in the conversation, recollecting the details of the splendid occasion. Inevitably, they wondered when next a ball could be held, recalling how much the previous one had been a focus of social life in the region.

Discussion of the ball, particularly of the militia officers who had been present, led to Lydia blurting out the fact that her mother had invited Major Thompson of Lord Mosley's Regiment, together with two of his lieutenants to dine that very evening. Daphne might well have let this pass without remark if she had not noticed that Lydia's imparting the information produced a look of consternation crossing Lady Marianne's face. Of course, Lady Marianne had no business inviting guests for dinner at Daphne's house, and she must have hoped to set a precedent that would make it difficult for Daphne to object in future. Daphne would have to nip this challenge in the bud.

"I quite understand your issuing an invitation when I was away," she began sweetly, "even though you might have realized that I would be returning today. But I expect that in future you will consult me first and, if I agree to what you propose, I will issue the invitation myself."

With that, Daphne rose from the table and headed upstairs to change into her riding clothes, leaving her newly acquired sister-in-law fuming and wondering what would be a suitable reaction to this laying down of rules. Daphne herself was reveling in having scored such an early victory, though halfway up the stairs, she realized that having officers and other single men to dinner might be one of the few avenues which could lead to a way to rid Dipton Hall of her husband's relatives. The most effective way would be for Lady Marianne to marry, but that would be most unlikely as long as she was encumbered with two unmarried daughters. It was possible that they could find some men who would be prepared to marry the girls even without dowries, but it would be ever so much easier if they did have something tangible to bring to a marriage. Daphne was well aware that Lady Marianne's father, the Earl of Camshire, was not about to step forward with money for the purpose. She would have to see if she couldn't persuade Richard that it was his duty. If her daughters were married, Lady Marianne might find a husband among the many well-off widowers in the area for whom the commercial source of their wealth prevented their rising much in society, a barrier that would be breached by having a wife who was the daughter of an earl, even if she had been thoroughly repudiated by her own father.

Daphne was sufficiently self-aware to realize that she was about to become as much the ruthless match-maker as any of the mothers of unmarried daughters in the area whose stratagems to snare a husband for their daughters had provided her with much amusement in the past. Indeed, she knew and was delighted that they had been astonished when Daphne herself had stolen the richest prize of all from under their scheming noses. Not that Daphne thought of Richard's wanting to marry her in that light.

Daphne changed into her riding habit, one of the scandalous ones that allowed her to ride astride rather than side-saddle. Though only a few days had passed since her marriage, she had been so busy beforehand that she had rather let her role as supervisor of the two estates slip. She was eager to catch up. First, though, she wanted to visit her father.

Mr. Moorhouse was, as usual, to be found in his library. He was quite happy to be interrupted by his daughter and was as keen to hear about her honeymoon as she was to tell him. Evidently, he thought, it had gone well, judging not only by how eager she was to tell him the facts but also by the way in which she regularly mentioned Giles, almost savoring his name and introducing it as often as possible in her discourse. He laughed with her at the spectacles she must have made being hoisted onto Giles's frigate with her skirts billowing in the wind and the sadness that came from having to part. He was immensely glad that the intimate side of marriage appeared to have gone well. Of course, he didn't ask, but he had been worried since he had been in no position to warn her of the pitfalls of being alone with her husband for the first time, and she had had no mother to inform her. But he could see from the twinkle in her eye and the somewhat dreamy look she gave him when talking about Giles that it must have gone well, especially when she remarked at one point that some of her friends, who had become married and had told her that the transition on the marriage night was painful and unpleasant, had been quite wrong and everything between Giles and her had been perfect from the beginning.

Mr. Moorhouse was amused at Daphne's handling of Lady Marianne's presumption and was sympathetic to Daphne's strategy to rid herself of the burden. But he was skeptical that Giles would provide large enough dowries to the girls to secure their marriages.

"I do not believe that he should provide such generous dowries that they alone would secure the girls' futures," he declared. "Captain Giles can't be expected to provide more than modest marriage portions* since it is really his Father's duty or those of Lady Marianne's older brothers to look after the girls. In no way is it Captain Giles's task, who himself was given virtually no assistance from his father in obtaining a well-to-do existence. Quite the contrary. Your husband, Daphne, has distinguished himself and can live very comfortably by his own merits, despite his father's lack of support."

Surprisingly to Daphne, Mr. Moorhouse refused to come to dinner that night to provide her with a male escort. "I may be a widower with more money than status," he said with a twinkle in his eye as he echoed Daphne's plans for her sister-in-law, "but I would never contemplate marrying Lady Marianne whom, quite frankly, I detest."

Daphne protested that she had not thought to include him in her schemes, just that she needed support in what could be an awkward dinner. "Try your brother-in-law," suggested Mr. Moorhouse, "there is no danger that he should fall victim to your marital strategies."

"Who?" asked Daphne.

"Lord David, of course. He's in your debt for taking off his hands the job of trying to keep Lady Marianne within her budget."

Daphne arrived at the vicarage to find Lord David about to have tea. After some polite conversation, she invited him to dinner. His response was to agree happily. "It will be a pleasure to dine out without having to avoid the not too subtle advances of people who think I should marry one of the young ladies present." Daphne hadn't realized that Lord David also saw through the many stratagems designed to install one of the many young ladies he encountered in the vicarage.

The dinner was a surprising success. The major was an older man who was a wool merchant in Leeds. Daphne suspected that he had bought his commission not only for the excitement that it might offer but also for the social prestige. He was well-spoken, though with a notable Yorkshire accent that told the world that he did not come from the gentry.

The two lieutenants were equally suitable targets for Daphne's schemes, being professional men whose accents revealed that they also were from the commercial strata of society. The one problem that seemed evident to Daphne was that they would appear to be of a level of society that would require a substantial dowry in order to set up house in the manner to be expected for the granddaughter of an earl, even ones with no close ties to the nobility or substantial fortunes of their own.

The conversation flowed smoothly. Of course, Lady Marianne had been married to an army officer, and she and her daughters had spent their lives in regimental towns. Furthermore, Daphne was surprised to learn that Lady Marianne and her daughters had been reading the newspaper that Mr. Edwards had arranged to have delivered to Dipton Hall. They were well able to participate when talk turned from camp life at Ameschester to the danger of invasion. Daphne became the center of attention when the officers learned that she had just returned from Brighton and Portsmouth. They plied her with questions about what she had observed about the state of readiness. Now she was glad that she had paid attention when Giles had commented on the coastal defenses they had seen on their walks and that he had pointed out army camps in the area. He had not been impressed by what he saw, and Daphne was able to repeat his opinion that, if Napoleon came in force, the existing forces would be hard put to counter the invasion. That opinion was hotly contested by the lieutenants. Daphne also could report on the large number of ships-of-the-line that Giles had pointed out to her at Spithead and his own feeling that the Navy should be able to prevent the French from gaining control of the Channel for long enough that an invasion might succeed. The overall effect of the discussion was to encourage the lieutenants in their wish that their regiment would be moved closer to the coast and for Lady Marianne's daughters to encourage them in their hopes of glory.

Daphne led the other ladies to the drawing-room when the meal was completed, leaving the men to their port. She rather wondered how Lady Marianne had intended to perform this ritual with no explicit host to manage the male conversation. The drawing-room conversation was largely centered on the officers' bravery who were so eager to see combat. Daphne was silent during this. For her, the talk of war had brought back that her concern was not Giles's winning distinction in battle but rather that of his surviving danger unharmed. She recognized, yet again, why he had to face danger, but she herself most certainly did not revel in it.

The men joined the ladies very shortly. With the numbers just right, two tables of whist kept everyone entertained until the men should leave. The card games were perfunctory, no one taking them very seriously. The three Crocker ladies and the officers fenced verbally in the time-honored rituals of flirtation. Daphne and Lord David discussed what he had found out about his parish and its challenges. He had no intention of getting a curate any time soon and was enjoying the task of meeting his parishioners.

Chapter IV

Lieutenant Ian Kirkpatrick had the morning watch. The wind had eased overnight and had backed into the north, but he had not been inclined to set more sail. The captain's orders had not required it and had not mentioned sailing a course closer to the north if the wind backed.

Kirkpatrick was still grumbling to himself about his treatment the previous day. That interloper from the Ordinance Board had seemed intent on making him look foolish. It was not his fault that the French could not build good gun carriages, and he could not be expected himself to examine them minutely. The Ordinance Board should have known enough to have changed them before *Impetuous* was commissioned. That business had kept him on deck so long that he had missed his supper and had had to make do with what his lazy servant could find.

It was almost four bells. First light would be just after six bells. The orders were to clear for action* at four bells. Probably the Captain would come on deck to witness the activity, and that lickspittle Milton wouldn't miss it. How the first lieutenant had aped the actions of the captain and the master yesterday instead of just enjoying being freed of his duties for a time. It was so unjust: Milton's commission was only three weeks ahead of his own. If Kirkpatrick's exam had been only one month earlier, he would by now be First Lieutenant of *Impetuous*. First Lieutenants were the ones who got their step*, not second lieutenants, especially not ones with no influence. It was only because that fool of a captain he had had at the time couldn't keep the dates straight that he had missed the earlier exam.

It was a pity that Milton hadn't been killed in that stupid attack on the French frigate when Captain Giles had succeeded in losing *Patroclus*. Milton was the one who had initiated the action against the French ship, even though it had been madness to attack with ships that had only one lieutenant on board and no other officers, as well as with untried and once-defeated crews, against a well-appointed enemy. Kirkpatrick was fortunate that he had been able to join the attack when it became evident that the other two frigates would be able to take the Frenchie without him after all. At least it had got him this appointment, and taking the French frigate had at least put his creditors at bay. Of course, he should also have shared in the money given for retaking the British frigates. It was all so unfair!

Kirkpatrick's mind turned to his lack of influence. Again his luck had been rotten. His father's cousin, the Earl of Blazy, had secured him his midshipman's birth and then had been instrumental in his getting his promotion and position as a lieutenant. He had been in rank long enough that he expected the Earl to get him his step, but it hadn't happened, and then the old fool had died. The new Earl showed no interest in securing his relation a better position and would not even use his influence to benefit the captains who had been the old Earl's clients. It was only because Captain Tomlinson hadn't realized that, with the old Earl dead, the Captain's own patron was no longer inclined to return favors that had secured Kirkpatrick's previous position.

"Captain's on deck, sir," murmured the helmsman. At least this crew was ready to warn him of the arrival of the Captain, not like those wretches in his previous ship. That commission had been a disaster too. They were sailing for the West Indies where prize money abounded when they caught a small French bark, trying to sneak into a French port from Martinique. He had had to take the prize into Portsmouth and then look for another berth. Some lucky midshipman, nephew to the Admiral most likely, would get his place and all that prize money that would go with it. Not that that would have happened anyway. The fool of a captain had run the frigate onto a reef as soon as he had passed through the Leeward Islands, so the ship had never even reached Jamaica. But that meant his prize money from the ship he had taken into port was all tied up in finding out who had survived the disaster and what their claims might be.

Kirkpatrick left the windward side of the quarter deck so that the Captain could start his exercise if he wished, but Giles came directly to him. Kirkpatrick gave the terse report of what had happened so far during his watch and what he knew of the frigate's position, course and speed. He was about to turn away when Giles ordered, "Clear for Action, Mr. Kirkpatrick. Do it quietly." What in the world was the Captain thinking? Undertaking the quiet version of the drill was just inviting chaos in the dark with a crew who had never undertaken the complicated task on this ship before. Well, it would be Milton's problem when he arrived on deck. Getting the guns ready, which was Kirkpatrick's task, would be simpler, especially after yesterday's drill.

Lieutenant Milton arrived and relieved Kirkpatrick even as the ship began to resemble a disturbed anthill with seamen scurrying around, often in opposite directions, the patterns only evident to the trained eye. After a short time, the hubbub started to die away, and Milton was able to report in a term of pleased surprise, "Ship's cleared for action, sir."

Giles had been watching the time. "Thirty-two minutes, Mr. Milton. We must do better than that in future."

Milton was shocked. In his previous ship, they had never cleared for action in less than forty minutes, and that after considerable practice and with a great deal of noise. His respect rose again for the crew and for the captain and first lieutenants who had trained these men. He was particularly surprised since he had learned from Mr. Brooks earlier that Captain Giles did not believe in flogging as a way to improve discipline and performance. This crew hadn't been driven to their task and seemed to have performed all the better for it. It was a lesson that went against all of Milton's experience.

The sky to the southeast was showing the first signs of daylight with a strip that seemed a bit less dark above a pitch-black base. The wind had been veering to the east in the last half hour, and *Impetuous* was now close-hauled on the larboard tack

"Land ho," came the call from the masthead. "Straight ahead, Cannot tell how far."

"Where do you think we are?" Giles asked Mr. Brooks.

"That should be the French Coast ahead, south of Boulogne, about three leagues*, by my dead reckoning."

"Let's hope you are right. Mr. Milton, furl the topsails, if you please, and shake the reefs out of the mainsail and foresail."

"Furl the sails, sir?"

"Yes, to make us less visible. The lookout at our masthead may be able to see a ship before they can see us. Now do it, Mr. Milton. And in future, don't question my orders before acting on them."

"Aye, aye, sir."

The light was slowly increasing.

"Deck, there. Ship ahoy! Two points to starboard. Two miles off, on a broad reach parallel to ours."

"Mr. Correll," Giles addressed the midshipman of the watch, "Get aloft with the telescope and see what you can make of her."

The midshipman raced up the ratlines and positioned himself in the top. After a brief consultation with the lookout and examination through his telescope, he shouted to the deck.

"Ship appears to be a brig*7 of war. She is flying English colors."

"Mr. Brooks, I want a course to intercept her."

"Aye, aye, sir... Our best course now, sir, is to maintain ours until we get close to her."

"Make it so, Mr. Milton, set the topsails. Mr. Brooks, I don't believe that the topgallants would make us faster. "

"Probably not, sir. And it would increase our leeway*, especially since we have such a shallow draft."

The two ships continued on their courses for a while. It became evident that they were converging and that *Impetuous* could control their meeting if each maintained her course.

"Deck," Mr. Correll shouted from the masthead. "The brig is tacking."

"That's suspicious," remarked Mr. Milton. "She won't be able to clear the land on her new course."

The ships were now on the same course, with *Impetuous* behind but to windward of the other vessel

"Mr. Stewart," said Giles. "Make the private signal with our number."

"Aye, aye, sir."

The carefully wrapped signal flags rose on their halyards and were released by a twitch when they reached their full height. There was no response from the brig.

"Mr. Correll," Giles bellowed, "Can you see any activity in response to our signal?"

"No, sir… Sir, there seems to be a very large crew on deck, even for a brig of war."

"Can you see any ships close to the land ahead?"

"Yes, sir, two small vessels. They are right in front of a battery on shore."

"This brig is probably a privateer," murmured Mr. Brooks. Privateers were not well-loved by men of the Royal Navy. "That accounts for her being shy of us. She probably thinks we would press much of her crew if we got a chance. Let's get that chance!"

"Deck," came a shout from above, "She has hauled down her jack… she is raising the French flag."

"Mr. Brooks, a course to catch up to her, staying to windward," Giles responded. "What are her chances of getting under the protection of that shore battery before we can catch her?"

"It will be close, sir. And that is presuming the battery won't simply try to blow her out of the water when she gets near. They may have seen her British flag."

"Follow her course. I must say, I am surprised how quickly we are gaining on her."

"It appears that she has a sail fothered over her hull near the bow, sir." Mr. Brooks pointed out. That would account for her slowness."

"Mr. Kirkpatrick," Giles called to the lieutenant who was in charge of the guns. "Load the foremost larboard gun with round shot and the rest of the larboard battery with chain shot and run out. If we fire into her, aim high for the rigging."

"Aye, Aye, sir," Mr. Kirkpatrick responded.

Impetuous was steadily gaining on the brig, and that ship, in turn, was steadily getting closer to the coast and the protection of the shore battery. Mr. Brooks was using his sextant to determine the vertical angle of the shore battery from *Impetuous*. "Sir, we will be in range of the shore battery in a few minutes."

"Mr. Kirkpatrick," called Giles, "use the foremost gun to put a shot across her bows."

The cannon boomed out, but it produced no effect on the brig, which held her course.

"Mr. Kirkpatrick, fire the larboard guns."

The broadside roared out. When the smoke cleared, those on *Impetus*'s deck could see several holes in the brig's sails. One was right against the gaff of the brig's spanker. As they watched, the gaff broke, spilling the wind from the sail. The chase yawed to leeward. Some furious rushing around on the brig's deck brought her under control. She lowered her flag, even as she backed her topsail. *Impetuous* also backed her topsail, so the two ships were stationary about one hundred yards from each other. A cannon fired from the shore. The ball fell just short of the brig.

"Bosun, we shall use the longboat and my barge to board her. Mr. Macauley, two squads of marines. Pistols and cutlasses for the seamen. Mr. Milton, take command of *Impetuous*. Mr. Kirkpatrick, come with me. Mr. Stewart, you will command the longboat. Let's not waste time. We don't want to give that Frog battery a chance to hit us when their guns warm up."

The two boats set off for the brig. The shore battery continued to fire, but even with their guns warmed, the shot fell short. Both ships were being pushed from shore by the wind.

Giles mounted to the deck of the Brig. The marines and seamen followed. A small group of officers came forward to meet him, led by a florid-faced, stocky man shaking with indignation. "I am George Hoxley, sir. This is a disgrace, sir. We are a British ship sailing under a letter of marque granted by King George himself. My backers are among the most eminent peers of the realm. One of them is the Earl of Camshire. You have no business coming to us with an armed boarding party. I order you to vacate this ship immediately."

Giles was not deterred by the claims of privilege, even by the invocation of his own father's name. "Captain Hoxley, you were sailing under French colors when we stopped you. You failed to respond to our order to stop. I have every right to stop your ship and ask for a full account of your doings. I require to see your letter of marque and your logs. Now!"

"Sir, I protest. We only evaded you because we knew you would try to press some of my crew. I only used the French flag as a ruse de guerre. I would have left the protection of the shore batteries as soon as the coast was clear, sailing for our home port of Harwich. I repeat, you have no right to board us, and my crew is protected by the most eminent authority. You most certainly have no right to see my logs. They contain information about the sources of my success, and I will not have that information bandied about in ports where French spies may transmit it to Bonaparte's forces."

This speech had the opposite effect from what was intended. It simply increased Giles's suspicions. "Captain. Hoxley, please let me have the key to your desk or lock-box and any other keys for locked objects in your cabin. No? You don't want to give them to me? Very well, I will just smash anything that is locked.

"Mr. Macauley, detail some marines to guard this man and the other officers while they are being transported to *Impetuous*. Mr. Stewart, take them now in the longboat and then return. Tell Mr. Milton to throw them in irons. Mr. Evans, get that gaff fixed. Mr. Kirkpatrick, take a gang of seamen and search the ship. You are looking particularly for a space where we can contain the crew with only one or two exits to guard. Also, make sure that no one is hidden below. Carstairs, get an axe and come with me."

Entering the Captain's cabin. Giles discovered a locked drawer in the desk and two wooden boxes with locks. Carstairs smashed open the desk and, in doing so, revealed a hidden compartment in the main drawer. But for the brutal way in which the drawer had been opened, this compartment might have escaped notice from someone examining the desk. In the secret space were several documents, the most important of which seemed to be the captain's log. There was also a list of what appeared to be the value of various ships and their cargoes. The documents did not include a letter of marque. Glancing through the captain's log, Giles realized that it was damning evidence of piracy, for, quite clearly, the brig had taken both English and French vessels as well as ships of other countries.

When Giles had removed all the papers, he realized that the drawer seemed to be too shallow. Further examination revealed a further hidden compartment in the drawer. It took some fiddling at the edges of the bottom of the drawer to open the compartment. When he did so, Giles found some papers.

They were in a different hand and in French. Examining the documents more closely, he realized that they appeared to be diagrams of the shore defenses around various parts of the English coast. Even though he could not read the documents, Giles realized that the papers must be the report of some French spy in England.

Setting the log and the papers aside for later study, Giles had Carstairs open the wooden boxes. The first one did contain a letter of marque for the vessel *Bountiful* out of Harwich, Captain William Hoxley. In addition, there were copies of share agreements for men who had invested in a venture whose purpose was to outfit and use *Bountiful* as a privateer. His father's name was indeed there as the owner of one share, which probably meant that the Earl had let his name be used as a sponsor without putting up any money. There was also a list of French vessels taken by *Bountiful* and the proceeds from the sale of the ships and vessels. There was also a version of the log of the *Bountiful*. It would all have appeared above board if one were investigating the English privateer, *Bountiful*. It only showed their French captures and only mentioned clear seas when *Bountiful* had been engaged in other activities.

The second box contained a similar-looking set of documents, but they were in French. Giles wondered what they were and asked Carstairs to summon Mr. Kirkpatrick.

"I believe you know French, Mr. Kirkpatrick." Giles greeted the lieutenant.

"Yes, sir."

"Have a look at these and tell me what they are."

"The engraved certificate is a letter of marque for *le navire* – I guess that is 'ship,' sir – *Généreux* out of Calais. And the book is the log of the *Généreux*, Captain Couchetard.

There is also a list of British-sounding ship names with some figures beside them. And what looks like a list of names of people. Sir, I was about to tell you that we found a name board in a locker on the after deck in the name Généreux and a port-name board saying 'Calais.'"

"Well, well, well. No wonder Captain Hoxley did not want to see us. Now that we know what he has been doing, I am sure that he will hang, and if the French had him and knew about this, they would guillotine him. Pity that he can suffer only one of those fates."

The cabin also contained a small, locked metal box. It was so heavy that Giles suspected that it must contain gold in some form or at least gold and silver coins. It would be better not to unlock it until it was turned over to the authorities so there would be no question about how large had been its content.

"What did you discover in exploring the ship, Mr. Kirkpatrick?"

"Sir, we found no other crew members or secret compartments below decks. The hold is empty, and it appears to have no access to the rest of the ship except for the two hatches. There is what looks to be a shot-hole about twelve feet to the rear of the bow, just at the waterline. Mr. Evans thinks he can plug it, but the sail they have fothered over the whole is limiting the intake of water so that the pumps can handle it easily."

"Very good. Mr. Kirkpatrick. We'll take this brig to Admiral Gardiner rather than to a port as is usual with prizes. I'll sail as soon as possible. I feel nervous drifting here near those guns."

"May I ask why you are not sending the brig into the harbor, sir?"

"Yes. That ship is likely to be known in all the likely ports. The papers have evidence that prominent investors were involved in her doings and that she was engaged in spying. It may be advantageous not to have her capture become general knowledge any sooner than necessary."

On deck, Giles quickly ordered Mr. Macauley to herd the brig's crew into the hold and leave a squad of marines to help guard them. He checked with Mr. Evans that he could probably plug the shot hole while underway and ordered him to stay with *Bountiful* with one of his mates to effect the repair.

"Mr. Osmond," Giles addressed the sailmaker, whom he had asked to come over to *Bountiful*. "I want you to start recutting the brig's sails, starting with the topsails, jibs, and staysails. Just to make her sails look different. "Use her spare sails to start with. I don't want her to be recognizable just from seeing her sails."

He then turned to Mr. Kirkpatrick. "Mr. Kirkpatrick. You will take station on *Impetuous*'s windward quarter. At night, I'll have a lantern on the taffrail, and you should have one on your bow. We expect to find Admiral Gardiner off the Goodwin Sands or news of where he is from a ship stationed there. I will have Mr. Brooks send over one of his mates with charts and courses in case we get separated. He can stand watches to relieve you. Be vigilant about the prisoners. Remember that they are very familiar with this ship and may have ways out of the hold that we could not discover. I am taking the precaution of removing their weapons to *Impetuous*."

By the start of the first dog watch, both ships were ready to proceed. The wind had lightened still farther but had also veered so that they could hope to reach the rendezvous on one long tack. Mr. Evans was still working to repair the shot-hole but reported that it should be easy to finish the job by nightfall. Mr. Osmond had the main and fore topsails recut already and was starting to work on the jib. To a sailor, they would look quite different from the sails they were replacing. He was now working on the foremast topsail. "No one will recognize *Bountiful* from the cut of her jib," he boasted. "And these sails should make her faster."

Lieutenant Kirkpatrick again had the morning watch, though now on a different vessel. His thoughts were much more cheerful than they had been on the previous day. *Impetuous* had already taken a prize, and while the prize carried no valuable cargo, their capture was a valuable ship. And he didn't forget the heavy metal box. With any luck, it would contain coins, maybe even gold. And his share of that – he reckoned it would be one twenty-fourth – should be a tidy sum. He even felt better about Captain Giles, who had not seemed to hold the fiasco with the gun carriages against him and who had answered his question about why *Bountiful* was to accompany *Impetuous* rather than be taken into harbor directly patiently, not taking umbrage on his questioning the reason for a decision. Captain Tomlinson, his previous captain, would have done so, vitriolically.

The sound of *Impetuous* clearing for action wafted across the open sea between the ships. They weren't using the silent drill this time. Kirkpatrick idly wondered how long it would take them to complete the drill. Yesterday must have been some sort of a fluke. He was glad that he would not be the one who would face the Captain's disappointment when the time taken was longer than that accomplished on the previous action.

Chapter V

The start of the forenoon watch found *Impetuous* drifting along in thick fog under a very light south-east breeze. *Bountiful* trailed along on her starboard quarter, like a dog at heel. Mr. Brooks' dead reckoning put them near the rendezvous with Admiral Gardiner's fleet. There were ships around them, though they could not see them. Giles had ordered a gun to be fired every five minutes and for a horn to be blown at one-minute intervals. They could hear similar cannon firings and horns sounding around them. It was impossible to tell in the fog how far away the other ships were or even exactly what was their bearing. Indeed, Giles could not even be sure whether the number of other ships was eight or nine. The Master had a man in the fore chains, and his voice came back to the quarterdeck every minute or so with, "No bottom with this line."

Impetuous sailed into an area where the fog was a little less dense.

"Ship on the starboard beam," called one of the lookouts. Just after this announcement came a call from the masthead, "Ship to starboard, one hundred yards."

The officers on the quarter-deck rushed to the starboard side. They could just make out a three-decked line-of-battle ship whose large guns were run out. The muzzles of her thirty-two pounders looked immense from where Giles stood. High above him, he could see officers on the other ship excitedly pointing towards *Impetuous*.

"What do you make of her, Mr. Brooks?" questioned Giles.

"A bloody great second-rate. It must be *Penelope*, Admiral Gardiner's flagship. Ninety-eight guns.

"Mr. Stewart," Giles called urgently. "The private signal followed by our number. Shake the flags out as soon as they are on the halyard so that they can be read even before they reach the yardarm. We don't want her to blow us out of the water."

The midshipman must have been expecting the order for the flags were attached even before Giles had ceased talking. There was an anxious pause as they waited for a response. It came in moments with the other ship raising the proper acknowledgment for the day, followed by the expected order, "Captain to report on board."

Giles decided to take Captain Hoxley with him in case the Admiral wanted to question the pirate captain immediately. The flag captain met Giles at the entryway with a serious look and the statement, "The Admiral wants to see you in his cabin immediately." Giles explained that Hoxley should be kept under guard, without specifying the reasons, and was shown by a midshipman to the Admiral's cabin. Admiral Gardiner sat behind a large table with his back to the windows. In the dim, fog-shrouded light, Giles could only make out his outline against the light. Giles had the fleeting thought that he looked like some pagan idol, shrouded in mystery, who was about to pronounce what the future would hold.

"Captain Giles," the Admiral began softly. "That was a good bit of navigation you and your master performed to find us in this fog."

"Thank you, sir."

"I see that you have a brig on your quarter." There was more of a rasp to the Admiral's voice.

"Yes, sir."

"And I suppose that the brig is a prize." The admiral did not seem pleased about the one-eighth of the value of the prize that would come his way.

"Yes, sir."

"Yes, sir," the Admiral mimicked in what was now a loud voice. "I'll have you know, Captain Giles, that I will not have captains pursuing prizes to the detriment of their orders. You were ordered to sail here directly from Portsmouth, were you not?"

"Yes, sir."

"Then how did you just "happen" to collect a prize on the way."

"Let me explain, sir," Giles requested. "With the wind as it was and the currents against us, it seemed best to make one long tack almost to the French coast before coming about to traverse the Dover Straights. We did indeed make the passage on just two tacks. We virtually stumbled on the prize just at dawn, a brig of war, sir," Giles knew he was prevaricating about how he came upon *Bountiful*, but not in any way that could be disproved by his or Mr. Brooks's logs. He just wasn't mentioning that the primary reason for crossing to France was to see if he could take a prize.

Admiral Gardiner seemed to be satisfied with the explanation. His next question showed that he had observed the prize carefully and was curious about some anomalies.

"Why is she just showing our British jack and not that flag flying over the French one? She is French, I presume."

"Not entirely, sir. She might also be regarded as British."

"How can that be? You surely didn't take a British ship."

"When we came upon her, sir, at dawn yesterday, she was on a converging course showing British colors. I made the private signal. Her response was to change course, apparently to get under the protection of a shore battery, and to change to French colors. We were able to catch up with her before she got near enough to the battery, and I persuaded her to stop."

"You *persuaded* her?"

"Yes, sir. A broadside into her rigging turned out to be very persuasive."

The Admiral chuckled at the turn of phrase. "And then?"

"I went aboard to see what she really was. The Captain upbraided me for firing at him, claiming that the French flag had been simply a ruse de guerre and that he had turned to the battery to avoid losing many of his crew to the press. He was claiming loudly that I had no right to stop him and that he sailed under the sponsorship of powerful English patrons."

"Did he mention any of them?"

"Yes, sir. He named the Earl of Camshire, sir."

"Did he! Camshire is your father, isn't he, Captain?"

"Yes, sir."

"Don't worry, I think we have all heard the story of how he has treated you. So, what did you do then?"

"I told the captain that I would examine his letter of marque and his log. I asked him to give me the keys to any locked material in his cabin. He refused, so I proceeded to his cabin and found several documents that were locked up there. I have brought them with me."

"Did he have a British letter of marque?"

"Yes, sir. I found it in a locked box together with a log and a list of names of shareholders in his venture."

Giles placed the documents from the first locked box before the Admiral, who scanned them. "I see your father is a shareholder. I am surprised he could raise the price."

"He probably didn't, sir. I would not be surprised if he were given the share as a fee for letting his name be used and possibly suggesting to acquaintances that they invest."

"Well, it all seems to be in order. I don't see why you seized the ship. You have presented me with a very nasty situation to rectify." The Admiral clearly was unhappy about the situation.

"Possibly, sir. But there was another letter of marque and log in a different locked box."

"What?"

Giles handed over the contents of the French box.

"I see—another letter of marque, and log, and what looks like another list of subscribers. Your captain Hoxley must have captured the *Généreux*. That would account for his having her license and log and documents."

"Yes, sir, I would have to agree. Except, sir, I found a third log for the *Bountiful* locked in the Captain's desk. It includes all the captures recorded in the English log, and those listed in the French log, and some others as well. When *Bountiful* was taking French ships, they do not show up in the French log, and similarly, her capturing English ships is not mentioned in the English log, and of course, neither of those logs mention her other captures."

As Giles suggested, the Admiral compared the three logs, getting more and more red in the face by the minute.

"This Captain Hoxley is nothing but a pirate! There is enough material for me to run him up to the yardarm right now. Where is he?"

"I brought him to the flagship with me, sir."

"Good. Mr. Arbuckle," the Admiral ordered. "My compliments to Captain Foster, and he can prepare for a hanging at eight bells of the morning watch."

"Sir, if I may," Giles interrupted, "there were still further documents that we uncovered. You may want to ask Captain Hoxley about their provenance before you tell him you are going to hang him."

"And all his officers too," sputtered the Admiral. "Mr. Arbuckle, belay* that last order. Now, what is it, Captain?"

Giles handed over the final documents. The Admiral started to skim over them, then stopped and seemed to return to the beginning to read them more carefully.

"My God! This is serious!" The Admiral thought for a few moments. "Do you suppose any other ships realize that you took *Bountiful*?"

"I don't know, sir. We only saw two distant sails before we raised the recut sails."

"Recut sails?"

"Yes, sir, I thought it might be advantageous if it was not generally known that we had taken *Bountiful*. Of course, the garrison of the French battery witnessed our capturing her."

"So there is no time to be lost if we are to catch whoever provided the assessment of the defenses and the sketch maps. Did you bring this Captain Hoxley with you?"

"Yes, sir."

"Lieutenant Arbuckle," the Admiral addressed his flag lieutenant, "bring him here."

Captain Hoxley entered, still sputtering with indignation at Giles's seizing his brig.

"Be quiet, Captain Hoxley, or should I say 'Captaine Couchetard?'" Captain Hoxley seemed to shrink with this evidence that clearly his different logs had been found.

"I should hang you and your officers right now. The evidence is overwhelmingly against you. But I do have some questions about this." Admiral Gardiner displayed the secret spy document. "If you tell me everything you know about it, now, where you got it, who you were taking it to, what you know about the network behind it, and so on, and will testify in court against any Englishmen involved in this matter, I am prepared to recommend that your sentence be commuted from hanging to transportation to New South Wales. The same offer will be made to your officers."

"And my crew? Will you hang them?"

"Of course not. They appear to be prime seamen. We'll press them. The Navy is always short of hands."

Captain Hoxley accepted the offer. He actually did not have very much useful information. He did know from whom he picked up the documents to be taken to France, a man called Mr. Dorset. Captain Hoxley suspected that that was not his real name. He could only describe him as a swarthy, older man with a pronounced French accent to be found at a certain house in Deal. He knew to whom he delivered the reports in Boulogne and at what location in the town. On his most recent trip, *Bountiful* had been carried beyond the port in the gale. *Impetuous* had intercepted him as he was trying to beat back to the port. He had been recruited for treason by one of the more prominent men on his list of shareholders. No, that man had not put up any cash for the venture. He was indeed impecunious, and Captain Hoxley suspected that he was getting additional funds for his treachery. Captain Hoxley said that he got the Earl's connection with the venture by promising to recommend the investment to others as a straightforward case of financing a privateer in the hope of large gains.

Captain Hoxley would be subject to much more intense questioning in the days ahead, but, for now, Admiral Gardiner thought it was important to act as quickly as possible. "Mr. Arbuckle, I believe that Richards, one of the topmen in the larboard watch*, is from Deal. Fetch him here, please."

Giles was amazed that the Admiral knew both the name and the origin of a seaman on his flagship. It was not long before the flag lieutenant returned with the man.

"Richards, what do you know of the house of Mr. Dorset in Deal?" Admiral Gardiner asked.

"Sir, I have never heard of Mr. Dorset. He must be someone new in Deal since I left the town."

"Possibly. Here is a description of the house. Please read it, Mr. Arbuckle?"

The flag lieutenant read from his notes the description that Captain Hoxley had given them.

"Sir," said Richards, "it sounds like Franker's Cottage. It's a bit to the north of the center of the town, about two houses back from the beach."

"Could you guide a party there?"

"Yes, sir."

"Thank you, Richards. You will be going over to *Impetuous* with Captain Giles. Just for this mission, of course."

"Aye, aye, sir."

"Now, Captain Giles. This is what I want you to do. Take *Impetuous* round to Deal now. Moor to the north of the center of the town. Before dawn, go ashore with a squad of marines and proceed to this Franker's Cottage. Richards will go with you to show you how to find the house immediately. Seize whomever you find there who fits the description we have been given and any other people who might be involved. Then take him, or them, or even no one if this part of your mission in Deal fails, to Walmer Castle* together with the documents you discovered on *Bountiful*. The Warden* of the Cinque Ports should be there, especially as he is no longer prime minister. He will know what to do with the traitor and the information you have."

Giles returned to *Impetuous,* none too happy with his new orders. Instead of getting on with the job of harassing the French, he would have to take *Impetuous* round to Deal and then seek out a politician for help in a matter that promised to bring scandal to his own family. Luckily the fog had lifted so that the first part of their journey around the Goodwin Sands was accomplished with adequate visibility. Nightfall came quickly before they could reach Deal, and the fog resumed, so *Impetuous*, under the guidance of a nervous Giles and Mr. Brooks, crept blindly to what they hoped was the appropriate anchorage.

Impetuous's boats were loaded with marines and seamen before dawn. Guided only by compass directions, they set off with muffled oars. The bow of Giles's barge, which was in the lead, grounded on the beach before they even realized they were that close to the land. The marines formed up in silence. The sun must have risen, but its only effect was to turn the fog from black to deep gray; visibility was scarcely improved. Giles and Richards felt their way gingerly up the beach. They were only three yards away from the structure when a substantial stone building loomed out of the fog.

"Do you recognize the building?" Giles whispered to Richards.

"I think so, sir," was the whispered reply. "I'd know better if we moved a bit to starboard ... Aye, Captain, we are seven houses to the south of where we want to be."

"Stay here. I will bring the others. Giles had used his pocket compass to make sure they had kept to a straight line as they ventured ashore, and he used the reciprocal course to find his way back to the boats. There he gave instructions to Mr. Stewart to select five boat-watchers who were to stay with the boats with the midshipman until their captain returned.

Giles led the remaining seamen, armed with pistols and cutlasses, towards the building, followed by the squad of marines under Lieutenant Macauley. When they connected with Richards, he led them across the fronts of other buildings until he reached the place to turn towards the suspect house. The fog was a little thinner here, and, before long, they could make out the shape of the target house.

Giles knew that he would have to use surprise and quick action to prevent whoever was their target from burning incriminating papers, and he also must prevent anyone from escaping from the back door. He sent the marines to guard the rear of the house and catch anyone trying to escape that way. He had his own group of seamen pull up a substantial fence post to use as a battering ram. Then he knocked loudly on the door with the hilt of his sword. There were scurrying noises behind the door, and Giles was about to order the use of the battering ram when the door creaked open, and an elderly servant started to speak. Giles pushed past him into the main room, where a well-dressed man was indeed about to throw some papers onto the fire. Giles simply shoved him aside, with the papers falling to the floor before the man could get them into the fire. Giles was gathering up the papers while topman Humphries held the would-be arsonist when the back door opened, and Lieutenant Macauley herded two civilians into the room. Their dress might have suggested superior servants, but their shoes, which were distinctly better than any servant would wear, gave away the fact that they were of a higher class. One of them had a pronounced bruise developing under his left eye, while the other one was favoring his right leg.

"These two came bursting out the back door immediately after you knocked on the front, sir," said Macauley. "They did not take kindly to my suggestion that you would like to speak to them. They do not understand much English, sir. They speak French."

At this point, the man whom Richards was holding found his voice. "I protest, sir, I protest. You cannot simply break into my home without a warrant. It is not the English way. What authority do you have?" This outrage was expressed with a distinctly French accent.

"I have every authority, sir. Who might you be?"

"I am le Comte de Fourcoup, sir. I am a guest of the English government, sponsored by Lord Lichgive. And who are you?"

"Captain Sir Richard Giles," replied Giles, surprising himself that he used his title. "I am acting under the orders of

Admiral Gardiner, whose duty it is to protect the English shores and prevent communications with the enemy. I have orders to take you, sir, and any others I find here to the Warden of the Cinque Ports. It seems particularly necessary in view of these treasonable documents that you were trying to burn." Giles thought he might be stretching the Admiral's authority a trifle and that of the Warden, but doing so might strengthen his position.

Only pausing to allow the Comte to don a greatcoat, Giles and Macauley set off with their supporting force, making sure that their prisoners had no chance to escape and that the main captive was well separated from the two they had found trying to escape.

It was only two miles to Walmer Castle. At first, progress was slow as they were still feeling their way through the fog. After thirty minutes, a breeze sprang up from the east and pushed the fog away. Ahead they could see the artillery fortress which had been established by Henry VIII at another time when England's coasts had needed protection.

At the castle, after crossing the moat, they were challenged at the gatehouse and had to wait until an army lieutenant with artillery patches appeared. He directed them to the Warden's lodging. The servant who answered the door led them, after checking with his master, to the breakfast room where the Warden and his long-time crony were finishing their meal.

"What brings you here, Captain Giles?"

"Admiral Gardiner's orders, sir. We have uncovered an espionage conduit for information about our defenses. He thought you would like to see what was discovered. On the way here, we captured, in Deal, the man who, we believe, collects and transmits the information. We brought him along with us."

"Let me examine these documents first."

The Warden started with the papers that Giles had discovered on *Bountiful*. As he read each page, he passed it on to his friend. His expression grew more and more distraught. He then looked at the papers that the Comte had been attempting to burn. These he also examined carefully, though speeding up when their nature became clearer to him so that by the end, he was only skimming over them.

"This is very disturbing, Captain Giles. It is very fortunate that you have been able to intercept these reports. Did your questioning of this Captain Hoxley reveal whether he had delivered earlier reports to France?"

"Yes, sir. He said he had been delivering them for the past six months."

"Damnation. I wonder how we can counter this if we can at all. What do you think of it, David?"

"I am puzzled. I was in Hastings two weeks ago, which is the period the first set of papers claims to cover..." The Warden's friend paused as if in thought.

"Yes?"

"Well, the report about the area between Hastings and Eastbourne – Pevensey Bay and so on – is all wrong. It indicates weak batteries or none at all where they are, in fact, strong or hidden from the sea, and strong defenses where there are virtually none. The strength of the troops posted behind the beaches is too weak since there are, in fact, many more soldiers. Also, this report states that they are militia while they are from a regiment of the line. And so on."

"What about here?"

"Let's see... Yes. The distortion is not as pronounced. But looking at the report in terms of using it to plan a landing would point to the wrong places as being the best sites to come ashore."

"Very interesting. I wonder if these discrepancies occur for the whole coast. You said that you had brought this comte, whom you caught, with you, Captain Giles?"

"Yes, sir."

"Haslet," the Warden addressed the servant who had originally shown Giles into the breakfast room. "Go and fetch the man Captain Giles brought with him. Who is guarding him now, Captain?"

"My lieutenant of marines, Lieutenant Macauley, and a squad of marines, sir."

"Bring Lieutenant Macaulay and a couple of his marines as well, Haslet. Leave the other prisoners behind."

Lieutenant Macauley arrived steering the Comte de Fourcoup by one elbow.

"Well, *Monsieur le Comte*," said the Warden, "this is very disturbing. To find out, after we have given you refuge and welcomed you to our country, that you are a traitor — an agent of the French government. What have you to say for yourself? Why have you done it?"

"I thought I had no choice, sir. Let me explain.

"When the Bastille fell, I was with my regiment in Alsace. We never returned to Paris. We did try to restore the monarchy. When that failed, I fled to England, where I had some resources, and I raised some funds by selling property in Holland. My family was trapped in France. I presumed that they had gone to the guillotine. I settled in Deal, not rich – nothing like what I had in France before the fall of the Bastille – but enough. I thought to return during the Peace of Amiens, but I realized it would be too hazardous.

"After the war resumed, I was visited by a man who represented the French government. He said my wife and daughters were alive and living in Boulogne, where we used to have a townhouse. He presented conclusive evidence. It would be easy to have them denounced and executed, even in these new times with Bonaparte as First Consul. If I didn't want that fate to befall them, I would have to co-operate with him. He said he had recruited others along the English coast to prepare reports on defenses and troops in the area. He needed me to obtain the information for the Deal area myself and collect their findings from some other people along the coast. I felt I had to agree. I could not sacrifice my family. The French agent left two men to make sure that I did not report his visit to the authorities."

"So, did you collect the information?"

"Yes. I am lucky enough to have a horse. No one pays any attention to me since I have been in Deal for so long. My contact gave me ways to recognize the others and a password to use to introduce myself. There are only five of us. I met with each of the others. Their stories are much the same as mine, though I think some of them are eagerly assisting on account of the money that was also promised. We were not all able to save as much as I could from the debacle."

"So you can identify the others?"

"Yes. Anyway, I went to meet each of them and started to collect their reports. One of them, the Conte d'Outrefort, who lives near Hastings, balked at giving accurate information. He was willing to risk the danger to his family of preparing a somewhat fictitious report. He altered his reports in ways that would be plausible, especially if these spies had other sources of information, but that would give a misleading idea of where it would be best for an invasion force to land. His daring may be helped by the fact that he is not devoted to his wife. He already knew that his wife has not been faithful and that the children are not his. He felt that providing false information might serve just as well as accurate information for getting them spared. I decided to take the same approach. I know that providing the reports at all was wrong and not denouncing the people who were recruiting us, but I couldn't condemn my family to certain death by refusing. So now you know it all. I expect you will hang me."

"Probably, but, first, I want more information. Haslet, ask Lieutenant Oxley of the garrison to come and take charge of the prisoners. Captain Giles, we are all indebted to you for bringing this matter to light. I will give you a letter for Admiral Gardiner with suggestions about actions he might want to take – I cannot give him orders, but I hope he will see the wisdom of my suggestions. I will just be a moment. I would be grateful if you can delay your return to your ship while I write the note. I had hoped to have a word with you sometime soon about Dipton, but it will have to wait for another time."

Giles found himself and his men unceremoniously ushered into a waiting room by Haslett. In minutes he was given the Warden's letter and was on his way. He was back on *Impetuous* well before the afternoon watch had ended and was able to sail almost at once. He felt a strong sense of loss and disappointment. He had seemed so close to matters of great and exciting import, and now he was back to his more routine activities as a frigate captain. He could only hope that Admiral Gardiner would have orders for him that would engage his talents.

Chapter VI

Daphne slept in. She awoke only when Elsie threw back the curtains to let in the first rays of the sun. The maid came with breakfast, having agreed with Mrs. Darling to delay the time when Daphne was normally woken.

"Elsie, why have you brought breakfast? I am not sick."

"No, my lady. I thought that that was how you would want to have breakfast now. I asked Mr. Steves and Mrs. Wilson, and they both said that the practice of married women was to have breakfast in bed, while unmarried ladies usually had it in the breakfast room."

"Is it? I didn't know. I don't like having breakfast in bed. I would rather be up and dressed before eating. No, no, Elsie. It's not your fault; you did what you thought best. Don't cry. And I will have breakfast in bed this once. We both have a lot to learn about the ways of married ladies, I guess. But I am not going to start doing silly things just because it is expected."

Elsie had hardly started laying out her mistress's riding clothes when Daphne set her tray aside and slid out of bed. She wanted to get on with things, not sit in bed where she might start to mope about being separated from her husband. Her appearance, so quickly after her tray had gone up, startled Steves. He was further disconcerted when she marched off to the stables to get her horse harnessed and saddled. He would have expected her to wait for the order that she needed the horse to be taken to the stables and the horse, when ready, brought up to the Hall for her to mount. Elsie whispered to him that Lady Giles would not even have thought it was necessary to have Steves arrange for the horse and that, in future, she would try to warn him if her mistress instructed her to layout riding clothes or came down to breakfast in them. However, Elsie thought that it might be best for Mr. Steves just to wait for the order. Lady Giles might well enjoy seeing what was happening in the stables before going riding. Mr. Steves shouldn't expect Lady Giles to be like any other mistress he had ever served, but she was sure that Mr. Steves would find that her ladyship was easier to serve.

Daphne spent the morning examining the four fields that her father had given to Giles as her dowry. She had not heard anything about her dowry before her marriage and had been so swept off her feet by Captain Giles that she had not thought to ask her father about what sort of a dowry he might be providing for her. When Giles told her about her father's gift, after they were already married, she discovered that the two men had spent some time bargaining over it, but not in the usual sense. Mr. Moorhouse thought his daughter should have a very substantial dowry reflective both of his own status and of the high value he placed on her. Giles had been equally adamant that he valued Daphne for herself and wanted no dowry. They had compromised on the transfer of property. The fields had become separated from Dipton Hall at some time in the past and acquired by Dipton Manor. Logically, especially in terms of improving them and the adjacent land still belonging to Dipton Hall, they should be part of the holdings of Dipton Hall. The two men had agreed that since Daphne would undoubtedly be managing both farms for the foreseeable future, the transfer would make for no change in fact, and the wishes of each man would be satisfied. Giles preferred to think of the fields as a wedding present from Daphne's father and not as her wedding portion*.

Daphne was delighted with the present. She had left improving the remote fields of Dipton Manor until the rest of her projects were underway since she knew that she would have to persuade both Captain Giles and her father that the work needed to be undertaken. Now she had been given the go-ahead, and she couldn't resist the temptation to survey the situation and talk to people who were more intimately acquainted with the ground. This took all day – Daphne was far too enthusiastic about what she was doing to stop for lunch – and she arrived at Dipton Manor just in time to have tea with her father. She then went home to change and have dinner with Lady Marianne and her daughters.

The meal was excruciatingly boring. Neither Lady Marianne nor either of her daughters had any conversation, at least none when they were with Daphne, and they showed no interest in accounts of Daphne's activities either in Dipton or in Brighton or in Portsmouth. In addition, they did not seem to be much interested in what news Daphne might have gathered about happenings in Dipton during her absence while she was visiting various people around the estate. Things were no better in the drawing-room after the meal, and when Daphne suggested that Catherine demonstrate the new piano-forte, all that was revealed was that, while the tone of the instrument was excellent, the performance revealed a lack of practice. Daphne escaped immediately after the demonstration to her room, and she, and therefore Elsie, enjoyed an early night.

The next day was much the same, though Daphne was concentrating on other parts of the joint estates. The only surprise was to learn that two ladies had called on her while she was out. One was Mrs. Butler. The other was Mrs. Oxley, the wife of a rather prominent landowner far enough from Dipton not to be part of the immediate Dipton community, though Daphne had heard that Mrs. Oxley was good friends with some of the grander Dipton families. The Oxleys had been at the ball that had been held at Dipton Hall before Daphne married, and they had been explicitly asked to the wedding. That might account for Mrs. Oxley wanting to make the usual *pro forma* visit to a new bride. Until she saw the visiting cards, Daphne had quite overlooked the possibility that, as the new wife of Captain Giles, she would be treated to such visits almost immediately after her return to Dipton.

The next day brought more cards of visitors whom she had missed by being away from the Hall. Daphne realized that having visitors calling on her unexpectedly might be a pattern for a while, and she did not want to snub anyone. She decided to stay home in the mornings. There were a lot of paper records concerning Dipton Hall to be examined. She had never felt the need to see them when she was managing the property as a stop-gap measure until Captain Giles could make more permanent arrangements for his estate. She had already squelched the belief, held by her father's bailiff and steward, that figures and calculations were beyond the grasp of women and especially of ladies. She had a flair for seeing what the dry numbers in ledgers and account books showed about what was going on and nipping any larceny in the bud. She would be doing the same things now for Dipton Hall.

Her immediate need was to have somewhere to examine the accounts. She thought of what she knew of the rooms of Dipton Hall and realized that she was not familiar with them at all. That could be easily changed. She explored the myriad of rooms on the ground floor. She hadn't realized how many there were or how sparsely furnished they were. The rooms were, in fact, waiting for the mistress of the house to decide on how they were to be used or, more likely, to get the advice of some house-arranger who then would furnish the rooms with only minimal input from the owner. That was not Daphne's way. She would take advice, but any decision would be hers! However, she would wait until her husband could be consulted before furnishing the rest of the house; she had to make sure that he thought of it as his, not as her house.

For the time being, she needed only a table and chair. However, she found on consulting Steves that even this minimal amount of furniture would be very difficult to obtain immediately. Apparently, Mr. Edwards had arranged only for furniture that would be required when the hall was occupied by Lady Marianne with a minimal amount for Captain Giles so that his taste could determine more accurately the rest of the furnishings. Daphne could, of course, start completing the furnishings she needed, but, right now, she required a table and chair for what would be her workroom. She decided that it would be best to forego the table that Steves offered from below stairs, largely because she suspected that it was Steves' own table that would be brought upstairs for her use. Instead, she dispatched two footmen and a horse-cart to Dipton Manor with a note for her father, knowing that he had several tables whose only function currently was to fill empty space.

Daphne decided that, since she couldn't yet examine the accounts, it would be a good idea to spend the time before luncheon at the piano. She needed to keep up her skills, indeed improve them, now that she played not only for her own enjoyment but, whenever possible, in duets with her husband. He kept assuring her that captains had nothing much to do on board ship so he could play his instrument regularly.

She had hardly started with some of the supremely boring exercises, which she was assured would improve the nimbleness and accuracy of her playing, when Steves announced that some more visitors had arrived. They turned out to be Lady Laura Dimster and her two daughters, Sophie and Deborah. Lady Dimster's husband, Sir Thomas, was a baronet with an estate about eight miles from Dipton, but the roads were such that it required a considerably longer journey to travel between them by coach. Sir Thomas's title went back to some service his Grandfather had provided to King George I. Exactly what that service was had been lost in time. Sir

74

Thomas's estate featured a rather pleasant house built at about the time the Dimster ancestor had been awarded the hereditary title, and it was said that its value, or maybe that of the incumbent, had been slipping in recent years. This latter information came from common gossip in the neighborhood: as far as Daphne could remember, she had never met Sir Thomas and Lady Dimster. They had certainly never visited her former home of Dipton Manor.

Daphne told Steves when he announced that visitors were at the door to suggest to Lady Marianne and her daughters that they might wish to join the visitors. The three women trooped in just after the initial greetings had been exchanged, neither side indicating that they had never been introduced to the other on previous occasions. Conversation was for a time distinctly sticky, there being only so much that one could find of pressing interest in the late autumn weather, but it picked up considerably when Lydia Crocker made reference to the ball that had been held at Dipton Hall. Somehow, the four young ladies gathered at one end of the room while the older or married ladies continued to occupy the other. Lady Dimster commented that they had not been fully aware of the ball at Dipton and so had not attended. Possibly the invitation had gone astray. Daphne, who was well aware that the invitation had not been received because it had not been sent, regretted that news that the ball had been open to all had not reached the Dimsters. Lady Dimster somehow indicated that she was particularly interested in the ball since she had heard that there had been a countess and a knight of the Order of the Bath in attendance. Lady Marianne was happy to inform her that the countess was her stepmother and, so, could be expected to grace Dipton Hall frequently in the future and that the knight was indeed her own brother.

When Daphne inquired about Lady Dimster's sons, the news was somewhat more interesting. Lady Dimster's older son, Thomas, had just been sent down from Cambridge for some offense that her ladyship most certainly had no intention of detailing. Sir Thomas was talking of buying him a captaincy in a fashionable regiment to keep him occupied until the time came for him to inherit the estate. Lady Dimster's younger son, Robert, was in Lincoln's Inn, articling to become a barrister. He would likely be home at Christmas time.

Daphne had never met either of Lady Dimster's sons and had asked only as a way to keep the conversation going. However, her ears picked up at the information about them. Here, indeed, were two very eligible young men who might be enticed by a suitable dowry to wed a granddaughter of an earl. She was starting to appreciate the dilemmas that faced the mothers of young ladies. They were typically domiciled in the country, and few of them would go to London for the season, while the corresponding young men were away and could only be caught at infrequent holidays or, possibly, very special occasions such as a ball that would induce them to return to their homes.

Her thoughts were interrupted by Lady Dimster's preparing to leave and mentioning that she would be delighted to have Lady Giles dine with them, possibly accompanied, in the absence of her husband, by her brother-in-law, Lord David. Daphne, feeling like a complete fraud, graciously indicated that she would be pleased to accept such an invitation, on her part based solely on the consideration that she could have a reverse visit that should include at least one of Lady Dimster's sons. Daphne wished that she knew more about the etiquette of inviting people to dine. Would she be expected to do so after she dined with them, and what interval should she allow to elapse before she could issue the invitation? She wished Captain Giles were here because he would know the answers, but she couldn't put that sort of an inquiry into a letter. What was really the case was that she just wished that her husband were there; she was still not used to thinking of him as Richard, even though she missed him with every bone in her body.

Daphne had only just sat down at the piano again when Steves announced the next callers. These were two gentlemen whose names were familiar to her, though she thought they had never been introduced to her. Their residences were on the other side of Ameschester, she knew. They must be prominent in society in the area for her to be aware of who they were. Why in the world could they be calling on her?

Her visitors had come with a purpose. Mr. Edward Summers and Major Ralph Stoner started by offering their congratulations on Daphne's wedding and to express their pleasure that Sir Richard and Lady Giles had settled in Dipton, their only regret being that it was not closer to their own estates. This was followed by comments on what a splendid house was Dipton Hall and, when that topic was exhausted, how the weather had been quite favorable for the time of year. The visitors then got down to the purpose of their visit.

"We are here in connection with the Hunt, the Ameschester Hunt. I am sure that you have heard of it," said Mr. Summers.

Daphne acknowledged that she had.

"It is one of the best hunts in the county," Mr. Summers continued.

"Very good sport! Very good sport, indeed!" added Major Stoner. "Very best people, too!"

"We were hoping that you might host one of our meetings," continued Mr. Summers.

"Yes. Splendid country for a hunt around here. Absolutely splendid, I say!" declared Major Stoner.

"You may know that old Gramley was not sympathetic to the hunt. Wouldn't even let us ride over his land."

"Damn shame! Terrible! What was the matter with the man? I have even heard that he instructed his gamekeeper to kill foxes. Can't have a good hunt if the landowners do that," pronounced the Major. He was single and often forgot to guard his tongue in the presence of ladies. His commission had been in one of the regiments in India, and it was said that he had returned to England very enriched. That sufficed to make him welcome in houses where his manners might not.

Daphne knew that her father had given the Ameschester Hunt permission to ride over his fields and woodlands, but she had never known him to participate himself. Apparently, old Mr. Gramley had gone farther.

"I am sure that Captain Giles would not object to the Hunt riding over our lands," said Daphne.

"We had more than that in mind, my lady," said Mr. Summers.

"You know, meeting point for the start of the hunt at a Great House, stirrup cups. All those things! Make for a great hunt!" elaborated Major Stoner.

"We also thought that you might be able to host the Hunt Dinner. It is, of course, men only, but your brother-in-law might be able to play host if Captain Sir Richard has to be at sea. There are, of course, no women."

"Don't women ride in the hunt?" Daphne asked.

"A few do, but not many."

"Damned dangerous for a woman! Riding side-saddle! Can't keep up! I wouldn't try taking a jump riding side-saddle myself. Damned dangerous! Women are better following the hunt in carriages if they want to participate in the hunt. Much more suitable!" sputtered the Major.

"I see," ruminated Daphne. "Women can ride if they want to but cannot attend the dinner?"

"Of course they cannot. It has always just been men."

"Quite right, too," said the Major. "Not suitable for women! Not at all!"

"I suppose not. But I am afraid that Lord David cannot take Captain Giles's place as head of the household for such an exclusive dinner. I will have to ask Captain Giles, of course, but I would not be surprised if he was reluctant to have the Hunt at all when he may not be able to be present. I know he doesn't want to do things halfway. If it was a more normal dinner, I imagine that I could be the hostess, but without that, I very much doubt that Captain Giles would allow the Hunt here."

"I quite understand, Lady Giles," said Mr. Summers, who most certainly did not. "Actually, the Hunt Dinner was only mentioned in passing. We sometimes hold the dinners in an inn if no suitable House is available. What I most wanted to inquire about is the Hunt Ball. Of course, women would not be excluded from that."

"I should think not! Can't have a ball without women! What a notion!" Major Stoner agreed.

"Yes. We do very much hope that you can see your way clear to hosting the Ball. Actually, the Ameschester Hunt has never had a ball."

"Damn shame," contributed the Major.

"Quite. There is no Great House in the area that could hold one except, of course, Dipton Hall, and the ball would occur too early in the year to hold it outside, so we have had to do without a ball all these years. The assembly hall in Ameschester really isn't suitable for a very special occasion. Having a hunt ball would certainly elevate the reputation of the Ameschester Hunt to what it should be. We have suffered in others' eyes for never having held one. Of course, unlike the hunt, or the balls at the Assembly Halls, the ball is not for just anyone. By invitation only you know."

"Quite right!" commented the Major. "One would want only the right sort of person at *our* Hunt Ball. Not that you need a ball to be a first-class hunt. It doesn't require a ball to elevate a hunt. Good terrain, not stopped by difficult landowners, and well-kept woods so that a fox can be started and started early. Not having a fox is far more serious than not having a ball," proclaimed Major Stoner.

"The ball would be a splendid contribution to the neighborhood," Mr. Summers added. "It would certainly establish Captain Giles as the leading figure."

Daphne had to hold back her immediate retort that Captain Giles was already the leading figure, and he had no need to hold a ball to curry favor from anyone. In any case, she already had experience holding a ball, and a hunt ball could not be much different. With its special prestige, a hunt ball would draw many young and eligible young men back to the area. She was secretly astonished how much the need to find husbands had entered her thoughts when earlier it had been one of the last things she was concerned about, but, of course, she had not had earlier the problem of getting the Crocker sisters and their mother married off, and she had not been eager to marry herself.

"Hosting the Hunt Ball might well be possible, Mr. Summers," Daphne declared. "Of course, I shall have to ask Captain Giles, and I don't know how long it may take for my letter to reach him and his reply to arrive at Dipton. His frigate is, as I am sure you know, engaged in the war with France, and neither his time nor his location is at his own choosing."

"Damn important service, ma'am, damn fine! Terribly important!" sputtered the Major.

"I quite understand," said Mr. Summers. "That is why we thought it wise to visit you so soon after your marriage, even though the Ball would not be held until late in March. Please do convey our respects to Captain Sir Richard when you write." Daphne was amused that Mr. Summers had not picked up on her using the title her husband preferred. She suspected that Mr. Summers was too enamored of the aristocratic title to refer to Captain Giles simply by his family name.

When her guests had departed, Steves told Daphne that her father had sent over a table and some chairs. She rushed into what would now be her own special room to find that her father had picked out the table she had used when studying the accounts for Dipton Manor, together with the chairs which had been in that room as well as some ornaments that she had had scattered around her former space. Her father had also sent a note in which he apologized for not having thought to send them earlier and asking her to dinner that evening. She would have to make sure that he realized that she had only expected a table that would be serviceable, not pieces of prized furniture from her father's home. She would make that clear to him when she went to dinner.

Luncheon with Lady Marianne and her daughters was a much more animated affair than usual. Everyone was excited about the news that they might host the hunt. The even more exciting news that they might have another ball at Dipton Hall was met with unalloyed enthusiasm. It was especially exciting that it might even be the Hunt Ball since that was certain to draw many more young gentlemen from elsewhere, especially London, than even a regular ball could. In none too subtle ways, everyone expressed the most intense desire that Daphne should persuade Captain Giles to hold it.

Lady Marianne recalled happily the hunts that had met at Ashbury Abbey. She was, however, extremely vague about the details and revealed that the Earl had ceased to hold hunt balls before she came out. She had only attended a couple of them elsewhere before all her ties to Ashbury Abbey had been severed and with them invitations to hunt balls. While the conversation had not been as dull as usual when the four women ate luncheon together, Daphne had no better idea of what might be involved in practical terms in having the Ameschester Hunt assemble at Dipton Hall when luncheon finished than when it had started.

Steves, when Daphne consulted him, also had only vague ideas of what would be needed. He had only been in service at townhouses in London where, of course, no hunt met. He would inquire around and try to discover what might be involved in having the hunt start from Dipton Hall. Daphne wasn't hopeful of Steves' learning all the details. She suspected that he would be consulting other butlers in the immediate neighborhood, and none of their houses had hosted the Hunt to her knowledge. However, she could probably deduce the requirements from attending one of the hunts herself. Ladies were allowed to ride, and the hunts themselves required no special invitation.

It was a crisp, sunny, autumn day and Daphne resolved to go for a long walk before returning to her accounts. Elsie had laid out her light blue walking dress, which fell comfortably from the bosom in the French style. It had a white trim at the hem and puffy sleeves. Over it, she wore a short jacket in a rich brown color. For someone who claimed to have no interest in fashion, Daphne had always dressed very elegantly.

The path that Daphne intended to take on her walk led first to the side of the well-kept gray stone Georgian house, where a good view of the red-brick stables could be had. She noticed that one of the stable boys was exercising Dark Paul, the hunter which Mr. Edwards had bought for Captain Giles. He was a handsome black stallion, a little taller than Daphne's own favorite mare, Moonbeam, and very much less placid. Daphne had ridden him a few times and had found him exhilarating, though a bit impractical for her usual trips on estate business because he was too high-spirited.

The Major's dismissive words about women riders in the hunt still rankled Daphne. She would just try to see how difficult it might be to ride a hunter cross-country with a side-saddle. She had ridden in that way for as long as she could remember. Only when she added the management of the estate of Dipton Hall to that of Dipton Manor had she adopted her current practice of riding astride. She ordered the stable boy, whose name was Timothy, to saddle Dark Paul with a side-saddle. He looked very doubtful about the order.

"Don't worry, Timothy. I can handle him. It is, after all, not the first time I have ridden Dark Paul."

"Yes, m'lady." Timothy had no choice but to obey. In moments the side-saddle was in place, and Timothy helped his mistress to mount.

Daphne realized that she seemed to be much higher from the ground sitting on Dark Paul than when she had ridden side-saddle in the past. And he was certainly a lot less placid than her other horses. But she wouldn't back down now.

She set off at a sedate pace, with Dark Paul well under control though he occasionally tossed his head, seemly impatient at not being allowed to run. She moved up to a trot, only to remember that trotting was much more difficult and uncomfortable when she couldn't post in the way she had become accustomed to while riding astride. So she turned the horse into a field and moved up to a canter. There was a small ridge of gorse ahead, and Daphne decided to see how it would be if she tried to jump Dark Paul. She turned him toward the barrier and gave him his head. He took the jump without difficulty or pause. Daphne found the jump hugely exciting, though she resolved that she would wear a quilted petticoat under her skirt, maybe two, if she rode this way again. She already envisioned herself joining the hunt in a scarlet, swallow-tailed coat and a buff skirt. She was slim enough that the extra padding would not make her look too unfashionably rounded.

This riding and jumping were not too difficult, and she was having great fun. She guided Dark Paul onto a slightly more challenging jump, and again he sailed across with his rider feeling increasingly confident as she maintained her seat without difficulty. A third jump, more challenging yet, was also negotiated without problem. Daphne was now fully confident of her ability. This would show that arrogant Major! She would do one more jump before heading back to Dipton Manor. To her left, down a gentle slope, there was a low hedge with the ground rising behind it. That would be ideal.

Daphne turned Dark Paul towards the point where she had decided to jump the hedge and set him in motion. He loved to run, and in moments they were rushing towards the hedge. He would have no trouble jumping the obstacle. The motion set her heart racing. This was magnificent!

Dark Paul soared over the hedge with no hesitation. On the other side, the ground was soft with clumps of gorse and juniper. Dark Paul's sudden arrival set off a grouse, which had been straight in front of him. The bird rose in a thrashing of wings, seeming to head straight towards them. Dark Paul swerved abruptly to his right, still going full speed. Daphne slid right off the saddle. She landed on her backside in some marshy land. She rolled, banging her elbow and somehow twisting her ankle. In trying to rise, she slipped, and when she again was able to rise, at last, she could feel a large smear of mud on her cheek. Surveying the situation, she saw that her hat was lying in a puddle, and her gloves were soaked. Her right knee hurt, and when she examined it, she found that her skirts and petticoats had not prevented her skinning it. She presumed that Dark Paul would have taken off when he had been startled. Instead, he was grazing a hundred feet off, obviously waiting patiently for his mistress to think of something else ridiculous to do.

Daphne started towards him. Her ankle could bear her weight and indeed seemed to improve with each step. When she had reached the horse, she realized that she had no chance of mounting him. She would have had difficulty with a regular saddle with stirrups, for they would probably be too high for her to mount without a mounting block. Of course, there was no block where she was and no one to help her up, and of course, this was a side-saddle which presumed that the rider would be assisted in mounting.

Across the field, she saw a tree stump near the edge of the wood. She led Dark Paul over to it, but it still was too low for her to mount the horse. Dipton Hall must be at least two miles distant, and she would just have to walk, leading the horse. Blast that Major for inciting her into doing something so stupid!

At the end of the field, they came upon a four-bared gate. After going through the gate, Daphne maneuvered the horse so that he was standing parallel to it, leaving a small gap between the horse and the barrier. Despite being hampered by her skirts – why, oh, why had she not worn her usual riding clothes, which were split down the middle? – she managed to climb to the top of the gate. She was then able to slide on her tummy onto Dark Paul's back. She was lucky that he was not as skittish as she might have expected at this treatment; he didn't try to throw her off. She was able to roll onto the saddle and set Dark Paul walking in the right direction.

Her track back to Dipton Hall ran right through the village. She succeeded in getting past the vicarage and the church without being seen. She was almost at the turn into the drive to Dipton Hall when who should step out of his front gate and turn towards her than Mr. Jackson, the apothecary and Daphne's long-time friend.

"Daphne Moorhouse, or should I say, Lady Giles, what have you been up to? You look an awful sight. Let me help you down. Come into my house."

"I was thrown by Dark Paul."

"Riding a fine hunter side-saddle. Do you have no sense?"

"I had to do it. Major Stoner suggested that it couldn't be done, and I wanted to see if he was right."

"Let's get you cleaned up, and warmed with a good cup of tea."

Mr. Jackson escorted Daphne into his house and through the front part to the kitchen. His cook rallied around, clucking over the state of Daphne's dress and face. She did what she could to clean up Daphne's face and hair and soon had a steaming mug of tea in front of her together with some fresh scones. Mr. Jackson himself insisted on examining Daphne's knee and ankle. The latter was a bit swollen, but Mr. Jackson's careful fingers could find no sign of more serious damage. He cleaned her knee, rubbed some sort of salve on it, and bandaged it. All the while, he was muttering about Daphne's stupidity, even as she related in more detail what had inspired her to such foolishness.

There wasn't much Mr. Jackson and his cook could do about Daphne's clothes and hair. He helped her onto her horse, and, before she set off, he said, "I hope you have learned from this escapade that elegant ladies and riding to hounds do not go together."

That wish rekindled all of Daphne's annoyance with Major Stoner. "I most certainly am going to ride in the next hunt," she declared, "and on Dark Paul."

"You'll break your silly neck, Daphne," retorted Mr. Jackson, "and that is one ailment I cannot fix."

Daphne had hoped to escape to her room without being seen by Lady Marianne or her daughters when she reached Dipton Hall. That was not to be. Just as she reached the landing on her way to her room, Lady Marianne and her daughters appeared at the top of the stairs. They pretended not to notice Daphne's disheveled state, but before she reached the top of the stairs, Daphne heard the unmistakable twitter of giggles coming from the two young ladies. Blast that Major and his vulgar ways! And blast her sister-in-law, who no doubt would be feeling seriously superior! Why she was nothing but the widow of an army captain in a nondescript regiment. He had probably been as uncouth as the Major.

Undoubtedly, Lady Marianne would think that Major Stoner's remarks were not offensive. They were made for each other!

Daphne's muttering stopped abruptly at that thought. Maybe the two were made for each other. He was rich and undoubtedly ill-born. She was penniless though well-born and might be used to men with rough edges. Maybe, just maybe, that might be the solution to her problem.

Elsie insisted that Daphne have a good, hot bath and have her hair washed, even though Daphne protested that she had had one just two days previously. When she had her mistress in the tub, Elsie made sure that all signs of Daphne's adventure disappeared from sight. Her bruises couldn't be fixed so quickly, but they would not be seen. Elsie thought that Daphne should go to bed immediately with dinner on a tray, but her mistress would hear none of it. She had a message sent to her father that she would have to postpone their dinner and warned Steves to delay dinner a bit. She insisted that Elsie arrange her hair, even though it was still damp, into an elegant coiffure and pick out her favorite dinner gown.

Daphne sailed into the drawing room before dinner, looking stunning, not in any way the worse for her afternoon experiences. As she told it, she had been so enthralled by Major Stoner's account of the role of women in the hunt that she had had to see how Dark Paul would serve as her mount. Major Stoner was such a nice man, very knowledgeable about the hunt and women's place in it, very helpful, indeed. Did Lady Marianne and her daughters know that he had served in India? It was said that he had done very, very well for himself before returning to England. Maybe a bit of a diamond in the rough, but such a nice man! Daphne had never seen it, but she understood that he had one of the best houses near Ameschester. But she digressed. Dark Paul had been startled by a grouse and shied away, and Daphne had to confess that she was thinking more about what the Major had said about the hunt than about riding and had slipped off. She would be more alert in future.

This account of Daphne's adventures occupied the time fully until dinner, and the hunt filled the conversation at the table for several dishes. Lady Marianne was sure that she remembered ladies only riding with the hunt until the view-halloo when the gentlemen went pounding away, leaving the women to follow at a more leisurely pace. Of course, the ladies would not want to be in at the kill, though it sometimes happened since foxes were notorious for their ability to turn back and cross their own tracks and thoroughly puzzle the dogs, and so those who had held back might end up at the finish.

Lady Marianne saw no reason why she and her daughters should not join the hunt on their own horses – Daphne uncharitably recalled that they were actually Captain Giles's horses that he was letting them use, though she said nothing to set them straight on the ownership of their mounts. Maybe, continued Lady Marianne, they would encounter the Major there. She realized that it was, of course, not possible for Daphne to invite the Major to dine at Dipton Hall without becoming better acquainted with him. Maybe the next hunt or so would provide the needed better acquaintance.

After dinner, Daphne settled down to write her nightly letter to Giles. It would be a long one, for she needed to inform him about the requests of the Ameschester Hunt, and she wanted to tell him about her other visitors. The account of her afternoon ride on Dark Paul was made even more of a credit to her as well as being more amusing than the one she told her in-laws. In this version, it sounded as if she had slipped off Dark Paul intentionally when he was startled, and the difficulties had arisen only when she tried to mount him again. She did boast of being able to jump him and how exhilarating she had found it.

Chapter VII

Giles was again standing before Admiral Gardiner aboard *Penelope*. The Admiral looked up from the note which the Warden had sent with Giles. "The Warden commends you for your initiative. He also wants me to send him Captain Hoxley and to keep *Bountiful* with me rather than send her into Chatham. I am not sure that the authority of the Warden of the Cinque Ports extends that far, but I think it wise to stay on his good side. I intended to buy *Bountiful* into the Navy in any case. Incidentally, my carpenter says your people did a very good job of repairing her, and she doesn't need to go into drydock immediately.

"Now to business. As you may know, the French are building boats for their invasion. All along the coast from the Texel to Cherbourg. All sorts of craft. To carry infantry, cavalry, supplies, even gunboats. They are trying to gather them together in ports close to the Strait of Dover. Mainly Boulogne, we believe, but also possibly Calais and Dieppe and St. Valery. None of them is a particularly good place to gather large numbers of craft. Boulogne may be the best since it is safest from storms, but it has a very narrow entrance. The French could not get all their craft to sea at all quickly. Bonaparte has massed some divisions behind Boulogne, we know. Indeed it's an army. But in general, our knowledge of what he is planning is not good. Maybe your discoveries will help change that.

"I am trying to disrupt their activities, especially their making the passages from the more eastern ports, where the Dutch are building these craft for Bonaparte, to the French ports from which the invasion would be launched. It is not easy. The coast is shallow, and there are many sandbanks offshore. Those banks are shifting with storms and tides, and there are often deeper passages close to shore along which the boats can move without its being easy for us to get at them. There are also many batteries of guns along the coast to which their craft can scuttle to seek safety from us. Some of the batteries are well-established permanent structures; others just consist of field artillery. Your master can consult our charts about the latest information about where the fortifications are and, of course, other matters concerning the latest news on the hazards on that coast.

"We mainly use smaller ships – sloops, brigs, and so on -- to harass the movements of the landing craft, but recently the French have sometimes sent frigates to guard them, so now we will be using frigates as well. You and *Perseus* will be used in that way. There are two things I want you to do. You are to disrupt the enemy's moving their craft along the coast. Also, you are to try to capture some of each type. Unfortunately, they are of no value to us nor as prizes, but we need to know what the French are building. Some of the ones we have captured in the past were hardly sea-worthy. We are particularly interested in their gunboats – small cockleshells of crafts with heavy guns, apparently to be fired at land establishments behind their landing beaches. Bonaparte was, after all, an artillery officer.

"Those gunboats seem to be particularly important to some of the people in charge of our defenses. Don't know why. They have gone so far as to send an official of the ordinance board to evaluate the guns and the gunships if you can capture any of them. If you cannot, he is to evaluate them from a distance. Foolishness, I think. My officers are perfectly capable of sizing them up. But, be that as it may, you are to take the official and try to accommodate his desires, though, of course, without putting *Impetuous* in any danger. He is a man called Hughes. I believe you have met him."

"Yes, sir. He has been very helpful."

"Amazing. The Ordinance Board should be under the admiralty and not a separate bunch of trouble makers."

"Yes, sir."

"You will have *Swan* both to further harass the French and Dutch, but mainly to convey to me any sightings of major warships who may slip out of the Texel or be coming from elsewhere. Can't trust the Russians or the Prussians not to ally themselves with the French.

"Well, that's it. Good luck. And, Captain Giles, I will not tolerate my ships, who are watching the coast, leaving their stations to chase after prizes. You will only take prizes that fall into your lap, so to speak, without your leaving the coast."

"Aye, aye, sir."

The task set to *Impetuous* was both boring and hazardous. The hazard came from the shallow and shifting nature of the off-shore sand bars, which had claimed many a vessel that had gone aground on them, and the need to stay close to shore even though fog banks were all too frequent. Often, indeed, *Impetuous* had to anchor and wait for the fog to dissipate. Giles could often see convoys of small vessels creeping along beyond the sand bars or in shallower water that prevented his ship from coming close to shore. At places where *Impetuous* might get at the landing craft, shore batteries made it impossible. The convoys were typically guarded at best by small sloops of war. Winds were light and variable. At the end of one long tack, *Impetuous* came up with *Perseus*, and Giles found out that Captain Bush had had no more success in capturing the invasion craft or even in disrupting their progress to the invasion ports. He decided that it was time to change his tactics for carrying out his mission of capturing the vessels.

Near dusk, just as the fog bank was forming again, *Impetuous* crept towards the coast, sounding* continually until she reached a depth that would ensure at least one fathom beneath their keel at low water. At that point, she dropped her anchor. At low tide that night, there should still be six inches of water over the concealed sandbank. Before the fog had obscured the coast, Giles had seen several landing craft creeping along close to the coast. He would try to surprise them and capture a few to satisfy the Admiral's curiosity.

Giles ordered each of Impetuous's boats to be filled with a mixture of marines and seamen. The seamen were armed with cutlasses and pistols and belaying pins*, which Giles suspected might come in handy. The sailors would also have their knives. He himself would go on the expedition, together with Lieutenants Kirkpatrick, Miller, and Macauley, as well as the midshipmen. The fog was so thick that Giles could hardly make out the bow of his barge from the stern. He ordered that the boats proceed in line ahead, with each boat's painter* being attached to the stern of the boat ahead. All oars were to be muffled, and anyone making a noise would have his rum ration canceled the next day.

They set off with Giles's boat in the lead. He was navigating by his compass and had a knotted lead-line going in the bow with the depths whispered back to him. Ten minutes after leaving *Impetuous*, they startled a raft of ducks that took off with a noisy beating of wings. Giles proceeded on the same course until the lead line* suggested that they had crossed the main sandbank and were now definitely in the channel between the bank and the shore. At that point, he turned so that they were rowing with the current. They could hear some muffled voices coming from ahead of them. The sounds increased, and they began to see a yellow glow looming ahead. They must be coming upon some craft where people were talking loudly in a gathering lit by lanterns. As they came near, Giles steered to larboard of the lights. Soon the whispered message was passed to the stern that there were boats ahead. Giles indicated that the rowing stop, and as the boat behind them caught up, he instructed that its crew do the same and pass the word back as each following boat came up. The little flotilla drifted up to the enemy craft ahead, which turned out to be one of the landing craft that they were looking for. It was rafted up* on each side to another boat of the same type. The glow of the lanterns to starboard seemed to be slightly higher than the deck of the landing craft.

Giles whispered that all his other boats were to stay where they were while he took the jolly-boat* to explore. Transferring to the smaller boat, he instructed Mr. Stewart, the midshipman in charge, to stand off from the landing craft until they could hardly make them out and then turn towards the lanterns. When they got near to the source of light, they realized that the illumination and the noise were coming from the waist of a sloop that must have been accompanying the group of landing craft. The sloop could hardly be considered a formidable foe. It probably had no more than six guns and only a small crew. It seemed that the crew of the sloop had assembled with the crews of the landing craft. Judging from the sort of noise that those in the jolly boat heard, the group must have broached a cask of spirits. The light was such that Giles could not make out the sloop's name. Continuing on past the ship, Giles found more landing craft, again with no one on board.

Giles turned back. When he reached the rest of his force, he ordered Lieutenant Miller and half his boats to join him in returning to the far side of the sloop. He instructed Lieutenants Macauley and Kirkpatrick to take the other half of his force across the intervening landing craft until they reached the one next to the sloop. They were to get ready to board the larger vessel and hopefully overwhelm the enemy crew without much trouble, but they were to wait to attack until they heard Giles's forces making a loud noise as they attacked from the other side. If they were discovered by the people on the sloop before that, they should attack immediately.

The jolly-boat set off again, this time accompanied by several other boats. They skirted the stern of the sloop and came back to the raft of ships three craft beyond the gathering on the sloop. The voices they could hear had become louder as time passed and were now interrupted from time to time by snatches of song. Giles assembled his forces. He warned again of the need for silence rather than speed, and then he led them across the intervening craft until they reached the side of their target. It was not so high that they could not easily climb onto the vessel from the gunwale* of the boat they were on. Just as Giles was about to order the attack, one of the men on the sloop came to the side of the sloop to relieve himself, apparently forgetting that it was closely moored to another vessel. Giles immediately yelled at the top of his voice and led the way aboard the sloop knocking the man, whose hands held no weapon, to one side. The sailors charged aboard, and their belaying pins made short work of the startled crews of the landing craft and the sloop. Simultaneously, the force from the other side attacked, also with large noise. In only a minute, all the enemy force were overwhelmed and taken prisoner, the only casualties being several who had received vicious knocks on the head from the belaying pins. They would be unconscious or groggy for some time.

Giles wasted no time in examining the sloop's papers. Now that he had captured the landing craft, he wanted to be away again as soon as possible. He did set some marines to guard the opened casks of liquor which had made the task of taking the sloop so much easier. A search was made of the ship to ensure that no hidden force was about to fall on the invaders. While it was being carried out, Giles had what was left in the casks emptied over the side together with two more that the search of the sloop found. Even with these steps taken, he noticed that several of the seamen, and possibly some of the marines, had succeeded in taking a very stiff drink from the guarded casks.

The landing craft had sweeps as well as single gaff-rigged sails so that even without wind, they could be moved. He would take them over the sandbank, and, when he had returned to *Impetuous* with them, he would evaluate fully just what he had captured. The sloop was a different matter. The obvious thing to do with the ship was to sink her on the spot. But she certainly had some value; indeed, she was the sort of minor war- vessel that was invaluable. No admiral had as many of them as he wanted. But to save her, she would have to be sailed along the coast to one of the channels through the offshore banks, and those openings were guarded by shore batteries. It was worth trying, especially since she could sail under French colors and was likely familiar with the shore batteries as a friendly vessel.

"Lieutenant Kirkwood. You will take command of the sloop. You may have Mr. Stewart with you."

"Aye, aye, sir. But how do I get her out of here? She cannot cross the bar, I believe."

"No. Of course not. You will have to wait for the fog to clear – or at least to be thin enough so that you can make out the coast. Then take her to one of the passes through the banks, whichever one is easiest to use at the time, based on wind and current."

"The passes, sir?"

"Yes. You did study the chart that Mr. Brooks laid out of this area, as I told you to, did you not?"

"Yes, sir." In fact, Mr. Kirkpatrick had only glanced at the chart, being sure that the whole venture that the captain had planned was a fool's errand, and he would have no need of any special knowledge.

"Those are the passages through the banks that are guarded by the more substantial shore batteries, are they not, sir?" Mr. Stewart piped up.

"Quite right, Mr. Stewart."

Kirkwood, for once, was glad of the midshipman's help, even though he regarded the remark as just another of the brown-noser's irritating efforts to ingratiate himself with the Captain. Well, he would give the boy enough to keep him on his toes while he was commanding the lad!

Giles proceeded to have the landing craft unrafted from each other. One of them, a miserable thing that had already half-filled with water from not being bailed while its crew caroused, he loaded with the captured sailors and told them to make their way ashore. A bit of a wind had sprung up, and the fog was starting to thin, but it was still too thick to navigate by anything but the compass and lead line. The moon had risen, and some of its rays were making the fog about them glow, but it was still too thick even to tell exactly where the moon might be.

Giles wanted to be across the bar before dawn, for he had no idea what other forces might be anchored near him or had ventured along the coast even in the fog. He did not have nearly enough officers to have one in charge of each of the craft, but he had plenty of experienced sailors who would have no trouble taking the boats over the bank and then to *Impetuous*. After telling the captives in the sinking craft to get ashore as best they could, Giles had his flotilla set off. They crossed the bar without any of the vessels grounding and turned to where they expected *Impetuous* to be. The wind strengthened, and, by good fortune, it was such that *Impetuous* should be downwind from them, which eased the effort needed to propel the boats. Giles was just beginning to worry that they might have passed his frigate unseen when the fog lifted to reveal *Impetuous* only half a cable away.

Giles wanted to get away from the coast as far and as fast as he could with the hope that the French would not be able to see just what he had captured. He had *Impetuous* raise her anchor and under a breeze that was increasing and becoming less fluky headed out to sea, trailed by his collection of landing craft. The fog bank remained between *Impetuous* and the coast, and after a couple of hours, he reckoned that it was time to examine his catches. They turned out to be a miscellaneous collection. As if to confuse the orders the Admiral had given, all the craft had single guns, from small field pieces on some to mammoth twenty-four pounders on two of them.

Similarly, they seemed to be designed for different tasks. The most lightly armed appeared to be either supply transports or infantry conveyances, the only difference being how easy it might be to scramble over their bows to get ashore. A third type was clearly designed to carry horses, having crude stalls for the animals. Whether they were for cavalry horses or draft horses could not be determined from their design. The fourth type of craft seemed to be gunboats; whether they were designed to fire at shore defenses or to engage ships that might interfere with an invasion was not clear from looking at them. All the boats were flat bottomed and sailed poorly. And each of them leaked copiously even though the waves were minimal.

Giles didn't have the men to send all the captured boats back to Admiral Gardiner without leaving *Impetuous* badly under-manned. He resolved to take the two heavy gunboats and select one each of the other three types. Since the only things of value on these craft were their guns, lightweight though they were, he resolved to transfer the guns arming the vessels he would not be keeping onto the ones he would take to the Admiral. Mr. Hughes helped immensely in that task, being much more knowledgeable than Giles on how to move guns in awkward circumstances. They were engaged in this task when the schooner under the command of Lieutenant Kirkpatrick appeared. She was limping along without her foremast, with a weird jury-rig on which not very appropriate sails were hung. She had obviously been under fire. Giles remembered hearing distant canon fire some time earlier, though he had not related it to his prize. He still didn't know the name of the vessel.

When the guns, together with their powder and shot, had all been transferred, Giles ordered Mr. Milton to sink the dozen extra landing craft that they were not going to take to Admiral Gardner. After that order was given, Giles could turn his attention to Mr. Kirkpatrick, who had just come aboard.

"What happened to you, Mr. Kirkpatrick?" Giles greeted the lieutenant.

"Sir, we raised anchor as soon as the fog thinned enough to see the shoreline. We ran down the coast until the point at which we needed to turn to seaward. The shore battery was silent, so the officers must have recognized us as one of the usual French vessels they had seen before. We turned to seaward, but Mr. Stewart ran us aground. Hard aground. We were still in range of the battery, and, before we could get off, the enemy opened fire. One of their shots hit the foremast. There is also considerable damage to the larboard side, some between wind and water*. I was able to get the ship off the sandbank and arrange for the jury-rigging."

"Arrange for it?"

"Yes, sir. I gave the order but left the implementation of the details to Mr. Stewart. I thought it would be good for him, sir."

"And the damage between wind and water?"

"We did not have a carpenter, sir. Only a carpenter's mate. And no supplies. I reckoned that it would be best to wait until we came up with *Impetuous*."

"You say that Mr. Stewart ran you aground."

"Yes, sir."

"How was that possible?"

"He had the watch, sir. It is all in my log."

"I see. Where is Mr. Stewart now?"

"He is still in the sloop, sir."

"What is her name?"

"I didn't have an opportunity to discover it, sir."

"Did you bring your log?"

"Yes, sir. Here it is."

"Very good. Mr. Kirkpatrick. I need to see Mr. Stewart. What you tell me is very serious! Please return to the sloop and send Mr. Stewart here. You must remember that Mr. Stewart has only been at sea a few months. And anyway, it was your duty to make sure that the rigging was in good order. You cannot set a midshipman to a task for a lieutenant without providing adequate supervision. Remember that in future. I'll send the carpenter with you to see what can be done to repair the damage quickly. And find out her name, Mr. Kirkpatrick. You can hardly command a vessel whose name you don't know."

"Aye, aye, sir."

Mr. Kirkpatrick turned away from the Captain to return to the prize, but not before Giles was able to spot a smirk of self-satisfaction cross his face. If the lieutenant thought he had transferred the responsibility from himself to the midshipman, he was sorely mistaken.

Mr. Stewart was soon in front of Giles. His story was quite different from Mr. Kirkpatrick's. He had indeed been given the order to direct the ship's progress when they turned to seaward, Mr. Kirkpatrick having said that the experience would do him good. The lieutenant had even relied on him to pick the appropriate spot to turn seaward. Yes, he had ordered the turn when Mr. Kirkpatrick had made no indication of when to turn. The lieutenant had not overruled him at that point. It was only when Mr. Stewart said that they should turn to larboard for the dogleg in the channel that Mr. Kirkpatrick had overruled him. Mr. Kirkpatrick said he knew of no dogleg, even though it had been clearly shown on the chart. Mr. Kirkpatrick said that he didn't recall there being a dogleg and said that the depth soundings they were taking indicated no reason to turn and that turning would expose them more to the shore guns. They had run aground soon after that. While Mr. Kirkpatrick was railing against the midshipman for running them aground, Mr. Stewart had had their anchor taken out to starboard, and they were able to pull the sloop off. It was while they were doing that that the fort opened fire and hit their mast. On orders from the lieutenant, Mr. Stewart had arranged the jury rig. Looking at it from the deck of *Impetuous*, Mr. Stewart said, "It's not very good, is it, sir?"

"No, it isn't. But I am sure that you did your best. Now, Mr. Stewart, you mentioned that you were doing something to determine the depth of water."

"Yes, sir. I found a lead line in the commander's cabin onboard *l'Avanture* and suggested to Mr. Kirkpatrick that we use it to get the depth. Mr. Kirkpatrick ordered an ordinary seaman into the chains to take soundings."

"Which seaman?"

"Daly, sir."

"Daly. He is an ordinary seaman, only recently rated that highly. I don't believe that he has ever taken soundings before. Did Mr. Kirkpatrick adjust for the fact that a French lead line may not be the same as one of ours?"

"Isn't it, sir? No, Mr. Kirkpatrick made no mention of that to Daly when he was sending him into the chains. Do the French not use fathoms in the same way that we do?"

"No, they don't. The knots are different distances from each other. What did Daly call out before you grounded?"

"Three fathoms, sir."

"I see ... Thank you, Mr. Stewart. You may return to *l'Avanture*."

Giles was not happy. In his previous command, he had been saddled with a first lieutenant who had more faults than virtues. Luckily, he had been able to trick that man into abandoning his commission. He couldn't expect such luck with Mr. Kirkpatrick, but a feckless second lieutenant could do a great deal of damage. He would have to think about how to minimize it without destroying the respect – at least the nominal respect – that his crew must show to their officers. He suspected that the crew already knew about Mr.

Kirkpatrick, though his behavior had not come to be such an issue that Carstairs had felt compelled to inform him.

Mr. Milton and Mr. Hughes had finished transferring the guns to the craft they would keep. Giles's next worry was what to do about the fifteen boats he was not going to keep. They seemed to be flat bottomed craft with no keels. He suspected that, even if they filled with water, they would not sink. He could just chop large holes in their bottoms so that they would fill with water, but even if this meant that they could not be rescued and repaired by the French, he was reluctant to leave such hazardous flotsam. Especially not in an area where he could expect *Impetuous* to cruise again. Any of the craft, wretched though they were, could cause serious damage if a ship ran into one of them, especially if it had filled with water but not sunk.

He mentioned his dilemma to Mr. Hughes when the artillery expert came to report the successful transfer of all the guns.

"Why don't you blow them up?" Mr. Hughes asked. "You can use some of the barrels of gunpowder we found with the guns. I can do it if you would like me to. Since the gunpowder has not been entered into your stores, you won't be charged for it. In any case, I cannot testify to its quality, so we might as well dispose of the barrels."

Giles told Mr. Hughes to proceed with his suggestion. If there was anything his crew enjoyed, it was seeing other ships blown up, and a series of fifteen explosions would be almost as much fun as an extra tot of rum.

The breeze was freshening. Giles ordered *Impetuous*'s anchor to be raised, and the little convoy set off to meet Admiral Gardener's fleet. The flat-bottomed craft made almost as much leeway as headway, so the broad reach which *Impetuous* was maintaining became a close reach for the others. *L'Avanture* was sailing hardly better. Giles saw through his telescope that Mr. Stewart was trying to improve the jury rig, aided, Giles suspected, by suggestions from Humphries, while Mr. Kirkpatrick seemed to be strolling about the quarter-deck giving the odd order to the helmsmen. The warning he had been given apparently had fallen on deaf ears.

The wind veered so that the landing craft could no longer make their course. Giles decided to tow the small vessels instead of having them sail themselves. This also relieved somewhat the problem that their seams were starting to work as the waves increased and they began to leak more seriously. Even dragging the five craft behind her, *Impetuous* was in danger of out-sailing *l'Avanture*, whose jury rig looked better and stronger than it had been but could not make up for the loss of her mast. Progress continued to be painfully slow, even as the wind increased. The craft being towed were leaking fast enough that their crews were kept busy pumping them. After another hour, the crews of the two large gunboats reported that they could not keep up with the water coming in and that they were afraid that their craft might break up.

Impetuous hove to. Giles was annoyed that a signal to *l'Avanture* had to be followed by bellows through the speaking horn before she too backed a sail to hold her in place. What in the world did Kirkpatrick think he was doing?

A quick survey by the bosun and Mr. Hughes established that they were most unlikely to bring the two gunboats safely to the fleet. With their guns on board, they would undoubtedly sink, and, even without them, it was doubtful that they could be rescued. Both Giles and Hughes were reluctant to abandon the twenty-four-pound cannon that each one carried. Each was hauled alongside *Impetuous*, and the ordinance expert demonstrated his skill in dealing with the monstrous twenty-four pounders by having them and their carriages lifted aboard *Impetuous.*

"Now, where do you suggest that we stow* these guns?" Giles asked Mr. Milton when the first of the cannon was safely on board.

"The aft hold would be best, sir, for the ship's trim," replied the First Lieutenant, among whose tasks was ensuring that supplies were used and repositioned in the order that best kept the ship floating evenly.

"Captain Giles," interposed Mr. Hughes. "I don't suppose that you would consider using them as bow-chasers."

"After what happened to *Patroclus,* Mr. Hughes? *Impetuous* does not even have the special strengthening needed to fire such guns."

"I talked to your carpenter, Mr. Evans, about that, Captain Giles. He thought that the reinforcing could be done quite easily. The problem would be lessened, he pointed out, because it would be possible to have the recoil extend quite a bit farther than was possible on *Patroclus,* so there would be less of a jolt when the gun reaches the end of its restraining tackle."

"And what would you do with the long-nines that are the present bow chasers?'

"Might I suggest using them for stern chasers, sir?"

"Go ahead with the changes. I don't know how happy the Admiral will be about this use of the captured guns when he finds out about it, but that is a problem for another day."

With the guns safely on board *Impetuous,* Giles swung himself over the side to inspect the second gunboat. Without its burden, it swam higher, and the pressures should not be such as to have the boat break up. It would still need constant pumping. Giles decided to continue towing the gunship landing craft with the others.

The wind ceased rising, and they made adequate progress so that at six bells of the afternoon watch, they spotted the lead ship of Admiral Gardiner's fleet. They came up with the flagship as daylight was beginning to fade into dusk.

Giles went aboard the flagship immediately to report to the Admiral. His initial reception was not warm. "Captain Giles. You seem to have trouble obeying orders. I ordered you to stay on station until I gave you orders to leave."

"Yes, sir, but you also ordered me to capture some of the landing craft making their way to the French ports."

"Is that what those miserable vessels, which you are towing, are?"

"Yes, sir. They would not have reached you if they were sailing alone."

"Why not? They do seem to have arrived here safely."

Giles outlined the deficiencies of the craft and the problem with the major gunboats. . The Admiral continued to be skeptical and announced that he would inspect the landing craft himself when there was enough light in the morning.

"Now, tell me about that schooner that accompanies you."

Giles told the Admiral about his capture of the schooner, a tale which also included his first description of the taking of the landing craft. He explained how the schooner was unable to cross the sand bars and so had to seek a channel to the sea. That requirement had put her under the French guns.

"I see," said the Admiral, "but surely the French would not fire on a ship they knew. Didn't she sail under French colors?"

"She did, sir, but she ran aground when she turned to the open sea, at which point the French battery opened fire."

"I guess that anyone could run aground in those waters. Pity. But she is still a valuable prize, I'll give you that."

"It's not quite that straightforward, sir."

Giles went on to recount how Lieutenant Kirkpatrick had tried to shift the blame to Midshipman Stewart because the lieutenant had not properly studied the chart and also how he had not allowed for the possible difference from what he was used to in the lead-line that was used.

"Are you saying that this Mr. Kirkpatrick shirked his duties, Captain?" asked the Admiral.

"I suppose so. There have been other problems with him."

Giles went on to tell about the problem with the gun carriages and why the rig of the schooner was so peculiar.

"I had heard that you had a very poor lieutenant, but I didn't realize it was this bad," commented the Admiral when Giles completed his narration.

"Heard, sir?"

"My coxswain makes a habit of talking with the coxswains of other ships when their captains come aboard the flagship. He picks up a great deal of information that way. No, he reported that your coxswain knew exactly what he was doing and thought it would be a good idea if the deficiencies of your lieutenant were known to me. Kirkpatrick was a client of Old Blazy, wasn't he?"

"I understand so. Apparently, the new Earl is not prepared to advance Mr. Kirkpatrick's career in the same way."

"Good. But you never know when this earl might pick up the strands of his father's spider web. Gad, sir, we can't do without influence, I suppose, but it harms the navy more than would an extra dozen French seventy-fours. Kirkpatrick's is a court-martial offense, you know, but it would be difficult to prove it and to find a court that was not hesitant about convicting a man who may still have powerful interests behind him.

"I'll think about what to do overnight, Captain Giles. I'll see you in the morning."

"Aye, aye, sir."

Giles returned to his barge, where he gave Carstairs a very significant look, one that said that he was not happy with his coxswain and would see him in his cabin shortly. He had hardly reached his quarters, after giving orders about the craft they were towing and their place in the fleet, before Carstairs arrived.

"Carstairs, I really didn't like finding out that the Admiral already knew about Lieutenant Kirkpatrick's weaknesses even before I realized how serious they are."

"Yes, sir."

"Well, what do you have to say for yourself?"

"Sir, there was nothing I could bring to you. Just a feeling among the crew about how Mr. Kirkpatrick avoided his duties. Nothing definite, rather a feeling. I didn't really have anything to bring to you, sir. But I thought it would be a good idea to let the Admiral know that there might be trouble, so he could deal with it promptly if it ever came to him."

"I know you meant well, Carstairs, but, in future, please let me know if there is anything serious enough to alert an Admiral."

"Yes, sir, but I didn't think there was anything you could do about it even if I had told you."

"Not quite true, Carstairs. For one thing, I would not have put Mr. Kirkpatrick in charge of the sloop. I am just lucky that that decision didn't get anyone killed. So, in future, let me be the judge of what I cannot deal with, Carstairs."

"Aye, aye, sir. Oh, sir, Mr. Carrell asked me to give you these."

Carstairs held out a handful of letters that must have been delivered while Giles was with the Admiral. Giles waved him away as he studied his mail. There were several from Daphne, one from his mother and one from Mr. Edwards.

He opened Mr. Edward's letter first, in case it contained some urgent news that he would have to deal with as soon as possible. It did not — just a summary of his financial affairs, revealing that he was even richer than he supposed. The mail from Daphne came next. She had written every day since she had returned to Dipton, and had numbered the letters so that it was easy to get them in order. He read them carefully, savouring every detail that she included. How he wished he could be with her as she went about the estates! How easily she seemed to have mastered the problems and opportunities which they presented.

When Giles came to Daphne's concerns about his nieces, he realized that he had unfairly left his wife to deal with a very awkward situation. He had insisted that Lady Marianne and her daughters live in Dipton Hall, rather than elsewhere, in order to try to keep a better rein on her spending. But now, he saw that he had placed a very unfair burden on his wife. Of course, she had not been his wife when he made the arrangements. Indeed, he had not even known of her existence at that time. How his life had been turned upside down by his meeting her and how happy he was at the change! He had been lucky in his career but far more fortunate in finding the perfect woman with whom to share his life! He'd have to do something about these dowries. What would be a suitable sum? Did Daphne know? He doubted that she did since she had never shown any interest in dowries to his own knowledge, nor had she ever thought how large might be her own. But maybe she did know. He would have to ask her in his next letter. Maybe Mr. Edwards would have the information. Would any of his officers be aware of the proper figure, and could he ask them without their thinking that he was asking how much it would cost him for them to take his half-nieces off his hands?

He continued his reading, reaching Daphne's adventure with Dark Paul. He could well see her riding joyfully on the hunter and pushing the horse to perform more and more exhilarating things. He already knew enough about his wife to guess that the spill she mentioned was more serious than she was making it appear. Should he forbid her hunting on Dark Prince? He knew she would obey, but he didn't want to try to limit her independence. Yes, wives should obey their husbands, but he liked Daphne's adventurous and confident spirit too much to want to curb it. He would just have to delicately point out that Dark Paul was a very large horse, and he was not sure how well trained the creature might be since he had never hunted on the horse himself. Maybe a suggestion that she buy a smaller mount for the hunt? As for hosting the Hunt and the Hunt Ball, he knew that was part of being a prominent landowner; he just wished he could share in the preparations and the event. He wondered idly why Mr. Moorhouse did not hunt. Anyway, he would have to reply to all her questions now so that his letter could be taken to the flagship for sending before *Impetuous* was dispatched on her next task. He had not slept on the previous night, but writing to Daphne was far more important than getting another hour of sleep.

112

Chapter VIII

Daphne woke to find that her hip hurt, her knee was stiff and burned, and her ankle was very sore when she first used it. That would teach her to take stupid risks on a horse! She struggled out of bed when Elsie drew the curtains letting in the weak, gray light that signaled it was just before dawn. She was tempted to return to bed. And why shouldn't she? She was in her own home and could do as she liked. But she didn't really want to lie around in bed, and she didn't want her relatives to think that her fall off the horse, Dark Paul, had incapacitated her.

When Elsie helped her remove her nightgown, and Daphne stood shivering as she waited for the first layer of her clothes, a glance at her hip revealed an extensive, dark-purple bruise. Her ankle looked a bit swollen. She couldn't see her knee since Elsie had renewed her bandage after her bath the previous evening. Even as she got dressed, the stiffness in her ankle and hip seemed to retreat a bit. She might hobble a bit today, but that wouldn't stop her from going about her planned activities. She would just have to stare down any knowing looks from her relatives and any others who had heard of her accident.

Daphne wanted to spend the morning with the accounts and other records for Dipton Hall, but again she was interrupted by visitors. This time it was Mrs. Sandforth from Deepling Hall together with her daughter Penelope. Her husband was a great friend of Daphne's father, and Penelope was one of Daphne's closest friends in Dipton. Mrs. Sandforth was also one of the women who had formed a very poor opinion of Lady Marianne when she first moved into Dipton Hall. Daphne felt very relaxed with her and Penelope. She saw no need to have Steves inform Lady Marianne that she had visitors.

The visiting ladies expressed their own happiness at Daphne's having married so well and their good wishes for the future. Mrs. Sandforth was quite open about her astonishment that Daphne had actually married and seemed to take at face value Daphne's claim that she was herself still surprised about it. Mrs. Sandforth's comments sounded suspiciously like a losing player congratulating one who had prevailed in a competition. The reason became evident when Mrs. Sandforth revealed that there had been a widespread misunderstanding about the desirability of Captain Giles as a match. This had made them delay having Mr. Sandforth visit the Captain at the Dipton Arms when he first appeared in the area. She laughingly congratulated Daphne on stealing a march on all the rest of them, acknowledging that the first time any of them had seen Captain Giles was at the ball where it was already very obvious that he had somehow become infatuated with Daphne. That view had been confirmed by Steves in conversation with the Sandforth's butler. Before Mrs. Sandforth and her daughter could concoct a strategy to get around this difficulty, they found that their schemes were no longer relevant. Captain Giles had persuaded Daphne to marry him.

Mrs. Stanford had a tongue, as Mr. Moorhouse often expressed his perception of her, which ran far ahead of her brain. In prattling on and coming to the subject that most engaged her interests, she revealed that Penelope now had her cap set on capturing Lord David, or failing him, Captain Bush. A red-faced Penelope, looking as if she wished the floor would open up under her, protested that there was no truth in her mother's allegations but with so much stammering that Daphne knew it to be true.

To Penelope's relief, Daphne turned the conversation towards the Ameschester Hunt. Mr. Stanford did, it was true, ride with the Hunt regularly, and he was invited and usually attended the Hunt Dinner. The Sandforths had even hosted the hunt but not the dinner and would be doing so again soon. Of course, Mrs. Stanford herself had never ridden with the Hunt. It was not her sort of thing at all! When Daphne revealed her interest in participating, Mrs. Sandforth warned her of the dangers of riding about the country in cold weather and told of the many accidents which she knew were the result of the dangerous sport. Penelope, by contrast, sounded eager to try hunting and speculated on whether her father would let her ride in the coming meet. As Daphne appreciated, Penelope, by the reference to her father's permission, had avoided her mother's being able to dismiss the idea out of hand.

This visit was followed by two others of women who had been, in the past, not nearly as close to Daphne and her father as had been the Sandforths. After they left, Daphne found that, once again, she had succeeded in doing little of what she wanted to accomplish in the morning. She also was beginning to appreciate how lucky she was that her father and now her husband encouraged her in activities that fully absorbed her interests. She had the feeling that the visiting women welcomed any breaks in their routines.

After lunch, Daphne again set off on estate business. She wanted to speak to some of the cattlemen and shepherds about the cull and the spring breeding, even though much of the cull had already happened. She knew that this was really an excuse to get out into the glorious fall weather, which she was sure would not last, but she felt no guilt at fooling herself. She also had no compunction about taking Dark Paul as her mount, though now saddled as was normal for her. She finished her business quickly and found that she had a good deal of time before she had to return to dress for dinner; she would skip tea as she often did. It would be much more pleasant to give Dark Paul his head on some of the open country of her estates, and, if it involved some simple jumps, so much the better. She made quite a sight gleefully pushing Dark Paul to see how he would go, her hair streaming out behind her like another horse's tail when she lost her bonnet, taking easy jumps with aplomb and laughing as the horse landed. It was only when, on one of the landings, she came down rather hard on her right hip, and she suspected that Dark Paul had again shied to try to unseat her that she realized this activity might be foolishness and reined in the stallion for a more sedate ride home.

Once Elsie had helped her change, Daphne had her carriage take her to her father's house. It turned out that he had invited Lord David and Mrs. Bush and her daughters to dinner. While they were waiting for the others to arrive, Daphne asked her father why he didn't ride in the Hunt.

"That is a long story, my dear," Mr. Moorhouse replied. "It has to do with some things I should have told you about years ago. We don't have time now. If you can forego roaring about the countryside on Captain Giles's horse for one day, come to tea tomorrow, and I will tell you all about it."

Normally, Daphne would have started to try to pry from her father a hint of what the mystery was, but she was interrupted by the arrival of the guests. Lord David opened the conversation by saying, "I performed a wedding today, my first after yours, Lady Daphne."

"Oh? Whose was it? I don't remember you publishing any banns recently," inquired Mr. Moorhouse.

"No, I haven't. This was by special license."

"Oh, yes? Tell us about it."

"Yesterday, Ted Miller came to see me to tell me that I would be needed at the church today about ten o'clock."

"Ted Miller, the Blacksmith?" Daphne asked.

"Yes. He is also the Parish Constable, and it was in that role that he visited me."

"Why"

"I was to marry Molly Trueblood to a man called Archer, George Archer. She is a milkmaid, and he is a gamekeeper. She was very definitely with child."

"So they wanted to get married?"

"Not exactly. Archer could either marry her or pay the parish to keep her and the baby or go to prison. After some persuasion, he chose to marry the girl. So I performed the ceremony. To my surprise, Mr. Miller paid me half a guinea when the wedding was completed. I never realized that the Parish could require someone to marry or that I would get a fee for doing it. I just presumed it was part of my duties, like holding services on Sundays."

"Oh, yes, such fees are standard for anything extra a clergyman does," remarked Mrs. Bush. "Weddings, either by license or by banns, baptisms, churchings*, funerals, they all carry their fees. As I know well. Mr. Bush's living was not a generous one, and we needed those fees to have some special treats or to meet some extra expenses. That is how we had enough money put aside so that we could get Tobias's – Captain Bush's – uniform and sea chest when he required them. Of course, in more wealthy parishes, these duties are passed on to the curate, who usually relies on them for much of his income. Are you going to get a curate, Lord David?

"Not immediately. I am enjoying the work. And Mr. Moorhouse tells me my sermons are becoming much better for not being so learned."

Over dinner, the conversation rapidly turned to hunting when Daphne mentioned the interest that the Amesbury Hunt had expressed in having the meet at Dipton Hall. Lord David indicated immediate interest. He had participated in hunts at his father's estate of Ashbury Abbey and had thoroughly enjoyed the sport. He did know what was usual at the meet. Namely, a generous stirrup cup sometimes supplemented with some sort of buns. The stirrup cup could be wine or often port. He himself felt mulled wine was best, especially if the hunt was occurring on a frosty day, and that was usually the weather in which hunts were held. Did Daphne know where next the hunt would meet and on what day?

Daphne had gleaned these pieces of information from Mr. Summers. That set Lord David off. "I have been thinking of hunting. I, in fact, have plans to buy a hunter. The stables at the vicarage are quite large and could accommodate the hunter as well as my regular mount and my carriage horse. I won't be able to get him before the next meet, of course. Daphne, could I borrow Captain Giles's hunter, Dark Paul, for the occasion? The exercise would do us both good."

Daphne was about to reply that she herself intended to ride Dark Paul at the meet. She was forestalled by her father.

"Daphne, isn't that the horse you had trouble with yesterday?" asked Mr. Moorhouse. "I heard that he threw you, and you could have been injured."

"It wasn't that serious," Daphne protested.

"That's not what Mr. Jackson tells me. He said that you were lucky not to break your leg or worse. I suggest that, for your first hunt, you ride Moonbeam. I will join you on my horse, Sterling, at the meet."

This was so out of character for Daphne's father that she changed the reply she had been about to make to Lord David, which had been to point out that the stallion would be in use that day.

"That is a splendid idea you have about riding Dark Paul, Lord David," she said. "We can make quite a party of the occasion."

In the drawing room after dinner, Daphne was again surprised when her father pressed Miss Carolyn Bush, Captain Bush's sister, to play for them. Miss Bush was now a good deal more accomplished than she had been on the previous occasion when Daphne had heard her play. She was even more surprised when Mr. Moorhouse urged Lord David to sing while Miss Carolyn accompanied him. Mr. Moorhouse had no ear for music, usually, though he had insisted that Daphne learn how to play the piano-forte as she was growing up. What in the world was her father up to?

Daphne made sure that she was the last person to leave the gathering. When it was her turn to express her farewells, she told her carriage to wait. "Father," she said, "I think we should talk now, not wait until tea tomorrow. I don't understand why you are now so interested in the Hunt when you never have been in the past. And why you are so keen to have Lord David ride Dark Paul instead of me."

"As to the latter, I think you don't realize that it is harder to control a spirited hunter than you think when your mount is excited by the other horses. You need much more practice. I don't want to lose my daughter. I would also like Lord David to enjoy being at Dipton. He is the best vicar we have had in a long time. Just look at the good-natured way he performed the unwelcome duty of conducting a forced marriage. And if he should marry Miss Bush, it is more likely that Captain Bush himself will settle here permanently, though, of course, Captain Giles is the main attraction. But I also have concerns about your riding with the Ameschester Hunt, and that is what I should tell you about."

Daphne and her father left the entryway where this conversation had taken place to move into Mr. Moorhouse's library, where a cheerful fire had dispelled all the autumn chill. Mr. Moorhouse poured two small glasses of brandy, one of which he handed to Daphne before settling into his favorite chair. Ladies did not drink spirits as a rule after dinner, but, ever since she had come out, Mr. Moorhouse had always poured Daphne a glass when they were in his library in the evening.

"Now, about me and the Hunt," he started. "For you to understand the situation, I have to go back a ways, long before you were born, my dear. And it covers matters about which I should have told you years ago, but when push came to shove, I never really felt like doing so because the circumstances are still a bit painful.

"My father was a gunsmith by trade, as was my grandfather and my great grandfather. Their business was making fine rifles and pistols for gentlemen. But they expanded into making Brown Bess muskets, just when the need for them was growing rapidly. My father increased the business much beyond what he had inherited from his father, and he became quite rich in the process. The demand for muskets has been growing in the last many years, and Moorhouse and Son -- that is the name of the establishment – kept expanding. Even in the intervals of peace, the company did very well, selling muskets to the East India Company and expanding their side-line of making nuts and bolts. He was an honest man and a rich one, but in no way was my father a gentleman, and that rankled with him.

"My brother George, your uncle, Daphne, do you remember him? He visited us once when you were about ten years old."

"Yes, I remember a big, red-faced man who spoke with a funny accent. He brought me a toy cannon to play with. He was very loud; I don't think I liked him very much."

"That's him. He is sixteen years older than I and was apprenticed to the gun trade even before I was born. He turned out to be just as good at the business as my father.

"My father had always been aware that gentlemen were automatically treated differently from him. He wanted his sons to be gentlemen, as befitted his wealth. It was really too late for my brother, a rough metal worker with a pronounced Birmingham accent. He would never be a true gentleman.

I was different, especially after my mother died when I was three. He got me a good nanny and sent me to prep school in Birmingham and then to public school. Not one of the great ones, like Eton or Harrow, but a respectable one, Cedarhurst. The students at the school were mainly the sons of professional men like lawyers or parsons, but also there were the sons of country gentlemen and minor aristocrats. Cedarhurst had a good enough reputation for its students to be admitted to the universities, and it made sure that we all spoke with the proper accent for gentlemen. From Cedarhurst, I went to Oxford, not one of the very fashionable colleges like Baliol or Christ Church, but a solid one with a penchant for serious studies. That is where I got my love of classical history and of hunting. Several of the men in my college were from country estates or parsonages, and they would ask me to go with them to their homes. You know that the university terms are not very long, so there were several opportunities to take up the invitations. There would be a hunt in the neighborhood of some of those visits, and I was asked to participate. I found I loved it. I also enjoyed the hunt dinners that often were part of the hunt. Men only, of course. And sometimes separate dinners for the younger and more boisterous participants from the more staid gatherings of their seniors.

"When I came down from Oxford, my father bought me Dipton Manor, an estate which had become available and was a good distance from Birmingham. He gave me enough money to live comfortably even if the estate did not bring in much income. At first, I was not well accepted here because of my roots. I didn't realize it at the time, but there was great resentment about someone buying Dipton Manor who wasn't really a gentleman but just a tradesman from Birmingham. That sort of prejudice still remains, though maybe it is not as strong as it used to be. I always tried to shield you from being looked down on, but I wasn't really worried about its effect on you since you are so strong. Anyway, soon after I settled here, I heard about the Ameschester Hunt and went to one of their meetings. Everyone, of course, is welcome. At the end of the hunt, I was riding with one of the men who seemed to have something to do with organizing it, and I asked about a hunt dinner. In very cold terms, he told me that they did indeed have a hunt dinner and that, of course, it was only for real gentlemen, so I was not invited.

"Oddly enough, the man who so insulted me was the father of the Mr. Summers who visited you about the hunt."

"How do you know about that?" Daphne demanded. "I haven't had a chance to tell you any of that."

"Tisdale told me. He had it from Steves, who, I am afraid, was boasting about how important a house is Dipton Hall. Anyway, I was badly hurt by the rejection and decided that if they did not want me, I would not have anything to do with them. But I do like hunting, so I was just chopping off my own nose to spite my face. And for all these years, I have not hunted."

"So why have you changed your mind?"

"It's been a long time, and I am much better accepted in the community, I think. And to give you support."

Daphne realized that it would not be a good idea to shock the gentlemen at the hunt by riding astride the first time she joined them, especially not when she was accompanied by her father, who was undoubtedly wanting a warm acceptance from those who ran the Ameschester Hunt. So she really should polish her side-saddle riding, even though she would be on Moonbeam. This was particularly true since she rarely rode the mare in the open fields as she would in a hunt.

Daphne found herself falling into a routine. In the mornings, she worked on the accounts when she was not receiving visitors. These kept coming. They were not only people whom she had known well before her marriage but also ones from outside her immediate neighborhood. Furthermore, there were ladies from the Dipton area who had been rather aloof from her in the past. Following her father's revelations, she realized that this might well have reflected her status in their eyes rather than any indifference related to her own personality or interests. She was amused rather than resentful that the only reason for their sudden interest was the title of her husband, for they did not know him, and she was the same as always.

Afternoons were given over to examining various parts of the estates and conferring with those who worked on them and with the tenants on their farms. Now she usually took Moonbeam for a canter over open country, riding side-saddle. She was teaching the horse to jump small impediments and found that Moonbeam, while initially very skittish, was beginning to take them in stride rather than balking at even slight obstacles. At the end of the afternoon, she would take tea at her father's home or her own and then usually dine at the other location.

On the day before the hunt was to occur, Daphne was overjoyed to receive a long letter from Giles. His practice was to start a letter to Daphne when the previous one had been mailed and then keep adding to it until another opportunity arose to send the letter to her. This one started with Giles's meeting with the Admiral after being ashore searching for the traitor and being to Walmer Castle. It seemed to end as Giles was returning from the raid on the French landing craft and talked of the emerging problem with Lieutenant Kirkpatrick. But that was not the ending, even though Giles left three-quarters of the page empty while his usual practice was simply to continue on the same page under a different date. Instead, when Daphne turned over the paper, she found that the letter continued.

> "I have just received your letters, Dearest Wife. How I love to hear all your news, though I am sometimes very alarmed at how daring you can be. I write in haste since it is very late and I must be up well before first light.
>
> There are two matters in your letter that I want to address at once. First, I am sorry about your having to share Dipton Hall with my sister and her daughters. I did not find Marianne a pleasing person when I was extricating her from the North. Quite the contrary, and I did not form a favorable opinion of the girls. But it is not my nieces' fault that their mother has made some serious mistakes, nor that their grandfather has not

seen fit to look after his own kin. I think, despite my father's shortcomings, or maybe because of them, that I should provide the girls with suitable dowries and if that makes it easier for them to marry – and it must – so much the better. I am afraid that I have no idea of what is the proper amount, either in view of their own status or in view of what may be necessary to attract a suitable suitor. I have in mind fifteen thousand pounds, but that may be too much or too little. I am assured by Mr. Edwards that I am rich. I hope he has sent you all my accounts, as I asked him to. You can judge better than I what we can afford. Mr. Edwards may have an idea of what is appropriate, or possibly the visitors you have told me about will talk about dowries, and you can infer what might be suitable portions for my nieces. I know that all aspects of getting married are a favorite topic among young ladies and their mothers when they gather together.

Now, the matter of the Ameschester Hunt. I am delighted that you were approached. Since I cannot commit myself to be at any particular meet or ball in the present circumstances, you have my enthusiastic support in having the meet at Dipton Hall when appropriate and to host the Hunt Ball. I know your organizing abilities quite outshine my own, so I expect that it will be a wonderful occasion. How I wish that I could be there, but I doubt that there will be a truce with the French just for the occasion.

I am happy that you are thinking of joining the hunt. How I wish that I could be there! I do hope that you will not ride Dark Paul. He is a very large horse with a hard mouth. I don't think I would have chosen him, but I knew that I would need a hunter when I am at Dipton, and I let Edwards pick him so that a hunter would be there when I got a chance to ride. I think you should get a smaller, well-trained horse of your own, maybe a mare, just for yourself. I, for one, do not care if you shock everyone by riding astride, though if you want to quiet tongues, it might be advisable to use a side saddle until you have some experience.

Now I must close. I love you, and I miss you.

Your Husband, Richard

What excellent news to receive just before the hunt! Daphne had realized that she had hardly any idea of what would be a suitable amount for the dowries, ones that would be enough to secure their purpose without being too extravagant. She suspected that Giles's guess was about right. She was even more pleased by his immediate acceptance and encouragement to take part in and to host the Hunt. Until reading his letter, she had considered that getting a hunter for herself would be a needless expense, but she realized now how deeply she desired one. If Lord David and her father were acquiring hunting horses, maybe they could help her find one soon.

The day of the hunt came bright and frosty. She met her father and Lord David at the end of the drive leading to Dipton Manor, and they proceeded at a gentle pace to Deeping Hall, where the meet was taking place. On the gravel in front of the portico, many horses were milling around as riders greeted each other and accepted stirrup cups from the trays carried by footmen. Daphne discovered that her cup contained mulled wine, just the thing, she thought, when waiting for the start. Mrs. Sandforth was in evidence greeting the riders as they arrived and seemed particularly glad to see Daphne and her father.

Daphne noted, as she had expected, that there were very few women mounted. They were all riding side-saddle and on horses that looked like regular mounts, like hers, not special hunters. She was somewhat surprised when Mr. Summers came over to greet them.

"Lady Giles, it is so good to see you out for today's hunt. The weather is most promising. Mr. Moorhouse, I was not aware that you hunted. I am very glad that you are here. I wonder if you are aware that we will be holding a hunt dinner at the end of the day. In Ameschester. At the Fox and Hounds. You must join us. And Lord David. So good to see a clergyman participating in the sport of his congregation! And what a magnificent horse you are riding! You, of course, must also come to the dinner. Come as my guests, both of you, please do."

Daphne was amused that her father agreed at once to accept the invitation and warmly expressed gratitude for the invitation. His previous resentment did not make him prickly about now attending a function from which he had been barred earlier.

Turning to Daphne, Mr. Summers continued in a lower tone, "I don't suppose that you have heard from Captain

Sir Richard, have you, Lady Giles? Or made up your mind about the meet at Dipton Hall?"

"Yes, I have, Mr. Summers. Captain Giles wished me to convey his disappointment that he cannot be here today and that he will likely miss other meets this season. His duties, you understand."

Mr. Summers face fell at the rebuff he was expecting, which gave Daphne an inner smile, knowing what she was about to add.

"Captain Giles, nevertheless, said that I could hold both the meet and the Hunt Ball if I wished. So, Mr. Summers, all I need to know is the date so that I can start planning to have a very successful day."

"Thank you very much, Lady Giles. That is splendid news," said Mr. Summers.

While they were talking, Major Stoner had drifted over and heard Daphne's last statement. "Jolly good!" he cried enthusiastically. "It is very good to see you here for the hunt, Lady Giles. Very good!" The Major had apparently forgotten his previously revealed attitude to women hunting. "And of course, you, Lord David," he continued, "and you, Mr. Moorhouse. I didn't know you hunted, sir, though we have had many a good chase over the fields of Dipton Manor."

Daphne wondered whether her father's now warm acceptance had more to do with his long-time status as a landowner in the community or with her own suddenly elevated social status. Her thoughts on this subject were cut short because two young men had drifted over to them while they were talking to Mr. Summers and Major Stoner. Now one of them spoke up, "Major, you must introduce us to this lovely young lady."

"Yes, of course. Lady Daphne Giles, may I introduce Captain Ralph Hicks and Lieutenant Geoffrey Charles of Lord Moresby's Regiment. And Mr. Moorhouse and Lord David Giles."

After the appropriate gestures recognizing the introduction had been exchanged, Major Stoner continued, "Mr. Moorhouse is the father of Lady Giles who is married to Captain Sir Richard Giles of the Royal Navy. Lord David is her bother-in-law and vicar of Dipton."

"Delighted to meet you," drawled Captain Hicks, and he and Lieutenant Charles drifted away again.

"Good men, those, good men!" exclaimed Major Stoner. "Add to the hunt! Captain Hicks has a high position in the family bank, I understand. And Lieutenant Charles is the eldest son of my good friend, Douglas Charles, who has a very pretty estate in Yorkshire, worth, I would guess, eight thousand a year. Very good family."

Daphne had been amused that the two men had lost interest as soon as they realized that she was not only a married woman but also was there with relatives. They seemed to be searching for a young lady to flirt with. She wondered if they could be induced to have an interest in her nieces. Hunting seemed to have unexpected social opportunities that she would need to pursue. However, she had little time to reflect on such matters as the huntsman chose that moment to start the hunt. He set the dogs to seeking a recent scent, and everyone else followed on behind. Soon the view-holloa was heard as a fox was spotted near a copse on the far side of the field beside which they were riding.

The hounds found the scent and headed off across the field, baying loudly. The pack was rapidly followed by most of the hunters, who galloped after them. A smaller, much more sedate group, consisting of all the women with various relatives or suitors accompanying them, followed along the lane they were on, intending to use existing paths, or routes across the fields leading in the direction of the huntsman's horn but in ways that would not require any jumps.

After a few minutes, Mr. Moorhouse said to Daphne, "I think we can do better than these hill-toppers."

"These what?" Daphne responded.

"This group who seem intent on following the hunt without any jumping or even crossing fields where the gates may not be evident. That is what they are called."

"I agree about this ride. It is a little unadventuresome, isn't it?"

Mr. Moorhouse turned off into a field and took a line more or less in the right direction, pushing his horse up to a canter. Daphne followed on Moonbeam. Their track was not as direct as that of the main hunt, for Mr. Moorhouse was going between fields in ways that did not require jumping hedges, and he dismounted to open gates rather than trying to jump them. Some low barriers he did jump, and Daphne had no trouble getting Moonbeam to follow suit. Even so, the sound of the hunting horn seemed to be getting more and more distant, and they could no longer hear the noise of the hounds and the horses. Daphne and Mr. Moorhouse were having a very refreshing ride, but they were not likely, it seemed, to be near the kill when it occurred.

After a while, judging by the horn, the hunt seemed to have turned towards them. Then they heard the sound that indicated that the fox had gone to ground and that the hounds had lost the scent. Several minutes followed before the horn told them that the hounds had found a scent again and were off again after the fox.

Soon it was evident that the hunt was coming towards Daphne and her father. They had just jumped a small stream running through a marshy field when they spotted the fox running from the woods at the side of the field they were facing. Moments later, the hounds burst forth hot on the trail of the fox. It was running right at Daphne and then faltered when it saw her, not sure where to go. That was fatal for the animal. The hounds were on the fox immediately and made short work of destroying it. Much of the hunt emerged from the wood soon after, having actually missed seeing the kill. The newcomers consoled themselves with the aid of the flasks they had brought with them and congratulated themselves on arriving at the right place when so many other people had gone astray, been thrown, or otherwise had reason to abandon the hunt. Daphne and Mr. Moorhouse received great credit and congratulations on having out-foxed the fox so that they were right at the kill. The more sedate group of riders, which Daphne and Mr. Moorhouse had left to pursue their own line, arrived on the scene still later. They might not have been in at the kill, which was just what they had expected, but at least they had not been forced to abandon the hunt either. Lord David did not appear, and several riders said that they had seen him showing obvious signs of having been thrown, heading towards the Dipton Vicarage and being in a mood that was quite unsuitable for a vicar.

Daphne and Mr. Moorhouse rode back to Dipton in the company of several neighbors. The conversation was easy, consisting of comments on the day's hunting and upcoming meets. The news that Dipton Hall would hold a Hunt Ball at the end of the season had already been spread among all the riders, and they expressed enthusiasm and curiosity about the details that kept Daphne busy until it was time to go their separate ways. The father and daughter stopped at the vicarage to find out how Lord David was. Only his pride had been injured.

"You were right to warn me about Dark Paul. He is a hard-mouthed brute, but it serves me right. I should have kept him on a tighter rein."

Lord David invited his visitors to tea. In the course of it, Daphne raised the question of the appropriate amount of dowries.

"Are you trying to marry me off, Lady Daphne?" asked Lord David." I am very well satisfied with my living which provides enough for all my needs. There are also all the little fees that are paid to me, which allow me all the indulgences I want. If and when I marry, the dowry will not be a consideration, though I confess more is always preferable to less."

"Do you happen to know what other clergymen of your age, but without such a favorable living, might need to be able to marry comfortably?" asked Mr. Moorhouse.

"Actually, I do. Several of us who were headed for the Church talked about it before we came down from Cambridge. Most seemed to think that a portion of seven or eight thousand pounds would suffice. Why do you ask?"

Daphne started to stutter some sort of an answer while Mr. Moorhouse remained silent. Suddenly Lord David smiled. "You are thinking of my nieces, aren't you? I can see why you might want them to get married. From what I have seen of my relatives, it must be very tedious living under the same roof with them and my half-sister. I would need a lot more than ten thousand to take on my sister as a mother-in-law. It is exceedingly generous of Richard to contemplate giving them quite undeserved portions. Of course, it would take a good deal more of a dowry, I would think, for anyone to take on my sister, and I would still think him a fool. Good luck with your schemes. You should try your snares on those two young officers we saw today. They looked satisfied enough with themselves that they would not notice that being an earl's granddaughter does not make a woman a pleasant mate."

"That is what I was thinking. Would you join us for dinner on Saturday if I can get those two and the major to come to dinner?"

"Why me?"

"You would add a touch of glamor to the event without providing a rival for Catherine and Lydia's affections."

"Oh, you are devious, trying to spend the dowries as soon as you have them. What a delightfully scheming mind you do have, Sister Daphne. And would I be wrong in thinking that you have your eyes on Major Stoner for Marianne?"

"Of course I do not!" Daphne lied, but the glint in her eye and the knowing smile on her lips showed her brother-in-law that he had hit the nail on the head.

"I shall be delighted to attend and see if you are catching your prey in your net."

Mr. Moorhouse changed the subject to whether Lord David felt up to going to the Hunt Dinner in Ameschester.

"Of course I will go. I don't want anyone to think that a little spill from my horse should be taken seriously," was the reply. Daphne and her father said their farewells to Lord David immediately after this exchange. They rode in companionable silence until they reached the point where the driveway to Dipton Hall branched off the main road.

"You know, my dear," said Mr. Moorhouse, "I think that in one day your presence has undone slights over which I have felt resentment ever since I moved here."

"Nonsense, Father," replied Daphne, "It is just that you have been too stubborn to realize that people have changed their opinion of you. It is now based on who you are and not where you came from."

Chapter IX

Impetuous was again patrolling off the Flemish coast. The Admiral's inspection of the boats that Giles had captured confirmed that they were worthless to the British cause, though he appreciated getting the guns. He wasn't helpful in other matters.

"There is nothing I can do about your Mr. Kirkpatrick, Captain Giles. I don't have a space for a lackluster lieutenant, and his offenses are none of them so clear-cut that he could be court-martialed for them. You'll just have to try to limit the damage and get him to hang himself more clearly."

The patrolling was a frustrating business. The winds were largely from the northwest and of such a strength that Giles felt he had to stay clear of the lee shore. When the wind decreased, he found that the procession of landing craft resumed before he could regain the shore. The craft seemed to be traveling in greater numbers than before and were more often accompanied by minor warships. He liked to think that that was the result of his raid but had to recognize that other commanders had also thought up similar ways of getting at the enemy.

There were places where *Impetuous* could get close enough to the shore to fire on the landing craft, but only at very long range. It was pure luck if her guns hit anything at all. That endeavor used up a lot of powder and shot for very little return.

There were places where the sandbar, usually hidden at high water, was narrow enough that *Impetuous* could have inflicted a good deal of damage to ships passing on the inside if only she could get at them. During much of their passages up and down the coast, the master, Mr. Brooks, could be found in one of the boats taking careful sounding to see where and how closely *Impetuous* could safely approach the shore so that the landing craft would be in range. However, most of these places were such that there were only a few hundred yards in which Giles's frigate could get close enough to do damage. Vessels creeping along the coast would see *Impetuous* approaching in enough time that they could avoid the stretch in which they were vulnerable by halting before they came in range of Giles's broadsides. In many other such places that were otherwise suitable, the French had built forts, often of a hurried or temporary nature, whose heavy guns would keep *Impetuous* too far out to sea for her broadsides to do any harm. Even a night attack was ruled out. If *Impetuous* snuck in to try to bombard the craft huddled under the protection of the battery at night time, her own gun flashes, supplemented by the blue lights* the fort was bound to send up, would render the frigate vulnerable to heavy shot coming from the fortress's guns.

Giles felt more and more frustrated. He was wasting his time while his prey was often just out of reach. He fixed on one particular part of the coast where *Impetuous* could get close enough to the shore do severe damage, if only it was not guarded by eight heavy guns – at least thirty-six pounders – on a somewhat elevated terrace. The redoubt* had a low parapet over which the guns would fire, and all the cannon could be brought to bear on any enemy venturing close to the shore. If *Impetuous* came close enough so that her broadsides could reach the craft huddling in the protection of the guns, she would be in easy range of the battery. This fort was a favorite place for the French landing craft and their escorts to gather in the late afternoon, waiting in safety under the shore guns until they could proceed in the morning. If Giles could only silence the fort while he crept close enough to the tightly packed craft, his broadsides would be bound to do a good deal of damage, even if he could not have much confidence in hitting any particular one of the craft.

Giles did not hurry his plans to take the redoubt. He, in fact, spent quite a few days sailing back and forth just out of range of the fort, sometimes coming close enough for the guns to open fire, though at extreme range, which meant that a hit was most unlikely. Giles spent much of these journeys high in the mast of *Impetuous* so that he could get a good impression of the layout of the redoubt and the anchorage in front of it. Based on his observations, he was able to form a plan that should have a good chance of success.

Giles intended to land his forces before dawn to take the redoubt so that they could attack at first light. He would wait to attack until the days just before the full moon when there would be no moonlight for a couple of hours before sunrise. The beach immediately in front of the redoubt seemed to be used quite extensively by boats from the anchored craft and the fort, so that area of the shore did not provide him with a good landing spot. Getting to that part of the beach would also expose his boats to the greatest danger of being spotted by the anchored craft. Those considerations ruled out attacking by the most direct route to the fort. Even though the gun platform was situated on only a gentle slope and the parapet was low enough so that the guns could fire over them, the height of the barrier that would have to be scaled in a direct attack was considerably higher at the front than at the sides. Should he attack from the east or the west? He could see no advantage to one side over the other. It came to him that it would be advisable to divide his attack between two separate forces, even though this was against his usual instincts. If his attackers on one side were observed before they could attack, they would draw defenders from the other side, and the still undetected force could sweep in and attack the defenders from the rear.

Impetuous would take up station just out of range of the guns of the redoubt. The signal for the attack on the fort would be *Impetuous*'s firing a broadside at the anchored vessels. They would still be out of range, but that cannonade should distract the garrison of the redoubt so that the landing parties could reach the walls of the fort before they were discovered. As soon as the redoubt was taken, *Impetuous* would move closer to the shore, and she would continue to fire on the vessels huddling under the protection of the fort. As they returned to *Impetuous*, the landing parties would try to start fires on the rafts of boats in the hope of further destroying more of the invasion vessels being moved to the chosen French ports.

With his plans laid, Giles only had to decide who should carry them out. Since *Impetuous* might be in danger from French or Dutch warships that could appear at dawn, he would have to remain on board. That, of course, was the usual procedure: the captain remaining with his ship while sending his subordinates on ventures off the ship. Giles realized that he had often not followed that course since waiting to see whether his plans would succeed, helpless to do anything about dealing with surprises while remaining in his ship, was far more difficult than taking part in a raid himself. He wondered if his past pattern had actually been sheer selfishness rather than a preference for putting himself in danger if he was ordering others to do so.

The attack on the southwest side of the redoubt would be led by Lieutenants Milton and Miller. It would consist entirely of seamen. The northeast expedition would have Lieutenants Macauley and Kirkpatrick in charge. They would be commanding the marines, who would be supplemented by a party of seamen. Both groups would be carrying ropes with grapnels* so that they could easily ascend the walls of the redoubt, even though these barriers were quite low at the points of attack which Giles had chosen. He congratulated himself for the foresight that had induced him to order Lieutenant Macauley to train his command in the skills of ascending and descending the rigging of *Impetuous* by all sorts of different routes so that the marines would not be trapped in the fighting tops if their usual route up the shrouds* should be made impassable by enemy action. Now they could put their climbing agility to other use

There were still three days until the moon would be best for the attack. *Impetuous* spent the time cruising back and forth along the coast in the area of the fort so that the observers on shore would get used to seeing her and might feel that she constituted no danger to them. The waiting weighed on everyone, with the officers snapping at each other and at the midshipmen, and the middies in turn not engaging in their usual larking in the rigging that tended to annoy their superiors even at the best of times. The same was evident among the crew too, who also felt unfairly picked on by the officers. Giles had to check himself when he was tempted to take his irritability out on those who could not snap back at him.

When the chosen night approached, Giles took *Impetuous* past the redoubt, keeping well out of range of its guns, and went along the coast until the fort disappeared just as night was falling. Then he reversed course. The night was overcast, with only a slight lightening of the clouds to tell where the moon was. Using the light of the fort and of the boats anchored in its shadow for guidance, *Impetuous* glided into position just beyond the range of the shore guns. She anchored with as little noise as possible, and Giles had a spring* put on the anchor cable so that he could be sure that his guns would bear on the landing craft when the time came. He also had the cable buoyed so that he could cast off the anchor with no delay but still pick it up again later. Looking through their telescopes, neither Mr. Brooks nor Giles himself saw any signs that the noise of their anchoring had been noted by the redoubt or the anchored craft. It wasn't until two bells of the morning watch that Giles ordered the landing parties into their boats and then waited anxiously for any signs indicating that they had been discovered. The night remained quiet. The overcast seemed to be thickening, judging by how the glow from the moon seemed to be diminishing.

It was almost six bells before the first slight lightening presaging the new day became evident. Giles studied the sides of the redoubt through his telescope, waiting until he could distinguish some features of the land in front of them before he launched his attack. Having his attackers stumble around in the dark was not likely to lead to success. What he had not reckoned with was that, with the sun rising behind the shore, *Impetuous* would be illuminated enough to be picked out by sharp eyes on the parapet of the fort. The miscalculation was made evident when the battery ashore opened fire at the frigate.

Giles still waited to fire his own broadside until the light ashore would be better, trusting his officers to wait for his signal before attacking. The cannonballs from the fort made splashes only a few yards from the frigate. *Impetuous* was too close to the shore. As Giles focused on the left-hand side of the fort, he saw a ripple of musket fire from the parapet of the fortification, suggesting that the group of attackers on that side had been discovered. He immediately ordered his own broadside to fire and to keep firing even as the flashes of light from the redoubt signaled the next cannonade from the fort. Even while waiting for the balls to arrive, it registered in Giles's mind that the two rightmost cannon had not fired. Could that be his other attacking party's doing?

One of the fort's guns must have had a double cartridge of gunpowder used for the second shot, for the ball did carry over *Impetuous* and by pure chance struck the foremast just above the fighting top. It played immediate havoc with all the rigging, and Giles spent the next few minutes issuing orders to get the wreckage cleared up and to jury rig the supports of the other masts. Another cannonball fired from the fort skipped off the water and slammed into *Impetuous* just above the waterline. In the dark, Giles had come too close to the shore. At least, he would not have to up anchor to move closer to his targets before bombarding the landing craft.

While he was engaged in dealing with the consequences of the fort's fire, a heavy rain shower engulfed *Impetuous*. This did not hinder the continued firing of the broadsides, though it did mean that what success they might have had could only be guessed at.

As the shower eased off only minutes after it had prevented observation in any direction, a cry came from somewhere near the bow of *Impetuous*, "Ship ahoy, one point off the larboard bow." Bearing down on them was a Dutch frigate, a small sixth-rate likely of twenty-eight guns. Giles had no time to wonder from where the enemy had come nor why no one on *Impetuous* had seen her earlier. His orders thundered out almost before he had time to formulate them. "Man the bow chasers, load and run out. Use the spring to change our heading to larboard. Bow chasers fire when you bear on the enemy."

The words seemed to be hardly out of his mouth when Mr. Hughes's twenty-four pounders roared out. The larboard one hit the edge of the attacker's bulwark, sending a cloud of lethal splinters over the foredeck of the approaching frigate. The starboard gun hit the bowsprit of the enemy close to the hull. That spar broke immediately, and the foresails all collapsed. The ship turned to starboard as a result of losing her jibs. She proceeded to run alongside *Impetuous*, larboard to larboard, with a mighty thump that reverberated through *Impetuous* when the Dutch ship hit her.

"Man the larboard guns," bellowed Giles. "Fire as you bear. Grapple the enemy. Prepare to board."

With half of *Impetuous*'s crew away attacking the redoubt, Giles did not have enough men to man both broadsides, but endless training took over as the crews of the starboard batteries secured their guns and dashed over to the larboard side to immediately fire the guns that Giles had had loaded previously, even though there had seemed to be no danger on that side. Grapnels were thrown as soon as part of the enemy's bow came next to *Impetuous,* joining the two ships together. With a huge roar of "Boarders away," Giles led his crew onto the enemy deck, followed by not only most of the ship-handlers but also by all the gun crews.

Giles's boarding took the Dutch crew completely by surprise. They had not prepared to board before their bowsprit was destroyed, and the change of course and collision with Impetuous had shaken them. Giles's landing party, all screaming like banshees, quite unnerved the crew who had no chance to grab their cutlasses from their racks. In moments, he was on the enemy quarterdeck accepting the surrender of the Dutch captain. The Dutch officers all gave their parole.

Giles gave orders to round up the Dutch crew and batten them down in the hold. He told Midshipman Dunsmuir to take command of the capture until the other officers returned from their shore adventures. The lad stood extra tall when given the responsibility, though Giles wondered how the young officer would do if another emergency arose. He had sent the other two midshipmen with the landing parties, presuming that, with Mr. Brooks on *Impetuous,* he had all the support he needed until the others returned.

Leaving a strong force of his own seamen to guard the prize and its crew, Giles returned to *Impetuous* to see how his land attack was progressing. It had taken less than five minutes to capture the Dutch frigate. One look through his telescope revealed that the redoubt was no longer a threat. Even as he watched, he saw members of his crew tip the last of the guns over the parapet. Soon, he could see them returning to their boats, the sailors scrambling down the slope in any old order, the red-coated marines marching as well as they could over the rough ground. As they neared the beach, the fort's magazine blew up, scattering debris wide and far.

Most of the landing craft were still rafted together. It appeared that in their haste to get away from *Impetuous*'s bombardment, the outer craft had become fouled with their neighbors. Their getting underway seemed to be hindered by the many craft that had been holed by the bombardment but were still afloat. The raft was still mainly intact. Giles ordered that the bombardment of the landing craft be resumed with as many guns as his depleted crew could man and settled down to await the return of his landing parties. It seemed to take an interminable time for the parties to assemble on the beach and take to their boats, even though Giles could see that the officers were organizing the departure with all reasonable haste. He was saddened to notice that several injured sailors and marines were being carried to the boats of the northeast group.

The boats shoved off from the beach. A glance at the hourglass told Giles that, in fact, the departure had been organized with great efficiency, and his ideas of reprimanding the lieutenants for tardiness died when he realized that the slowness had been entirely in his own head. When each of the parties approached the raft of invasion craft, they announced their presence with a fusillade of musket shots. They then boarded some of the outer craft and set them alight before resuming their journey to *Impetuous*. Soon a pall of smoke rose from the raft, joined by sudden flashes followed by muffled booms as powder kegs on some of the boats blew up. Giles realized that with the destruction by fire added to the effects of his earlier bombardment, he had probably destroyed since dawn more of the pernicious vessels than in all his previous time on the coast. Nevertheless, he might still do more damage with his guns.

The boats of the landing expedition began to approach *Impetuous*, those from the southwest coming first. Lieutenant Milton reported crisply. His force had got into place well before dawn, successfully feeling their way up the slope until they were just outside the redoubt. They had been aided by lights from the fort and from the rafted invasion craft. No, there was no indication that they had been spotted by the guardians of the fortification. Just as it was starting to become lighter, they heard a good deal of chatter and scurrying around from the fort, and in a few moments, its guns opened fire – on *Impetuous*, they presumed. Almost immediately, they heard musket fire from the far side of the fort and shouting. Lieutenant Milton decided to attack at once. His men swarmed over the parapet and quickly captured the guards. They then swept over the guns, leaving previously selected groups to secure each cannon while the remainder moved on to the next one. After they had captured the last gun, they came upon enemy soldiers lined up along the parapet. They appeared to be firing at the ground near the fort, presumably aiming at some of the attackers whom Giles had sent against the redoubt. Lieutenant Macauley's marines were arriving at the same time from the right, so the two groups quickly captured the defenders along the parapet and returned to the guns. They spiked the cannon and then levered them over the parapet. When that task was complete, Midshipman Stewart took a group of men who laid slow match* to blow up the magazine after the forces had withdrawn. His success was evident, marked still by a wisp of smoke from where the building had been.

Giles dispatched Mr. Milton to relieve Midshipman Dunsmuir on their new capture. He turned to Lieutenant Macauley.

"What happened to Lieutenant Kirkpatrick?"

"He was killed, sir, by musket fire from the fort."

"I see. A pity. But why did he get killed?"

"Mr. Kirkpatrick insisted on keeping our groups separate and assigned Mr. Correll to accompany me. He seemed to think that we would not be able to complete our task without naval oversight."

"Yes?"

"I can only suppose that Mr. Kirkpatrick mistook the guns firing from the fort to be the guns of *Impetuous*. When they fired, he leaped to his feet, waving his sword and screaming, "Attack, attack." This drew the attention of the guards on the parapet, who had not spotted us until then, and Lieutenant Kirkpatrick was killed by musket fire. Since that group was already discovered, I led my marines to the edge of the parapet and attacked, from the side, the group firing at Lieutenant Kirkpatrick's men. The minute Lieutenant Kirkpatrick was shot, I sent Midshipman Dunsmuir to try to keep the rest of his force undercover until the attention of those on the parapet was distracted. While I was dealing with the defenders, Lieutenant Milton arrived, and we completed the capture of the Fort."

"I wonder what in the world Lieutenant Kirkpatrick was thinking of. My orders, as you know, were to approach the redoubt as silently as possible while the defenders were distracted by *Impetuous*'s fire. Jumping around yelling 'Attack' hardly corresponds to my orders."

"I don't know, sir. I don't like to speak ill of the dead, but Mr. Kirkpatrick often did not seem to pay attention when orders were given to a group and had to be told again by one of us what had been said. Maybe he misunderstood your orders."

"What other casualties were there?"

"One man was killed, and two were injured. One of them, Howes, sir, got a musket bullet in the leg. I am afraid it may be broken. I had him taken to the surgeon as soon as we boarded *Impetuous*."

"Very good. Did you examine Lieutenant Kirkpatrick's body?"

"Yes, sir. He was shot several times in the front. None in the rear."

"Thank heavens. I was worried."

"That's why I examined the body, sir. He was stupid, but it wasn't one of our people who brought him down."

"Very good, Mr. Macauley. Now Mr. Milton could use some marines to secure our prize."

Mr. Evans, the carpenter, was the next to demand Giles's attention. "Sir, I found a good spar to replace the foretopmast and was able to save the rest of the fittings for the foremast. It is now finished, though it will not bear as much pressure as the original. We should replace it when next we are in port. The damage from the collision from the frigate is not serious, though it will take planks that we do not carry to repair the damage properly. The ball that hit us from the fort is more serious. It stove in* one of the strakes* and revealed that the wood was rotten. I have fixed it temporarily, but it will take a dockyard to do it properly."

"Very good, Mr. Evans. Now see what you can do about the prize, which has lost its bowsprit."

"Aye, aye, sir."

"Mr. Carrell," Giles summoned the midshipman who had been waiting patiently for orders since he had come on board *Impetuous.*

"Sir?"

"Lieutenant Macauley tells me you did very well when Lieutenant Kirkpatrick was killed."

"I tried to do my best, sir."

"And a good best it was. You are now acting lieutenant. Third, of course."

"Thank you, sir."

"You are also nearly nineteen, as I recall."

"Yes, sir."

"I want you to take the lieutenant's examination as soon as can be arranged so that your appointment can be made permanent."

"Thank you, sir. Sir, I don't have enough sea-time to be made a lieutenant yet."

"We'll see what can be done about that. How much time are you short?"

"Five months, sir."

"I see. If I can't get the age requirement waived, you will still be able to drop the "acting" in five months. That will cost you five months' seniority, I am afraid. Anyway, you had better start studying for the examination and make sure all your papers are in order."

"Aye, aye, sir."

Giles turned to see how his guns were doing. The raft of invasion craft had pretty much broken up. The few that were still navigable had succeeded in getting out of range. The rest were sinking or in the last stages of being burned. "Cease firing," he ordered the gun crews. They gladly swabbed their cannon for a final time, lowered the gun ports, and bowsed them up to the bulwarks, fastening them tight so that there was no danger of their breaking free.

For the first time in what seemed like ages, Giles had no pressing business to attend to. He decided to check on the progress being made in repairing the prize – what was she called? – Oh, yes, *Medea*. Odd name for a warship.

He found Mr. Milton on the quarterdeck, apparently idle since Mr. Evans and Mr. Shearer, the bosun, seemed to have the jury-rigging under control.

"The carpenter and the bosun tell me, sir, that they will be finished in less than an hour."

"Very good. We will take the prize back to the fleet and let the Admiral decide what to do with her. You will be in command."

"Aye, aye, sir. There is one other thing, sir."

"Yes?"

"The prisoners. They have already found one way to escape from the hold. Fortunately, Mr. Stewart realized what was happening, and we were able to contain them again. I was thinking, however, that maybe we should just put them ashore."

"Why is that, other than because they are very inconvenient?"

"They are Dutch, sir, and probably none too happy to be fighting for Bonaparte. If we take them with us, they will end up in a prison hulk, awaiting exchange. That is not likely to happen quickly since the Dutch have not been capturing many British sailors. I think it will simply be a drain on the treasury keeping them prisoner."

"What about the officers? Would you put them ashore too?"

"That is a rather different matter, sir."

"Why?"

"Captain van Teckle – that is their captain's name – Captain van Teckle, asked if I thought that they could refuse to be exchanged if that was their desire. I think that he and at least some of his officers are serving Bonaparte under duress, and they fear reprisals against themselves if they are returned to the Batavian Republic – that is what they call Holland now, sir."

"Yes, yes, I know. Get on with it, Mr. Milton."

"Well, sir. They feel that they and their families might be safer if they remained prisoners in England. Captain van Teckle even indicated that he might be willing to join us."

"I see. Well, I will dare the wrath of the Admiralty if this is not what their Lordships want. It would be convenient just to land the Dutch sailors and take the officers to Admiral Gardiner. We'll keep their boats—boats always come in useful. We can use all our boats, Mr. Milton, and theirs to get the prisoners ashore quickly. Use the marines to guard them until we are rid of them. Of course, we will not release the petty officers. They are, after all, the real core of a navy."

"Aye, aye, sir."

"And send this Captain van Teckle over to me in a few minutes. I shall be in my cabin."

"Aye, aye, sir."

The Dutch captain was an older man, possibly over forty, with a wind-beaten face and iron-gray hair.

"Captain, I congratulate you," he greeted Giles in perfect, though accented, English. "I expected to catch you by surprise, but you surprised us with how quickly you adjusted and overwhelmed us."

"Thank you, Captain. Mr. Milton tells me that you do not want to be returned to the French or the Batavian republic."

"That is correct. We only serve under duress because Bonaparte rules the Batavian Republic, as he calls my country, and there would have been severe repercussions for our families if I, and my officers, had not served. Now that I have lost my ship, the repercussions are likely to be the same whether I am exchanged or not. The same is true for my officers. Some of us may want to serve in the English navy if you will have us."

"You suggested setting your crew ashore. Won't they just return to fight us?"

"Most will not. They will just disappear into Flanders and are unlikely to be discovered. They have no great wish to serve in the Batavian Republic's navy."

"Very well, we will set them ashore – all except the petty officers. Whether you can stay in England or must await exchange will be up to higher authorities than me, but I can at least encourage them to let you stay with us. I trust you will join me for dinner."

"Gladly, sir, though Lieutenant Milton mentioned that he intended to invite us to the, what did he call it? -- the wardroom? – for dinner. He mentioned that he would be inviting you also."

"In that case, Captain, I shall look forward to seeing you in the wardroom."

Giles turned to writing his report on the day's activities. They would likely find the fleet on the morrow, and his report would be needed. He was interrupted by the information that the needed repairs were finished. He decided to let Lieutenant Correll command *Medea* with a small crew. Giles consulted Mr. Brooks about the right course to steer in order to find the fleet and made sure that the master's mate who was to sail with Mr. Correll was told how to find the fleet in case *Medea* became separated from *Impetuous* in the night. Then he gave the order for the anchor to be raised, and they were underway. He was interrupted again by Mr. Milton, who came to invite him to celebrate the victory in the wardroom. Giles finished the report just before it was time to join his officers and their guests.

The wardroom celebration was a boisterous event, for all *of Impetuous*'s officers had come through peril safely, and the death of Lieutenant Kirkpatrick did not dim their spirits at all. He was surprised how happily the Dutch officers took part in the celebrations, though that was explained by a rather drunken explanation from *Medea*'s first lieutenant that they were relieved not to be fighting any more for the man they all regarded as the oppressor of their country.

Giles left the gathering early to write to Daphne. He had a lot to tell her, all about the long day and the various successes that had accompanied it. As he described how the dawn raid was discovered, he felt a slight unease. It somewhat disappeared when he got to the Dutch frigate, but it reappeared to nag him as he got to describing the celebration in the wardroom. He put down his pen and considered what the source of his unease might be. He found that it stemmed from Lieutenant Kirkpatrick. His initial reaction to the news of his officer's death was relief that a problem had taken care of itself. Yes, he was glad that Kirkpatrick was dead and was relieved that the lieutenant had not done more damage. But, somehow, those feelings did not seem to be appropriate. Shouldn't he have done something to enhance his subordinate's performance? Why had he ordered Kirkpatrick to take command of the sailors in the northeast assault? He was only lucky that more of his people were not injured by the untimely actions of the lieutenant. Shouldn't he have kept his subordinate with him and used a midshipman instead to command the sailors, or shifted Mr. Miller to go with Mr. Macauley and given Mr. Milton another midshipman?

Giles found that his pen had written these thoughts and doubts in the letter to Daphne even as he was formulating them. Surely, he shouldn't burden her with these things. How could she respect him if she knew the doubts that sometimes assailed him? Surely it was up to him to maintain a sure confidence in everything so that she would know that she could always rely on him. But she had shown him that at times she had doubts about her decisions concerning the farms. They had succeeded during their few days in Brighton in stripping away much of the formal attitude of self-confidence and sureness that was a large part of their upbringings, especially Giles's. Did he really want to slip back into that mask of self-confident sureness in the correctness of his actions and opinions, even though, in reality, he had strong doubts? No, he would risk showing his hesitations. That way, he might even get support for overcoming them.

Having wrestled with himself over the matter, Giles did not remove the page with the account of his worry, even guilt, about how well he had handled the problem which the lieutenant had presented. He would take his chances that showing his vulnerability would not lessen him in Daphne's eyes, even though it went against all his upbringing to take the gamble. Instead, he brought the letter to an affectionate end, ready for posting in the morning.

Chapter X

Daphne put her dinner scheme into practice on returning to Dipton Hall. After taking another bath, over Elsie's protests that it was not healthy to bathe so often, she wrote notes inviting Major Stoner, Captain Hicks, and Lieutenant Charles to dine with her on the coming Saturday.

Next, she joined Lady Marianne and her nieces in the small drawing-room before dinner. Talk of the hunt and who had been there occupied them not only until dinner was announced but also during the first part of the meal. At that point, Daphne mentioned meeting the three military men and inviting them to Dipton Hall. She found herself positively grilled about the three guests by her nieces and Lady Marianne, who was particularly interested in Major Stoner. Daphne portrayed him as a diamond in the rough, though her real opinion was that he was just quartz that would not take well to cutting and polishing. She waited until they had withdrawn into the drawing-room to mention that she understood that Captain Giles intended to give the two girls modest dowries. She indicated indirectly that she didn't know the amount, which was true. Still, Daphne was not going to let on that the first notions of her husband and the figures which she was herself thinking about would undoubtedly be considered to be very generous as a wedding gift to compensate for a young lady's having no real influence or access to the higher levels of society. The announcement was greeted with unbridled excitement by her three listeners. They knew that even a modest sum could make the difference in whether marriage to them would be feasible for many very respectable young men of limited income. Their speculation about the army officers whom Daphne had met also revived.

The enthusiasm was used by Lady Marianne to get her two daughters to perform on the piano-forte. This rather grated on Daphne's nerves, for the girls were not accomplished musicians. She realized, however, that this disadvantage might be partly because they had had no realistic expectations of ever getting a genteel husband to whom such a skill might be attractive. The promise of a dowry, or a wedding portion as they called it, even a modest one, might make it worthwhile to pursue an ability to attract men through music. Indeed, after a bit of playing, each one took a turn singing while accompanied by her sister. Daphne got an early escape on the basis of pleading fatigue as a result of the hunt, though, in truth, her main reason was to escape the cacophony which had taken over the drawing-room.

Daphne had trouble falling asleep that night, even though she was exhausted by the day's activities. She was reflecting on the effect of her announcement on the others in the drawing-room. For the first time, she realized how the prospect of a dowry could turn hopes and dreams, which up until then had had little chance of fulfillment, into possibilities that needed to be pursued. She had been regarding her companions as at best a nuisance that had unavoidably been forced on her as part of her marriage. Now she realized that they had probably been no happier with the situation than she was. Indeed, their situation was worse. They had no real assurance that their step-brother would keep supporting them and their prospects otherwise were grim. Marriage would have been but a distant possibility since any suitor would have to be able to take on the expenses of a wife without any recompense from her dowry. A long, unfulfilling future lay before each of them. No wonder they were not the most entertaining of people to share her home with! So far, she had regarded her thoughts of match-making as only a way to get rid of a nuisance. Now she realized that it would be an act of charity as well. With that comforting thought, Daphne fell asleep.

She was surprised the next morning that her first caller was Lord David.

"Did you enjoy the dinner last night?" was Daphne's first question, said in a tone with a bit of an edge to it.

"Immensely," Lord David teased her. "I have never seen so many pompous old men gathered together. Quite put my college's high table to shame."

"No, seriously, was it enjoyable?"

"Yes, on balance, I would say it was. There were some good chaps there, and many had useful things to say about the area and people. I even found out where to buy good hunting horses – and other horses, for that matter."

"Oh?"

"It's near a village called Salton Masham, on the other side of Ameschester. It is rumored that the stud farm may be closing down. The owner died, and his heir apparently is a London man with little interest in horses. That, actually, is why I am here."

"Here? Why?"

"The man I was talking with suggested that it might be wise to see what horses they have for sale if I am interested in getting a hunter, in case they are about to sell off the stud to someone who wants to raise horses themselves. Your father and I are intending to ride over there today, and we wondered if you would like to accompany us."

"I would certainly enjoy that. Just let me get changed. I won't be a minute."

The time taken was more like thirty minutes than one since Daphne first had to summon Elsie from the bowels of the house where she was cleaning the clothes that Daphne had worn on the hunt, and Elsie had to make sure that Daphne's riding boots were cleaned and ready. It also took time for Elsie to help Daphne out of her morning gown and into her riding clothes and to brush her hair again. Elsie was used to her mistress arriving home looking disheveled, but she would not allow her to depart in less than perfect order. At least Lord David and Daphne did not then have to wait for Daphne's horse. As soon as her plans were known, word had been sent to the stables to saddle Moonbeam. The mare was at the portico along with Lord David's mount when they emerged from the front entrance of Dipton Hall. Mr. Moorhouse was already on horseback at the end of his drive when the other two came along.

It was market day in Ameschester. Progress through the streets was hardly hindered by crowds until they came to the market square itself. There, a crowd had gathered in the southwest corner of the square. The trio of riders eased their way towards that corner, for that was where their road exited the square. They were blocked near the corner by the crowd. There were several other riders who, like them, were looking on to see the source of the blockage. Lord David recognized one of the mounted men from the Hunt Dinner.

"What is going on?" he asked.

"Dick Hanks is trying to sell his wife, Martha. That's him with a bridle around Martha's neck."

Daphne could see that there was indeed a stout, red-faced woman dressed only in her shift, with a rope bridle around her neck which was held by a small man. He seemed to be shouting at another man near to him, though the hubbub of the crowd made it difficult to make out his words.

"Sell his wife?" asked Lord David. "And if she bosses him, why is she wearing that bridle?"

"Yes, that is what he is doing, and the bridle is necessary for the action, as is her being dressed only in her shift. The two of them have been fighting together ever since they were married, and that was five years ago. She is a complete shrew and leads him a dog's life. When he tries to control the woman by hitting her, she just hits him back, and she is better at it than he is. That harridan definitely runs their household. The bridle is only to show that she is his in law if not in fact and so he can sell her, and the shift says that she is bringing nothing with her – including his debts."

"So he is really is going to sell her?"

"The story is that he called her a useless scold in the tavern last night, and he would happily sell her if anyone would buy his woman. She responded by daring him to try. She just declared here that she would happily sign the paper for anyone who would buy her off him. Her words were actually 'if anyone will buy me off of this turd.'

"What makes it particularly interesting is that it is said that in the tavern last night, two men were teasing him on not being able to control his woman. He responded that they certainly would not be able to do any better if she belonged to them. The two who were ridiculing him were arguing that Martha would make a very good wife for anyone who could control her, and Dick said just let them try. If they liked her so much, they could buy her. She was worthless to him, but she must be worth a few shillings.

"So here he is, and he has been daring the two men to put some money where their mouths were. The crowd is encouraging them, and Dick is saying that they won't buy her because they know she will put them under her boot just like she did him. She will, too, I'd guess. But their pride is involved. In response to the taunting, one of them offered sixpence, and the other offered a shilling. They have a bidding contest going on, and her price is up to half a crown and still rising."

The three riders from Dipton watched in fascination as that bidding continued with much taunting and insulting of the various men's abilities and manhoods into which the auctioned woman joined with passion. The price rose to seven and six, whereupon one of the men who was bidding yelled, "That's too dear for me. You can have her, but don't come to me if she controls you the way she does Dick Hanks."

The crowd broke up with the entertainment at an end, and Daphne and her companions were able to resume their journey.

"Is that legal?" asked Lord David.

"Probably not," replied Mr. Moorhouse, "but it is the only way the poor chap can get a divorce. He can't just abandon her, not unless someone else will take her on. The Parish wouldn't allow it. The money, and the document of sale they sign, is a commitment to support her. The law says she is her husband's property, but it also says that he has to support her whether or not he wants to."

"I am certainly learning things that they don't teach at Cambridge," remarked Lord David.

"They didn't teach them at Oxford either," Mr. Moorhouse rejoined.

The three riders continued on in companionable silence until they reached Salton Masham, where they were directed to the horse farm of Masham Grange. The house itself was large but not imposing, probably dating back to the time of King Charles II. The stables were newer and were adjacent to several paddocks, some quite evidently fitted out for breaking and training horses. There was a good number of steeds to be seen, grazing in nearby fields, while, in the training areas, several horses were being put through their paces.

They were greeted at the stables by a middle-aged man in riding clothes who introduced himself as the stable master, Griffiths by name, and apologized that the owner was not at home. He would be happy to show them the hunters that were ready to be sold. Normally, they would be sent to auction, but with the impending changes, they could also be sold for a favorable price immediately.

Daphne asked about the impending changes. Mr. Griffiths explained the situation. Mr. Audley, Mr. *Daniel* Audley, the former owner, who had been very committed to his stud farm, had died. His heir, Mr. *Stephen* Audley, who was only a second cousin, was from London and had no interest in horse breeding. He thought the stables ugly and would tear them down and replace them with a much smaller establishment and felt that the paddocks as laid out distracted from the beauty of the grounds. As a result, Mr. Audley – Mr. *Stephen* Audley – was going to sell all the horses. Indeed, he might look favorably on an offer for all the horses together and all the moveable equipment used for the stud farm, just to spare himself the trouble of dispensing with it all piecemeal.

Mr. Moorhouse and Lord David listened to this explanation impatiently, but Daphne was enthralled. What was involved in running a stud, she wondered, and on being given a quick summary by Griffiths, she asked a question that surprised both the stable master and her companions.

"How profitable is a stud, Mr. Griffiths? Is it a business or a hobby?"

"It is both, my lady," was the reply. "There is a good demand for horses of all types, especially with this war on, though heaven only knows when any of the cavalry mounts will see action. That side is highly profitable. But much of the passion that Mr. Audley, Mr. *Daniel* Audley, that is, had for the stables came from breeding exceptional racehorses and trying to improve the breed. That can be a much more speculative venture. I am not sure if Mr. Audley made a profit from it, but financial return didn't seem to matter to him on that part of the venture."

"I see. And it is all for sale?"

"Yes, my lady."

"Well, I would have to examine the accounts before I could to be truly interested in it as a venture."

"I have never heard of a woman owning a stud farm, my lady."

"Haven't you? Well, there is a first time for everything. But if we were interested in the venture, it would be owned by my husband, Captain Richard Giles, of course. But really, we are here to look at your hunters, Mr. Griffiths."

"Yes, my lady. I knew the name sounded familiar. Dipton Manor. But Captain Giles already has a hunter, does he not, Dark Paul? A fine horse, though not very well trained, as I recall. He would take a very firm hand to control him, though some of his worst habits come from his trainer. That man is not really very good at his job. But why would Captain Giles want another hunter?"

"This horse would be for me, Mr. Griffiths. Dark Paul is more than I can handle easily. Furthermore, my father, Mr. Moorhouse, and Lord David here both need good hunters."

"We surely have some mounts that should interest you. Would you tell me your experience and what sort of horse you are looking for, my lady?"

"I have almost no experience hunting, especially not in following the hunt directly. So I want a thoroughly trained horse that will not try to be too daring on its own."

"Not like Dark Paul, I would think. I believe that we may have just the horse for you. Almost as good as the mare you are riding. Of course, your horse is not a hunter, but she is an extraordinary example of horseflesh. You really should breed her, my lady. May I ask where you got her?"

Daphne laughed, "We bred her ourselves. Not intentionally. Our stable boy put her dam into a field with other horses when he should have isolated her. Moonbeam was the result. No pedigree at all."

"Sometimes accidents turn out better than our best-laid plans, my lady. Though I would never confess that to other breeders. And you, Lord David, what sort of hunter are you needing?"

Griffiths rapidly discovered the extent of Lord David's experience and drew the same information from Mr. Moorhouse. He sent a couple of stable boys to gather several horses.

"I am afraid, my lady, that I only have the one mare that would be suitable for you. She is a little small, but she is a very good jumper and full of energy, even though she is fairly easy to handle for a high-spirited mount. I expect you intend to ride astride since that is how you have come here today. I do not think she has been trained to the side-saddle."

"That is correct, Griffiths," broke in Mr. Moorhouse. "I don't want her to break her neck trying to follow the hunt side-saddled."

Daphne laughed but did not contradict him. The horses were brought, and each of them tried the mounts that Mr. Griffiths had thought would be most suitable for them.

Daphne fell in love immediately with the mare he had selected for her. She was lively yet responsive to the reins, required no use of the crop, and, when Daphne took her over some hedges, her take-off and landing were as smooth as butter. Her companions, with a couple of horses to choose from each, for Mr. Griffiths had determined that their needs were quite different from each other, were each placed on the horns of dilemmas, for in each case, they felt they preferred the horse they were riding to the other one, no matter which horse they were on. They promised to return shortly to see if they could make up their minds. Daphne also promised to return, but more to allow some bargaining in which her position would be weakened if she wanted to purchase immediately.

As they were about to mount up to leave, Daphne turned to Griffiths.

"Mr. Griffiths, I would like to see the accounts of the stud farm."

"Yes, my lady, I can have them delivered to your man of business."

"No, I was thinking of looking at them myself."

"Yourself, my lady? Oh, yes, of course. I can have them brought over to Dipton Hall tomorrow if that is convenient. Keep them as long as you need to."

"Thank you, Mr. Griffiths."

The three companions rode off. As they turned onto the road that would lead them to Ameschester again, Lord David broke into laughter.

"Lady Daphne, you could charm the birds from the trees."

"Whatever do you mean?"

"Mr. Griffiths. *Mr.* Griffiths. The poor man has never been called that before by any of his customers. He expects to be called 'Griffiths' by such as us if we can remember his name at all."

"I don't see why I shouldn't call him Mr. Griffiths. He holds a position of responsibility. He may not be a gentleman, but he is certainly a man with a profession."

"I don't disagree. It is just that calling him 'Mister' quite overwhelmed the poor man. Especially since you are 'Lady Giles', not just 'Mrs. Giles'."

"Well, I'm not going to change my ways, even if they cause you to laugh."

They stopped for tea in Ameschester, in the tea rooms that had been doing record business since Lord Moresby's Regiment had encamped in the area. Indeed, they met Captain Hicks just leaving as they entered.

"Lady Giles. Thank you for the kind invitation. I am sure that I speak for Lieutenant Charles as well when I say that we look forward eagerly to the evening."

As they sat down, Lord David again broke out laughing. "Lady Daphne, I see that your lure has already hooked a trout. Now your only problem is to land it."

"That is the most difficult part, Lord David. I am assured by several ladies, who thought you might have taken their bait, that it takes more to land a trout than to hook it."

Night was falling as they left the tea shop. It was cold but clear, and a gibbous moon gave them plenty of light in which to ride to Dipton. Daphne realized that she might feel uncomfortable recounting the day's adventures in choosing horses to those with whom she would dine. They could hardly expect Captain Giles to buy expensive special-purpose horses for their use when he had already done more than they might reasonably have expected in providing horses for each of them to ride. She concentrated, instead, in recounting how she had seen a man sell his wife. It turned out that Lady Marianne had heard of the custom in the North, though she had never known of an actual instance and had doubted that it ever occurred. Daphne also stressed how eager Captain Hicks had been to visit Dipton Hall.

The girls again performed in the drawing-room, and there was evidence that they must have spent a good part of the day practicing on the piano-forte. Daphne also noted that they showed much more interest in their needlework than they had in the past. A little hope, she reflected, seemed to go a long way.

Daphne took great care in writing her letter to Giles that night. She wanted to prepare him in case she felt that establishing a stud farm would be a worthwhile venture. It would be a large change in the estate that belonged to him. As she prepared her thoughts on how best to phrase her reflections on the subject, she wondered if her sudden interest was actually wise. She knew little about breeding horses, but she did know that it was a business with substantial risks. On the other hand, farming itself had considerable risks from bad harvests. Would the risks offset each other?

Then her thinking took a different direction. She remembered that these decisions were rightfully her husband's, not hers. She did not want him to feel that she was always pushing him. She regarded him more as her partner than as her master, but that was not the usual relationship in marriage. She wasn't really sure that Giles would not automatically assume that he, himself, would take all the important decisions and that she would be lucky if he even bothered to consult her. That was how decisions were made in all the better houses in the neighborhood. Indeed, she was discovering that much of the conversation among married women was about how to get their husbands not only to agree to something the wives wanted but also to get the men to think it was their idea in the first place.

Daphne hoped she would not sink to that level of duplicity, but she really should make sure that Giles felt he was in charge, at least to the extent that he wanted to be. The memory of the man selling his wife in the marketplace at Ameschester came back to her. Of course, at her level of society, husbands did not sell their wives, but she never wanted Giles to wish he could. Gentlemen were certainly known to take mistresses, presumably when their wives were unsatisfactory. She had had broad hints from some of her visitors that one could hardly expect a naval captain to be faithful, and the shocked, but intrigued gossip, about Admiral Nelson's scandalous doings with Lady Hamilton, was used to reinforce the point. He had openly taken a mistress when he visited Naples. Amazingly, the strumpet's action occurred with her husband's apparent concurrence, even though he was the British Ambassador to the Kingdom. It was even alleged that Admiral Nelson had said that all men were bachelors east of Gibraltar, or so the whispered reports maintained, which were given in drawing rooms while the ladies waited to be joined by the gentlemen after dinner.

Daphne did not know her husband all that well; she still had facet after facet of his character to explore, and she should not presume that they would always agree on how things should be ordered. Indeed, exploring their differences as well as their shared interests was something to which she was looking forward eagerly. How to make decisions that affected both of them was a subject that they had never considered. There would be more to married life than what had occurred on a brief and ecstatic honeymoon, and Daphne would be wise to go slowly on presuming that they would make decisions in unconventional ways that suited her entirely.

After these reflections, Daphne modified what she was going to write so that she only mentioned in passing that the horse-breeding aspect of the farm was for sale. She added that it would be a pity if the breeding moved far from Dipton since it was so convenient to be able to ride over to Salton Masham to inspect their horses. She finished the letter by telling him again how happy she was that he had encouraged her to buy a hunter and how much she wished he was in Dipton to share her activities and help her choose a horse.

Chapter XI

Admiral Gardiner had given up admonishing Captain Giles for returning to the fleet without being summoned. This time the Captain had returned with a Dutch frigate as a prize, albeit a small one, and an obviously damaged *Impetuous*. The Admiral did not pretend indifference to having his own wealth increased by one-eighth of the value of a small frigate. As always, the interview took place with the admiral seated in front of the stern lights of his cabin while Giles faced him standing across the table.

"Captain Giles. Another prize, and more damage to *Impetuous*, I see. Tell me about how you captured your prize and the rest of your doings."

"It's is all in my report, sir."

"I am sure it is, but it will be quicker if you just tell me now."

Giles outlined his actions in destroying the fort and most of the landing craft rafted in front of it. This was met with approving grunts from the Admiral and a distinctly unfriendly glare when the captain had to admit that *Impetuous* had gone too close to the fort in the dark. The reduction of the fort was applauded, and Giles mentioned that the Dutch frigate had been hidden from them by a rain shower, and its arrival could not have been anticipated.

"You know as well as I do, Captain Giles, that if *Medea* could see you, you should have seen her," the Admiral objected. "But the encounter seems to have ended well. It sounds as if your Lieutenant Kirkpatrick was responsible for his own death. It does neatly solve one of your problems, does it not? Now you need a new lieutenant."

"I have promoted my senior midshipman into the position of acting lieutenant, sir. He will need to take the lieutenant's exam, but he is ready for the promotion."

"I see. Well, you will have to go into Chatham for repairs and supplies. I am going to order that a lieutenant's exam be held at the Nore* in the next few weeks, and he can take it there. If he passes the exam, I will confirm the appointment. If not, there are several lieutenants in the fleet who would welcome the position on *Impetuous*. I suppose that you are also low on supplies."

"Gunpowder and shot, primarily, sir."

"Yes. Well, I have a small job I need you to do with *Impetuous* before you go to Chatham. It will only take a few days."

"Sir?"

"You remember Captain Hoxley and *Bountiful* or, maybe, for what I have in mind, I should say Capitaine Couchetard and *Généreux*?"

"Yes, the pirate captain and spy."

"I don't know where the idea came from – the Warden or the Admiralty – but they want to send him into Boulogne one last time, allegedly to deliver the latest reports and to get any new instructions."

"How can you trust him?"

"The Admiralty seems to think that they have enough of a hold on him that he can be relied on."

"Won't it be known that I took his ship?"

"We hope not. She was, after all, sailing under the British flag, so they may believe that her true purpose was not discovered. But it may not matter. The scheme will be to send him in with false reports and then use *Bountiful* as a fireship to burn the landing craft that are already jammed into Boulogne."

"But won't the French then know that we had discovered Captain Hoxley's duplicity?"

"That is the beauty of the scheme. The report will actually give fairly accurate information on our defenses. We suspect that the French have other ways of discovering what they are and must be puzzling over which set of reports to believe. Sending in an account that they will believe is our work, designed to confuse them, will make them give more credence to the earlier reports brought by Captain Hoxley – and most of them were actually false. Where the others were true, they will be given misleading information that could be taken as a reasonable change in our plans."

"And my role?"

"*Impetuous* will supply the men to crew *Bountiful* in this venture. Captain Hoxley will appear to be in charge, but we don't want him disappearing with his ship if left to his own devices. We have various levers over him to secure his loyalty for this one voyage, or so I am assured. *Bountiful*, commanded by one of your officers, will take him to the quay in Boulogne and wait a limited amount of time there for him to return. If he takes too long, or the French realize that *Bountiful* is no longer what she seems, she will immediately assume her role as a fire ship and abandon Captain Hoxley to what I presume will be a quick termination caused by a meeting with the guillotine."

What is *Impetuous*'s role in all this?

We intend her to approach Boulogne from the south while *Bountiful* – disguised as *Généreux* -- approaches from the north. There are batteries along the coast between Calais and Boulogne. If they open fire on *Généreux*, we will know that she has been discovered, and she will sheer off and go into Boulogne after dark. Otherwise, *Impetuous* will arrive from the south and appear to chase the French ship into harbor. In either case, it will also be *Impetuous*'s task to pick up the boats with the crew after they have set the landing craft on fire. If all goes well, Captain Hoxley will go to the house to meet the French agent and give him the reports prepared for him, designed to confuse and mislead the enemy and return with new requests for information. Captain Hoxley's – or should I say Couchetard's? – treachery will be revealed when *Généreux* attacks the landing craft, but that should cast doubt not only on the report which he brings, which includes several items that are true but on others they may have received from other sources.

"So good luck, Captain Giles. You will have noticed that *Bountiful* is in the center of the fleet. She only has a skeleton crew on board under a midshipman. Select the men to man her from among the members of *Impetuous*'s crew and similarly the officers, and have them taken over to her so you can get away as soon as you can. Report back to me when you finish before going into Chatham."

"Aye, aye, sir."

Giles returned to *Impetuous* to organize the foray. He selected a small crew for *Bountiful* and took them over to the brig together with Midshipman Stewart. They were replacing a rather lackluster crew selected from the men who had been forced to serve in the Navy by being caught by the press-gang. That collection of misfits could man the prize while the Admiral decided what to do with her, but they would not be suitable for a serious mission.

The Admiral's written orders had not been very explicit about Giles' assigning the command of *Bountiful* to one of *Impetuous*'s lieutenants, though Giles knew that the Admiral had presumed that this was what he would do. However, commanding the brig in carrying out their plan would be far more hazardous than commanding the frigate, and it would require better judgment, or so Giles told himself. He also was reluctant to send an officer into danger if he could assume the role himself without jeopardizing his command or the mission. Memories of his guilt over Lieutenant Kirkpatrick's death, groundless though he knew it to be, made him reluctant to assign the command to either Mr. Milton or Mr. Miller. He would captain the brig himself.

Giles realized that there was one major problem with the crew he had picked. They were proud of *Impetuous* and dressed smartly. They looked like navy men, not like the sailors one would expect on *Généreux*. They certainly did not look like the slovenly crew who had been manning *Généreux* when he had captured her, whether one supposed her to be a privateer or a smuggling ship. It would be even better if somehow they looked like a French crew. Probably, Captain Hoxley had had his crew dress as Frenchmen when he entered French harbors.

Giles wondered what had happened to the clothing that the original crew would have worn when going into a French port. When he mentioned his problem to Midshipman Stewart, the lad stated that he had found out where they had been kept when he had explored the ship after it was first captured. He dashed off and returned to report that the clothes were still there.

Giles returned to *Impetuous* with Mr. Stewart to pick up clothes more suitable to their own disguise. Giles would look like a rather ineffective mate for the ship, while Mr. Stewart would impersonate a ship's boy. After checking that

Mr. Milton thoroughly understood his role, Giles went on to the flagship to pick up Captain Hoxley. He returned to *Bountiful* to find that the ship appeared to be manned by about as tough and surly a crew as one could want. Some of them even seemed to delight in spitting on the deck – a flogging offense on most British ships of war. Giles had picked for the mission some of his Cornishmen who, he knew, spoke passable French and some others from Kent. In both cases, the French, he expected, had been learned in the smuggling trade before the seamen had been induced to serve in the Royal Navy. Those of the crew who did not speak French could growl in a sufficiently threatening manner that their true origins could be hidden from casual observers when the brig was tied up in the enemy port.

The two ships made their way across the Channel on an easy broad-reach using a wind from the west. Soon after midnight, they separated so that *Impetuous* could take up her position to the south of Boulogne while *Généreux* would steer so that dawn would find the ship a few miles to the north of Calais.

Généreux was just where Giles wanted the ship to be at sunrise, with the coast of France north of Calais just off their bow. The wind had stayed steady, and they shook out a couple of reefs in the sails in order to reach the rendezvous with *Impetuous* at the right time. Giles could only hope that Mr. Milton and Mr. Brooks had been equally successful in positioning the frigate.

After they passed Calais, Giles chose a course that would bring them within range of one of the coastal batteries. It would be the test of their disguise. If the fort opened fire, Giles would have to do his best to get out of range and vary his course so that the brig would not be destroyed. He would then have to take the brig out of sight of the shore batteries and try to sneak into the harbor after dark. He stationed several hands so that the boats they were pulling behind them could be dragged up to his ship as quickly as possible if *Généreux* were seriously damaged by cannon fire.

The fort remained silent, though Giles could see officers studying his ship through a telescope. He wondered if he should dip his flag as a greeting to the fort, but Captain Hoxley told him that that was not their custom. As *Généreux* neared the next fort, *Impetuous* appeared from the southwest. Giles ordered that the course be changed to bring *Généreux* under the protection of the battery. Mr. Milton, he saw, had been over-eager. *Impetuous* would come up with *Généreux* before she was safe. However, *Impetuous* would have to tack before she could catch the brig. The frigate turned into the wind. Giles wondered if somehow Mr. Milton had received a message to call the expedition off, but that did not seem reasonable: surely he would have just signaled in that case. The puzzle was resolved when *Impetuous* missed stays and was taken all aback. By the time the frigate had sorted itself out and had gathered enough speed to try again to tack, *Généreux* was safely close to the fort. Since *Impetuous* had never missed stays since they first determined how the ship handled, Giles realized that Mr. Milton had been play-acting to make their ruse seem more convincing.

Impetuous turned away, a frustrated hound that had somehow been interrupted just as it was about to catch its rabbit. *Généreux* carried on to the entrance to Boulogne harbor. "I had better take over here, Captain Giles," said Captain Hoxley. "I know this harbor like the back of my hand, and we need to dock smoothly. With this wind, we can turn and slide into the quay without trouble and be facing the right way to leave quickly. Have the line handlers ready and make sure that those who handle the sails speak French, for that is the language that I will use in my commands."

Giles had already designated his French-speaking Cornishmen to handle the mooring lines, and they and his Kentish men to respond to the sail and helm orders. He had also told the crew members who only spoke English to stay out of sight or on the starboard side once they had docked so that their nationality should not be evident.

Généreux slid up the harbor, passing a large raft of landing craft that had been assembled, presumably in preparation for the invasion of England. Captain Hoxley picked his spot on the quay and proceeded far enough up the harbor so that he could turn the brig and slide directly into the berth. The mooring lines were thrown. Idlers on the quay caught them and snugged them down to bollards* that studded the dock every few yards. As the mooring lines tightened and groaned, *Généreux* was pulled to a halt.

The man, who had caught the bow line, called something to Tremethyk, the Cornishman who had thrown it. The seaman gave a reply that produced a laugh among the idlers who then lost interest in the brig. The laugh was joined by the French speakers on *Généreux,* including Captain Hoxley.

"What was that all about?" Giles asked the privateer in a low voice.

"The man on shore asked your crew member where was Leclerc, the seaman who usually throws the bow line. The answer was that Leclerc had caught the clap in some brothel and had missed the ship so that he could spread the same joy among all the other -- ugh – nightingales – ugh -- in the whorehouse. Now, I had better get on with my task. If all goes well, I should be back in time for us to push off before dark. Try to hide how well you are prepared, but be ready to cast off at a moment's notice in case something goes wrong."

With that, Captain Hoxley left the ship and walked down the quay in a purposeful, but not hurried, manner. Giles and the crew pretended to be engaged in minor tasks about the ship even as they were on tenterhooks awaiting the return of Captain Hoxley. After about an hour, Giles saw the ship's master at the end of the quay, strolling along as if he didn't have a care in the world. As he worked his way towards the brig, he even stopped to talk for a few moments to acquaintances. Only when he came aboard did he suddenly become more businesslike. He shouted out a stream of orders in French. Though he didn't understand a word of the commands, Giles inferred that they amount to, "Come along, you lazy fellows. Man your stations to leave the dock. We don't have all day," though Giles figured that this was probably a much milder translation than a literal one would have been.

Taking their cue from how the Captain had acted, the crew members drifted more than jumped to their stations. A string of orders, accompanied by what sounded like well-directed invective, had the mooring lines taken in, the sails set so that the slight breeze shoved the brig away from the quay before the sails were trimmed so that they could proceed down the harbor. At the appropriate moment, a seaman sliced his knife across the jib sheet, and the resulting loss of the headsail and a compensating turn of the wheel had *Généreux* falling off, apparently out of control, right into a raft of landing craft. Several seamen promptly swung down onto the decks of the two craft they had bumped into and secured several lines as planned. Even as they swarmed back onto *Généreux*, several barrels of gunpowder from which protruded fairly short fuses already burning were lowered onto the craft, and smoke began to waft from *Généreux*'s companionway, indicating that the brig had been set alight. The two boats that had been trailing astern were brought to the starboard side, and the crew rushed to fill them. Last to leave *Généreux* were

Midshipman Stewart and Captain Giles. The boats shoved off from the brig, and their oars bit into the water to get them away from the ship and out through the harbor mouth as quickly as possible. Unfortunately, one of the fuses must have been cut too short for a barrel of gunpowder exploded before the boats reached the harbor entrance. As the boats approached the defenses at the mouth of the harbor, the guns opened up. Luckily, the boats presented a small and moving target, and the first salvos only soaked the men in the boats without doing any damage. Even as he encouraged his crew to pull with all their might, Giles noticed that *Impetuous* was sailing towards the harbor entrance and was continuing into danger when she should have turned away from the batteries that guarded the harbor mouth. People in the forts must have noticed the frigate as well, for the guns ceased to try to sink the two boats attempting to escape, presumably so that they could lever their guns around to fire on the frigate.

Impetuous held her course for several moments more until Mr. Milton must have judged that the frigate had come as close to the defenses as he dared, for she fired her two, especially large bow-chasers, before spinning around to head back to sea. The shots from *Impetuous* fell short, but they did kick up large clumps of earth that sprayed over the guns that were being lined up to destroy her. The first two retaliatory salvos from the battery were misdirected and luckily only caused large splashes in the water beside the frigate without hitting her. The next shot was high. The following one was low, but two balls skipped off the water rather than sinking, and they struck *Impetuous*'s stern. One of them destroyed part of the windows of Giles's cabin. The other thumped into the ornate board, which had her name emblazoned on it. Both shots probably did further damage, but they had missed the rudder. The next shots missed the frigate altogether, and, after that, it was evident that the ship had sailed beyond the range of the guns. At that point, *Impetuous* luffed up to wait in the hopes that the boats from *Généreux* would be able to reach her.

The guns were again directed at the fleeing boats. Their aim was not good, with most of the balls missing their targets by a large margin. Some, however, came disturbingly close. One, indeed, hit one of the starboard oars on Giles's boat and the impact drove the handle into the chin of its rower. Giles could not pause to attend to the man, his only reaction to the hit being to starboard his helm a little to compensate for the imbalance in the number of oars that were still pulling the boat.

One other ball seemed to fly past within inches of Giles's nose. There was a sound to his left, and when he glanced that way, he saw that Captain Hoxley's body was splayed across the side of the boat, his head gone, presumably having been carried away by the cannonball. Despite the bile that rose in his throat and his horror at the sudden fate of the pirate, Giles's training made him seem indifferent to the sudden slaughter. "Steady, steady, pull hard," he growled, the order primarily directed at the rower nearest him who had vomited into the bilge at the sight of the headless corpse. Giles diminished the immediate horror by tipping the corpse out of the boat. Amazingly, given the large number of shots that the battery had taken at the boats, there was no other damage, and both boats were able to escape to *Impetuous*. The only person killed in their foray had been Captain Hoxley. Penprase, the rower whose oar had been hit, had only been knocked unconscious and had his jaw broken. He had not been killed. The surgeon claimed that the Cornishman would recover though his jaw would have to be bound up; sustenance and water would need to be poured carefully into his mouth until it healed.

As Giles ascended the side of *Impetuous*, he debated how best to reprove Mr. Milton for putting the frigate in danger in trying to rescue Giles. He found it particularly difficult since he knew that he would have done the same thing if their roles had been reversed. That was not really comparable, however. He would have sent Mr. Milton into danger, and Mr. Milton had certainly not sent Giles. What Mr. Milton should have done was to turn away. However, Giles realized that he would not truly want to serve in a Navy where such a cold-blooded and calculating approach to comrades' danger would be taken. Mr. Milton was wrong, yes; he probably knew that he was, himself; Giles would simply thank him, not give him a tongue lashing.

The damage to the ship was not serious. The stern windows would have to be rebuilt, and the other ball had cracked an underlying plank. *Impetuous* was getting more and more banged up and would have to go into dry dock soon. Giles would have to report to the Admiral that his ship was hardly seaworthy. Then, surely, his superior officer would send them into Chatham for supplies and repairs. With any luck, the repairs would take quite a while, and he would be able to visit Dipton while the work was being done. Giles was already anticipating seeing Daphne again. But first, he would have to have another interview with Admiral Gardiner.

Chapter XII

The records from Salton Masham arrived on the morning following the trip to evaluate hunting horses. Daphne spent some time studying the accounts. She had learned basic arithmetic at the dame school she had attended, as it was an accomplishment that ladies were thought to need in managing their households. That had kindled an interest in figures which was furthered when her father allowed her to assume much of the running of Dipton Manor. She found that she had a knack for seeing what numbers said about how things were being run and that they even showed how improvements might be made. She could do quite complicated calculations in her head and keep track of several numbers from different pages simultaneously to illuminate a larger picture.

The accounts revealed that the stud farm had been quite a profitable enterprise until the past year when its expenses seemed to be getting out of hand. It would take more investigation than Daphne was prepared to put into the records to determine whether this was due to inefficiencies or to thievery that had crept into the operation with the death of the owner.

The stud record was written in quite a different hand, suggesting that the writer was not comfortable with a pen and had possibly learned to write as an adult. From the context, it appeared to be Mr. Griffiths, who recorded in detail and precision all the breeding activities and results of the farm. It was the work of someone who clearly knew his business. To Daphne's surprise, while it listed where each colt had been sold as well as its characteristics, it never mentioned the price. That, Daphne surmised, had been the domain of someone else.

The accounts did little to dull her attraction to the stud farm, even though caution would be needed to discover the reason for the recent increase in expenses. However, before Daphne got too lost in dreams of turning Dipton Hall into a famous breeder of horses, her resolve of the previous evening caught up with her. She would be risking too much to undertake such a radical change in direction even with permission from Captain Giles if he had not himself examined what was involved. Only if the opportunity was still there when once more he returned to Dipton, and only if he came to the conclusion on his own that this would be a good direction for the estate, would she take any steps to accomplish the change. She, instead, should make sure that all was in order for the dinner that night, not dream of an unlikely change whose realization, she had resolved, would not occur at her instigation.

The dinner to initiate Daphne's scheme to provide futures for her house companions turned out, in her opinion, to be a shrewd maneuver. It started well by her asking Lieutenant Charles what had been his occupation before he joined the militia. The answer was that he had been at Cambridge but had been sent down for some unspecified prank. He seemed to think that this dismissal was a great joke. Daphne's heart sank as he reported that he had been up at the university only a short time because she had visions of Lord David and Lieutenant Charles going into a corner to swap reminiscences of their student days. Fortunately, however, the lieutenant turned the conversation another way by adding that he had intended just to have a good time after being sent down, living in London and spending an allowance from his father. His parent, however, had quite other ideas about how his son should occupy his time. He had bought his son a lieutenant's commission in Lord Moresby's Regiment, where he hoped his offspring would learn responsibility. Lieutenant Charles complained that, really, his father should have bought him at least a captaincy. This gave an opening to Miss Lydia Crocker to comment on how stingy rich relatives could be, citing the case of her own grandfather. They were sitting together, and somehow their conversation drifted away from the others as Daphne turned to Captain Hicks with much the same question as she had directed at Lieutenant Charles. As she expected, he explained that he had a position in the family bank.

To keep the conversation going, Daphne stated, rather untruthfully, that she knew there was a bank in Ameschester, but she wasn't really sure what they did. Despite a serious, sudden case of coughing from Lord David, who was well aware of Daphne's financial acumen, Captain Hicks proceeded to explain how banks could take deposits, and people could write draughts on them, and how banks would make loans and issue bills of exchange that could be cashed at their correspondents' offices. How did that work, Daphne asked, while really hoping that Catherine Crocker would show some interest in the conversation. The Captain explained, again not overly coherently, how you could put money into one bank and then have the bank give you a piece of paper that could be taken by someone in another town to the bank there and get the money. At that point, Miss Crocker suddenly showed a keen interest in the mysterious world of banking about which Captain Hicks was so well informed.

"How, Captain Hicks, can that be? How do they know in advance to which bank to send the sack of gold coins?"

Daphne was sure that getting this conundrum sorted out would surely take the two young people until dinner was announced. She turned to get her third project underway.

"Major Stoner, did you know that Lady Marianne's late husband was an army officer?"

"No, I did not. Lady Marianne, what was your husband's regiment?"

As Daphne hoped, that got the two of them engaged in comparisons of army life in India and in Yorkshire and how, while some challenges were quite different, others were the same wherever there were soldiers.

Lord David winked at Daphne, much to her annoyance since she did not like having her stratagems recognized so easily. They then started to discuss the adequacy of the vicarage's stables and of Lord David's groom if he were to acquire a first-rate horse for hunting. Lord David spent quite a bit of the conversation on the relative merits of the two horses he had under consideration, and they agreed that the choice should not be made without another chance to ride the two mounts again.

After dinner, when the other men had thoroughly bored Lord David by exchanging tales of life in barracks while indulging themselves with copious glasses of port wine, the opportunity presented itself for the ladies to exhibit their musical talents. Luckily the army men did not seem to have much of an ear for music, and things proceeded even better when the men themselves were induced to sing. As the most accomplished pianist, Daphne was pressed into service to accompany the men, which she did more than adequately. Lieutenant Charles had a light tenor voice which he controlled excellently so that his singing of familiar love songs seemed to have Miss Lydia almost swooning. Captain Hicks provided a rougher baritone, though it seemed to please Miss Crocker immensely. Finally, Major Stoner persuaded Lady Marianne to play while he sang some well-known military songs. What they lacked in technique, for Major Stoner had a harsh voice and sang off-key while Lady Marianne's precision in hitting the right notes was rather wobbly, they made up for in enthusiasm. They only grated on the nerves of Daphne and Lord David, for the other possible listeners had moved to the end of the drawing-room and seemed to be engaged in good-natured banter that was not hindered by their elders' efforts.

Lord David took the opportunity to discuss once more the horses that they had examined. He was eager to see them again and to choose one in time to have some experience on the horse before the next hunt. His unpleasant ride on Dark Paul still grated on him, and he wanted to avoid any chance of a repeat. Daphne sympathized and felt that she would also like to get used to her horse before displaying her skills to the jaundiced eyes of the men of the hunt who, she was sure, believed that women in a hunt should merely follow meekly along in order to admire and praise the actions of the gentlemen. Discussing horses and agreeing to examine them the next day did something to give relief to the enthusiastic noise-making that was occupying Lady Marianne and the Major.

After the guests left, Daphne could congratulate herself that the first steps of her plans were off to a flying start. Of course, it was still very early days, and the course of true love was not supposed to run smoothly. But that had not been her own experience, and she wasn't sure that true love was really what she could expect from her scheming on behalf of her in-laws.

It was still nearly pitch dark when Elsie drew the curtains in her mistress's bedroom the next morning, though a pink line along the horizon indicated that dawn was at hand. The scullery maid had been in a couple of hours earlier to lay the fire in Daphne's grate, so getting out of bed was not the torture that it might have been otherwise. Daphne wondered how she should occupy herself in the coming day. The farm tasks had ground to a halt except for the chores needed to maintain the livestock. She was now well versed in the financial accounts. She would read, and play the pianoforte and possibly take a brisk walk for exercise. She was about to instruct Elsie on the proper clothes to get out to match her intentions when she remembered her agreement with Lord David. She ordered Elsie to bring her the special writing desk for use in bed, which, in fact, she had not yet used so that she could write a note to her father to suggest that he join them in the expedition. With that dispatched, Daphne bounced out of bed to don her winter riding clothes before going down to breakfast.

Daphne was surprised to find that her nieces were already at the table. Normally they slept later. They also seemed to be having a much less substantial meal than was their norm. Daphne suspected that this self-denial might have something to do with the men who had attended the dinner the previous evening, and that suspicion was strengthened when the first topic of conversation raised was the dowries that Daphne had indicated might be forthcoming. Daphne confirmed that there would be dowries, but she indicated that the amount could only be determined by Captain Giles. She rather hinted that it might be a subject of negotiation between the captain and any suitor. That made the girls realize another problem that they had never considered. At their age, someone had to consent to their getting married. Could their mother do that, or did it require some man? And if so, which man? Was it their grandfather, in whom they had no confidence, or could their half-uncle be the one to give permission? Daphne had no idea what the answers were, but she indicated that she imagined that their uncle's permission would be sufficient, especially if their mother agreed. The girls then began to pester her about when the Captain might be returning, a subject on which she had no information.

Lord David was announced at nine-thirty. He was impatient to get going. The ever perceptive Steves had ordered that Moonbeam be saddled and brought up to the house as soon as he had been told that Lord David had been spied riding up the drive. Soon the trio was again on their way to Salton Masham. Lord David wanted to stop at Drucker's Bank in Ameschester to determine how he might pay for the horse he wanted to buy. He knew that Mr. Edwards, Captain Giles's man-of-business, had set up an account for him in the Bank on which he could write cheques for his expenses, but he was not sure if he had enough money on deposit to pay for the horse. Daphne teased him that he should have listened more carefully to Captain Hicks's explanation of banking, to which Lord David replied that if he had not been confused before the Captain's discussion, he surely would have been after, except that he had paid no attention to the presentation. Daphne also didn't really understand how these accounts all worked. She knew that Mr. Edwards regularly forwarded bills of exchange drawn on Coutts Bank in London to Drucker's Bank. She had been assured by Mr. Edwards that virtually any amount that she might spend would be paid by the Bank without worry. He had also arranged for all her accounts for regular purchases to be paid directly when she had approved them. It had never occurred to her to wonder just how the money was transferred from London to the people who would receive it.

Mr. Drucker, the owner of the bank, assured Lord David that even quite large draughts on the bank would be honored. If there were an over-draught, which he explained happened when a request to have the bank pay out more money than was actually in the account was honored by the bank, there would be a small amount of interest charged. Daphne wasn't at all sure that Lord David really understood the details of the ins and outs of banking, even though Mr. Drucker's explanation was a great deal clearer than had been Captain Hicks's. However, she was sure that he got the main point which was that he could certainly pay for the horse and not have to worry about finding himself in difficulties over the payment.

The three travelers had a pleasant luncheon at the Fox and Hounds, which served a fine Welsh rarebit and plum duff and a tankard of excellent ale in a warm room, removed from the common bar. The men assured Daphne that the fare was a good deal better than what had been served at the hunt dinner. Their further conversation turned largely on hunting and horses. All three were used to having horses in their lives, but the nearest they had come to how horses were reared was the auction ring, except for the accidental breeding of the sort that had produced Moonbeam. Mr. Moorhouse was also riding a horse that had arrived on his estate by an accidental mating of his horses, and it was also a good horse, though not as good as Moonbeam. Mr. Moorhouse teased Daphne that she should consider breeding horses as part of her agricultural activities. That led to a long discussion of what made a horse a good one and how one might plan to raise superior mounts.

They proceeded happily on to Salton Masham. Mr. Griffiths was more than pleased to let the two men try the horses again while he and Daphne entered his office to complete the transfer of the mare she had chosen, whose name was Serene Masham. Mr. Griffiths explained to Daphne that he had been told to set the price at £120, but he also had been told that he should accept, if necessary, £90. Daphne realized that Mr. Griffiths was too honest for his own good and decided to offer £95. They struck an amicable deal at that price and then turned to discussing the stud farm, whose books Daphne had returned.

"I was intrigued by the detailed records you keep of all the horses you have bred and even the results of unsuccessful couplings," Daphne commented. "They were certainly well kept, Mr. Griffiths."

"Thank you, my lady. Raising horses is my passion as well as my trade, and I get great satisfaction just looking in the book and seeing, in my mind's eye, all the horses that have passed through these stables. There have been some steeple-chase champions and some that were famous for usually being in at the kill while hunting. Of course, these sorts of result also depend on the rider, but he cannot win without a winning horse."

"I suppose so. And will Serene Masham be one who will stay in your mind?"

"Oh, yes, my lady. Such fine lines and so good-natured. I will be sad to see her go."

"What will happen to you, Mr. Griffiths, when the stud activities are sold?"

"I don't know, my lady. There will be no need for a horse breeder and trainer at Salton Masham Grange after the stud is sold. Or at any other estate near here. My wife doesn't want to leave, but I don't think we will have a choice. I will just have to look for work as a stable master somewhere else."

"Well, I am afraid that Dipton Manor and Dipton Hall both already have adequate stable masters since neither estate breeds horses. There is another side to the accounts that I should mention to you."

"What is that, my lady?"

"I could not understand why the expenses seemed to rise suddenly in the last year while your activities did not. Did something change?"

"Of course, young Mr. Audley took over, and he brought in his own bookkeeper. Young Mr. Audley shows much less interest in the farm than did his father. I confess that I don't really know how to interpret all those figures in the records, but I am surprised by what you tell me. We have been running as tight a ship as in Mr. Daniel Audley's day, even though the owner isn't as interested. But you would need someone better able to interpret the numbers to explain what was going on."

"I suspect that the new bookkeeper has been slipping some money into his own pocket as an expense," said Daphne. "But I only looked over the accounts quickly, so I can hardly accuse the new man."

"Yes, my lady. I'll try to keep an eye on him."

Their business finished, Daphne and Mr. Griffiths chatted on about horses and farming and how uneven the past summer's harvest had been, and even how the war was affecting their different prospects. Mr. Griffiths was particularly distressed that the demand for cavalry mounts and other horses for the army had lowered the standards for good horses. Of course, he added, that had little effect on the Navy. He just hoped that that service could keep this man Bonaparte on the other side of the Channel.

At last, Mr. Moorhouse and Lord David had made their choices, though Mr. Moorhouse had had to end Lord David's dithering by riding both of the vicar's possible mounts and choosing between them. Despite Lord David's continuing confusion about banking, Mr. Griffiths was happy to accept their draughts on Drucker's Bank. The three decided to ride their new mounts home.

They set off to return to Dipton. It began to sprinkle soon after they passed through Ameschester, and before long, it was raining heavily. They all stopped at Dipton Manor to have tea, partly in the hope that the downpour would ease up before Daphne and Lord David had to proceed to their own homes. It was a distinctly damp trio that assembled in front of the roaring fire that Tisdale had had the maids build in anticipation of Mr. Moorhouse's return. The warmth of the fire, added to the hot buttered scones that were part of the tea, kept them cheerful as they planned to give their horses a good workout before the next hunt. The meet was scheduled to be held in only three days' time.

It was raining even more heavily as Lord David and Daphne emerged from Dipton Manor. They did not tarry in riding to their respective abodes, but, even so, Daphne was soaked through by the time she reached the portico of Dipton Hall. She directed the footman, who emerged to hold her horse as she dismounted, to have the animal taken to the stables. She rushed into the house. The heavy, homespun wool riding clothes, which could protect her from more normal rain, were hanging on her as a heavy, sagging brown load in which she could hardly move. She stood shivering for a moment before a concerned and open-mouthed Steves, as a puddle formed on the marble of the entrance floor, before trudging up the stairs to shed her clothes. She just hoped that a fire was burning in her room, for her teeth were beginning to chatter.

192

Chapter XIII

Admiral Gardiner looked very angry. He had asked for the full story of the attack on Boulogne, more detailed than the written report that lay before him as yet unread. Giles had reached the point in his narration where *Généreux* and *Impetuous* diverged from each other so that *Généreux* would appear from the north while *Impetuous* would seem to be coming to Boulogne from the south. It was also the point at which it was clear that Giles would be going into Boulogne on the brig while leaving Lieutenant Milton to command *Impetuous*. The Admiral said nothing as Giles continued his presentation, but it was clear that he was not pleased as he glowered at Giles during the rest of the story. When Giles finished, the Admiral's first comment was, "Why in God's name did you take command of *Généreux* yourself, Captain Bush?"

"It seemed best for me to command the most difficult part of the attack."

"Best? Best? How could it be 'best' for you to put your valuable frigate in the hands of your lieutenant and take command of the hazardous venture, where any number of things could go wrong that were quite beyond your control, in a ship that was going to be destroyed anyway?"

"Lieutenant Milton did very well, sir. I would never have thought of the ruse of missing stays to allow the brig to seem to escape."

"Maybe not. But remember that he brought *Impetuous* into range of the shore guns just because you needed rescuing from your arsonry. It was only sheer luck that the French aim was faulty so that their guns only took out your cabin lights. *Impetuous* could easily have been sunk."

"Yes, sir." Giles was not about to protest that he would have taken the same actions if Mr. Milton's and his own roles had been reversed. He knew that Mr. Milton had been in the wrong, and the fact that he would have done the same did not change that evaluation.

'Well, all's well that ends well," said the Admiral with a slight grin. "You do have a knack for getting rid of bothersome people."

"Sir?"

"Captain Hoxley. I don't know what we would have done with him if he had lived. These papers he collected are likely to be quite valuable, but the man himself was a bloody pirate, nothing more. He should have been hung! At least, now, he cannot be rewarded for his perfidy. Was he really your only casualty?"

"Yes, sir."

"Remarkable! Especially after the way you got rid of that lieutenant, what was his name, Kirkpatrick?"

"I protest, sir. I in no way intended Lieutenant Kirkpatrick to be killed – or Captain Hoxley, either."

"I suppose not. But luck trumps cleverness every time. Now, I imagine that *Impetuous* needs the attention of the dockyard more than ever."

"Yes, sir, and supplies."

"Go directly into the dockyard at Chatham; don't wait in the Nore for them to summon you. It's all done on the basis of influence or worse there. I have sent word that you will be coming and that there will be all hell to pay if *Impetuous* is not attended to immediately. Even though Boney* is not likely to invade in the depths of winter and his invasion craft are still being assembled, and you have just dealt them a blow, I need you back on patrol to harass him. And Captain Giles, use your title when you deal with the Dockyard. I know that you don't normally use it in the Navy, though I see no reason why you shouldn't. It will emphasize that you are a quickly brightening star in the Navy's firmament, and they may not know how little influence you really have as yet. Furthermore, with the acquisition of Dipton Hall, you may well be more important than you realize.

"Good luck to you, Captain Giles. I presume that your Mr. Milton can supervise the repairs and that you will return to Dipton while they are going on. Give my regards to Lady Giles. You do know that you will have to return some time before the repairs are supposed to be finished to chivy the Dockyard to keep working on *Impetuous*, do you not?"

"Yes, sir." Giles, in fact, had not thought of that complication. He secretly admired how the wily Admiral had neatly countered any tendency for Giles to tarry longer than wise at Dipton.

"There is one other matter, Captain Giles."

"Yes?"

"With the promotion of Mr. Correll, you must be short of a midshipman."

"I am, sir."

"If you have not yet filled the position, I have a suggestion for you to consider."

"Yes, sir?"

"My sister's grandson. Her daughter is married to Lord Merville's son, his second son. Their boy's name is Ian

Maciver. He's a good lad, just fourteen. He would like to go to sea. He has been on *Penelope*'s books for the last two years, but the truth is that there really is no room for him here. He hasn't been on board yet. It is time, though, that he went to sea if he is really to progress in the Navy. He would learn much quicker on an active frigate than on a flagship that never goes anywhere. You would be doing me a great favor if you could find room for him in *Impetuous*."

"With pleasure, sir. I will look forward to meeting the young man. It would be a good idea if he reported to the ship in a couple of weeks. Give him a chance to become familiar with the ship while she is not bouncing around in a storm."

So that was how it was done, Giles reflected, as he made his way back to *Impetuous*. Do a favor by pushing the Dockyard to give prompt service, and get a favor in finding a position for a relative. All very logical, but he had never really seen so clearly the system at work first-hand. He couldn't say that he approved of this way of running the Navy, but if that were the game, he would be more than happy to play it.

Chatham Dockyard sprawled for a mile along the Medway River. Giles had never been there, at least not on business, though earlier in his career, he had been on ships in the Nore. Fortunately for him, Mr. Brooks had experience with the establishment and confidently took *Impetuous* right up to a jetty close to the Superintendent's office. Luckily, Captain Smythe, the superintendent, was not away, though he often was, and Giles had word sent in that Captain **Sir** Richard Giles wished to speak with him. Whether it was on account of the Admiral's warning, Giles emphasis on the title, whose details he had no doubt that Captain Smythe looked up before asking for Captain Giles to be sent in, or simply that the Superintendent was exhibiting unusual competence for someone working in His Majesty's Dockyards, Giles was shown into Captain Smythe's room after hardly any wait. Of course, *Impetuous*'s needs would be given high priority. Most important, definitely most important. Admiral Gardiner had stressed how critical were Sir Richard's requirements. Why Captain Smythe would dispatch his senior shipwright immediately to survey *Impetuous*'s needs. Giles returned to his ship and was followed in half an hour by a Mr. Cornwell, a rather rotund, red-faced, cheerful man who announced that he was the master shipwright sent to examine the frigate's needs. Giles turned him over to Mr. Evans and Mr. Shearer, *Impetuous*'s carpenter and bosun, to make a thorough examination of the various bits of damage that the frigate had suffered as well as a more general assessment of her needs. Giles settled at the table in his cabin to catch up on the never-ending stream of paperwork that accompanied the running of a naval ship and to read and reread the latest letters from Daphne that had reached him after *Impetuous* docked.

It was well into the first dog watch before the marine sentry announced that Mr. Cornwell, Mr. Evans, and Mr. Shearer wished to see him. The news was not entirely good. Mr. Cornwell was particularly worried about where the cannonball from the fort had struck the frigate near the waterline. She would require dry-docking to examine the damage properly and to replace any strakes that had been broken or weakened. Mr. Cornwell would need to do some calculations and consult dockyard schedules before estimating how long the work might take. If Captain Giles would visit the Superintendent's office after ten o'clock the following morning, the Superintendent should be able to give an estimate of how much time would be required before the frigate could be released. In the meantime, it would probably be best if *Impetuous* anchored out in the river to free up the jetty. Giles noted with amusement the confidence with which the shipwright was able to give what amounted to orders to a post-captain. He must have found that his control of the repair process gave him a distinct edge in dealing even with officers of that lofty rank

The following morning found Giles in the Superintendent's office again together with Mr. Cornwell and a couple of other senior functionaries. Yes, the damage was serious, possibly more so than Sir Richard had realized. *Impetuous* would certainly need dry-docking, and that had to be fitted into a busy dockyard schedule. It would take at least ten weeks before the frigate would be ready for sea, and it might be longer if they found more serious weaknesses. It was a pity that the standards of French shipbuilding had so deteriorated with their revolution.

Giles feigned horror at the estimate. He stressed the importance of the work on the frigate and the urgency of getting her back on station. He wondered if Admiral Gardiner had emphasized how important was her role. Why, just before coming to Chatham, *Impetuous* had been responsible for destroying a large number of Boney's invasion fleet. And that was an expedition undertaken partly at the urging of the Warden of the Cinque Ports. Of course, the Superintendent knew his own work best, but Giles was sure that his father, the Earl of Camshire, would be delighted to hear that the Superintendent had succeeded in cutting the period required to four weeks. Of course, Giles would have to tell him about the situation, when he saw him, to explain why he did not have to return to his ship so soon. The Warden would, undoubtedly, be concerned to hear for how long the frigate would be out of service.

The officials conferred together in lowered tones so that Giles could not make out what exactly they were saying. It seemed to consist of guessing which parts of the overall schedule of the dockyard could be put back without too much loss in broken promises. They finally agreed with each other, and the Superintendent turned back to Giles. They had been able to rearrange the schedule so that repairs on *Impetuous* would only take seven weeks. The Dockyard officials could only hope that this rearrangement would not have serious consequences for England's safety. Giles decided he had probably got all he could hope for in concessions from the Superintendent, especially as he had already used all the names that he thought might have an effect, and, in the case of the last two names, it was all a sham: He would not be seeing his father and even if he were to talk with the Earl, discussing *Impetuous*'s repair schedule would not be on the agenda.

He returned to *Impetuous* to explain to Mr. Milton what would be happening. There was no point in keeping the crew on the ship or in barracks while she was in the dockyard. Most of them could be given leave for the next six weeks. Mr. Milton must just make sure that enough petty officers and experienced hands were on hand for any necessary work not done by the dockyard. That part of the crew, too, should be given leave, but on a rotation basis. Mr. Correll would have to stay with the ship until a lieutenant's exam was held. Mr. Milton and Mr. Miller could divide the responsibilities of staying with the ship and taking leave. The same would be true of the two midshipmen. Oh, and there was a new midshipman who would be joining in the next two weeks or so, a Mr. MacIver, as green as grass. Help the lad get his bearings. And, of course, if there was an emergency, send post-haste to Dipton Hall.

Carstairs had been investigating the ways to get to London quickly. With a rising tide and a steady east wind, the best way would be by water. Carstairs had already found the boatmen and packed Giles's sea chest so that he could head to the entry port as soon as he had finished giving his orders. Just before he got to where the marines were lined up to mark his departure from the ship, he saw Midshipman Stewart.

"You must be looking forward to seeing your family again, Mr. Stewart."

"Yes, sir, but I switched with Mr. Dunsmuir as to which of us would go first."

"You are going second? Why?"

"I want to see as much as I can of the dockyard before going, sir. My father will have any number of questions when I get to Butler's Hard."

"I suppose he will. I had forgotten your origins, Mr. Stewart. Keep an eye on the dockyard men while you are here, and mention anything that might be amiss to Mr. Milton. And my respects to your father when you see him."

"Aye, aye, sir."

Giles's boat made good time up the river, and he reached London Bridge just after sunset. It was too late to take the coach to Ameschester that night, so he and Carstairs went to the inn near Charing Cross at which they had previously stayed. There Giles ran into two other naval captains that he had known slightly when the three of them had been lieutenants in Jamaica. The evening was spent with good food, much wine, and talk of the naval doings. Giles's head was none too clear, and Carstairs also seemed the worse for wear when they caught the coach to Ameschester. Both demonstrated the ability of naval personnel to sleep anywhere even before the coach clattered through the outskirts of London.

They reached Ameschester as night was falling, and the rain became harder, quite unaware of the trio of riders who had passed through the town on their way to Dipton just before their arrival. Giles hired a coach to take him to his estate and soon set off on the last leg of his journey. As the coach neared Dipton, he started to recognize things and his anticipation became acute as the conveyance turned into the drive leading to Dipton Hall. The rumble of the arriving coach produced a footman who dashed to open the door of the coach. Giles was out of the vehicle just as soon as the door swung wide and rushed to the entrance. There he found Steves, surprisingly somewhat flustered by the unexpected arrival of the master of the house, and was about to ask where Lady Giles might be when a large brown object, seeming more like a bear than a woman, came surging down the stairs and ran right into him.

Daphne had just dragged her sodden figure around the bend in the stairs after arriving from her visit to Salton Masham when she heard noise from the entryway and Steves saying, "Sir Richard." She spun around and started to race down the stairs. Unfortunately, the speed of her descent and the soaked nature of her clothes made her trip over the hem of her riding clothes and rush totally unbalanced into Giles's chest just as he turned to see what the commotion was all about. That collision, in turn, toppled Giles into Steves, who sat down on his backside as a result of the impact. Had there been an uncommitted bystander to witness this collision, they would have noted that it is possible to sit down with a thump on the floor with dignity. Steves accomplished the feat as part of the comedy act.

Giles had often wondered what his first moments at Dipton Hall might be like; indeed, it had been one of his favorite last thoughts before he would fall asleep at night. Never had he imagined the welcome he had just received. Even as Daphne started to wail, "Oh, no! What have I done?" Giles began to chuckle. Daphne started to see the humor in their tangle and began to giggle. Soon the chuckle and the giggle turned into hearty laughs. Elsie, who had come to the bend of the stairs to see what was causing the ruckus, was smiling broadly even before she spied Carstairs entering with the Captain's sea chest on his shoulder. Steves gave up his attempt to look solemn. The footman was having a hard time keeping a straight face as he rushed to help extricate his three superiors from their tangle. He knew, however, that if he joined in the merriment, his position might disappear when Steves recovered his dignity.

The first person to speak was Elsie, who cried out, "Lady Giles, you must get out of those wet things, or you will catch your death." Daphne turned, intending to ascend the staircase in her sodden riding habit, but that was interrupted immediately by Giles. He picked her up, seemingly without effort, and started up the stairs. He had never had the chance to carry his new bride over the threshold of Dipton Hall, but he made up for it by carrying her all the way up the stairs and into their bedroom. Daphne found that being carried by her husband, with her arms wrapped around his neck, was an unusual pleasure that she would be glad to have repeated, though preferably when not wearing heavy clothes and being soaked to the skin. Unfortunately, the pleasure did not last long. All too soon, Giles had carried her to her room and set her down for Elsie's attention while he himself went to change.

Dinner was delayed while the master and mistress of the house were getting dressed. Their good manners were restored by the time they were seated in the dining room, and the conversation was general. The girls and even Lady Marianne showed substantial interest in Giles's naval adventures, which he did make less graphic than he had in his letters to Daphne. The young ladies, in turn, recounted much of the gossip of the neighborhood, and Giles was good enough not to tell them that he knew most of it as a result of Daphne's letters or that her accounts included the more salacious tales that his nieces were omitting.

The girls left the subject in which they were most interested to the end of the meal when a spotted-dick* pudding was served as dessert.

"Uncle Richard," ventured Lydia, who, as the younger sister, had been chosen to ask the delicate question in the belief that she would be less likely to cause offense, "Aunt Daphne told us that you would provide us with marriage portions."

"Not marriage portions, Lydia," Lady Marianne interrupted. "You have no claim on your uncle's estate. It will be a dowry or a wedding present if your uncle is kind enough to make you such a gift on marriage."

"Yes, Mama. But Uncle, will there be a gift?"

"Yes, Lydia, there will be. I haven't decided on the sum yet. But I am sure that it will smooth the way for your suitor to make the commitment. However, I will have to make sure that the amount is not so large that you will need protection from fortune hunters."

"Oh, thank you, Uncle Ricard," burst in Catherine. "I don't think we are in danger of being snapped up by fortune hunters, but you are right. A lot of wonderful men cannot afford to marry without some contribution from the bride's family. I don't know if we will ever attract men. So far, no one has really been interested in me."

"It is early days, yet, Catherine," said Daphne. "I didn't have any offers of marriage until I was much older than you."

Giles had to hide a grin at this statement. He knew perfectly well that Daphne had not had any earlier offers of marriage because she had actively discouraged them. He was still amazed that he had won her hand.

Giles did not stay in the dining room when Daphne rose to lead the ladies into the drawing room. He had no need of port wine, especially not when Daphne would not be with him as he drank it. He rose at the same time as the ladies to accompany them into the drawing-room. Only Steves was disappointed with this development. He had specially chosen an excellent bottle to decant and had hoped for Giles's approval. Not that this setback would prevent him from taking the long-established prerogative of butlers to make thoroughly sure that the wine had not deteriorated in the decanter before sealing it away.

Giles and Daphne found excuses to leave the drawing-room almost immediately after entering it, pleading tiredness and the strenuous nature of their activities that day. Daphne dismissed Elsie as soon as possible, only making sure that the bedroom fire was blazing warmly. Giles was equally efficient in sending away Ralph, the first footman. Steves had designated him to serve as valet since Captain Giles had not yet appointed someone to fill that position. Steves had finally realized that Carstairs was not a valet. Strangely, given the urgency of the couple to get to rest, Elsie found in the morning that the candles in Daphne's room had burned down completely and must have guttered out.

Chapter XIV

Elsie waited an extra half hour beyond the usual time before going into Daphne's bedroom the following morning. Even then, she did not throw open the curtains, as was her usual practice. Instead, making enough noise so that her mistress could not possibly sleep through the racket, she turned and left the room for half an hour. On her return, she found that her intention of sparing Captain Giles – or her mistress – any embarrassment had been for naught. She was greeted by Captain Giles sitting up in bed wearing a red flannel nightgown and nightcap. He asked her in a friendly tone what sort of a day it was.

Elsie replied that the rain had passed away and that it promised to be a sunny day, a bit warmer than the previous one.

If Captain Giles was supposed to be embarrassed by being found in his wife's bed, he certainly didn't show it. Instead, he turned to Daphne and said, "Come along, sleepyhead. There are too many important things to do for us to spend more time in bed."

With that, he bounced out of bed, looking more like an oversized elf than a post-captain in the Royal Navy.

"Ralph is waiting for you in your dressing room, sir," Elsie told him demurely.

"Thank you, Elsie," he replied. And then, in a voice that easily reached the topmast in a gale, he cried, "Out of bed, Lady Giles."

Giles left, and Daphne emerged from the bed, still sleepy-eyed. "Good morning, Elsie. Riding clothes again today."

"The warm ones are not yet fully dry, my lady."

"Well, the next warmest. You said it will be a warmer day."

"Yes, my lady." Elsie knew enough not to contradict her mistress when she was in her 'get things done' mood. Daphne washed in the rapidly cooling water Elsie had brought and started to get dressed. "Did you see Carstairs yesterday evening?"

"Oh, yes, my lady."

"And everything is still fine between you?"

"Oh, yes, my lady!"

"Good. Let's hurry. I know Captain Giles does not take long dressing."

"Yes, my lady."

When Daphne entered the breakfast room, she was surprised to see that her nieces were there ahead of her. Giles was just completing his plate at the sideboard. The two girls revealed why they had risen early as soon as Giles sat down.

"Uncle Richard, did you know that the Hunt is meeting tomorrow?" asked Catherine.

"Yes."

"Are you going to ride in it?"

"Yes, your Aunt Daphne and I are intending to do so."

"Can we go too?" broke in Lydia.

"Just going with those who take the easy way, not following the hounds directly." Catherine elaborated.

"What do you think, Lady Giles?" asked Giles, in an attempt to avoid a responsibility he had never considered being his own.

"I think you should ask your mother," Daphne prevaricated.

"But she has no interest in hunting," wailed Lydia.

"That doesn't mean that she will not let you go," said Giles, hoping that this would end the discussion. It did since Daphne and Giles immediately rose to leave the table. Daphne took Giles's arm.

"This is getting to be more complicated than I expected," remarked Daphne.

"In what way?"

"I hadn't thought that inviting potential suitors based on meeting them at a Hunt meeting would, of course, get the girls interested in hunting."

Giles laughed. "Maybe Lady Marianne will also develop a sudden passion for hunting. Didn't you say she was getting on very well with Major Stoner from the Hunt?"

The two spent the morning examining some of the many projects that Daphne had been telling Giles about in her letters. He was enthusiastic about the progress that had been made, being amazed at how much she had accomplished in a few short weeks despite there having frequently been unfavorable autumn weather. As they were riding back to luncheon, Giles stated, "I think we should spend the afternoon on the hunting horses."

"Why do you think that?" queried Daphne.

Giles was not used to having his suggestions questioned. He was about to react negatively when he recalled that one reason he had chosen Daphne was that she was so independent and not afraid to let her ideas be known. He decided that it would do no harm to explain his thoughts.

"Your mare, Serene Masham, looks like a splendid animal, but you haven't had much experience on her back."

Daphne was about to protest that she had thoroughly tested her mount before buying the animal, but her protest died as Giles continued, "I'll be riding Dark Paul, and I have had no real familiarity with him. We were too busy for that when I was last here. He has already thrown two riders who have had him jumping, and if I am going to ride him, I'd rather be thrown today than in front of everybody tomorrow."

Daphne held her tongue. Giles was right that the horse had thrown her, even if she had described the incident as her slipping off the horse. Her husband should get some familiarity with his horse, and she certainly would not mind getting to know Serene's habits better. After luncheon, they mounted the hunters and set off. Their route started over the ground where Daphne had tried to ride Dark Paul with unfortunate consequences. In fact, Giles, who was in the lead, tried to make the same jump where the stallion had unseated Daphne. Dark Paul shied on landing in exactly the same way in which he had got Daphne off his back. He almost succeeded with Giles, even though this time his rider was astride. Unphased by this failure, the horse allowed Giles to put him to a gallop towards the next hedge. Just before he should jump, he dug his forelegs into the ground in an attempt to throw Giles. It almost succeeded; Giles had to loosen the reins to grab the pommel of the saddle to catch himself. Dark Paul took the opportunity to get the bit between his teeth.

Even before Giles thumped back into the saddle, Dark Paul took off at a wild gallop. He headed towards a large oak with low branches on the other side of the field. Giles saw that the horse intended to scrape him off by going under a branch with not enough room beneath it for the rider as well as the horse. He swung himself to one side of the horse, quite out of the saddle, using only his left foot in the stirrup and a hand on the pommel to keep connected to the horse. He ducked low, and the branch passed harmlessly over him.

As soon as they were beyond the limb, Giles pulled himself back into saddle. Dark Paul reared in frustration; Giles stayed with him; indeed, he used the horse's annoyed whiney to pull the bit back behind the horse's teeth. Now he was in charge again.

Dark Paul set off, still at full gallop, towards a hedgerow marking the edge of the field. He sailed over it and continued at full speed for the next hedge and the next. Giles was now guiding the horse over the jumps, and when Dark Paul started to try to slacken his pace, Giles used his crop to keep him going full out. Before long, Giles was setting the pace completely, and the direction, and the jumps, with a tiring Dark Paul forced to do his master's bidding.

Giles directed them back towards the field where the horse had first taken control. He kept him at a gallop and forced Dark Paul to make all the jumps again, though coming from the opposite direction. When they reached the starting field, Giles let the horse slow to a canter and then a trot. He looked ahead to where the horse had first tried to throw him expecting to see Daphne. She was not in sight. He looked to each side and, out of the corner of his eye, spotted her beside him just one or two steps behind.

"How did you get there?" he asked.

"Serene is a remarkably fast horse, and we took the inside of your circle," came the reply.

The next day, the party from Dipton caused quite a stir at the meet. There were seven of them because Lord David and Mr. Moorhouse joined the riders from Dipton Hall, including Lady Marianne. Any number of people came over to greet Captain Giles, even though most of them had not met him earlier. Mr. Summers was particularly welcoming, repeatedly asking Giles to come to the Hunt Dinner that night. After a glance at Daphne, Giles gave his regrets, stating that with only a short stay at Dipton being possible, he preferred to dine with his wife. Major Stoner was notable for moving over to Lady Marianne after the briefest of introductions to Giles.

The hunt started off at the signal of the huntsman. Daphne noted that Lieutenant Charles strove to be among the leaders. Earlier she had observed that he had succeeded in downing three stirrup cups, which were generously filled with mulled wine. She and Giles started out near the end of the group as a result of still being engaged with well-wishers, so Daphne could see, to her surprise, that both Captain Hicks and Major Stoner chose to stay with the hill-toppers. She hoped that Catherine's enthusiasm for banking would last the full day.

The hounds took some time to find the scent. When they did, the hunt took off after the sounding hounds. A few good jumps started to thin the field as horses balked at various barriers or were turned aside by riders who doubted they could safely make the jump. Daphne was not surprised to see that Lieutenant Charles was the first to be thrown off as his horse stumbled on the first jump, but he was soon up again and riding recklessly to get to the front. Just after he passed Giles, his horse refused to jump a hedge at an ill-chosen place, and Lieutenant Charles sailed unaccompanied over the barrier. Daphne saw him stand as she was about to rein in Serene after the mare had cleared the barrier, so Daphne gave the horse her head so that she would keep going.

Daphne marveled at how smoothly Serene picked her way over the uneven ground and how effortlessly she seemed to skim over barriers. It occurred to her that she could have ridden side-saddle and then reflected that being accompanied by a genuine war hero probably meant that all her eccentricities would be forgiven by others. Serene was keeping up effortlessly with Dark Paul and would have passed him if Daphne had not made it clear to her mare that they were riding in company with Dark Paul and Captain Giles.

Dark Paul was giving Giles more of a problem. He suspected that the horse had not yet given up the idea of ridding itself of its rider, and he kept a tight rein and watched not only for safe lines to take over the rough ground but also for places where Dark Paul might try one of his stunts. So far, Giles was quite clearly doing the better in the contest, and he was beginning to sense that Dark Paul was accepting that his rider had control and would keep it.

The hunt lasted a much shorter time than the previous one, the fox being not nearly as cunning and so was much more easily run down by the dogs. Giles and Daphne were in on the kill, and Lord David and Mr. Moorhouse were close behind. The foray to Salton Masham had clearly been a success in terms of their all obtaining excellent mounts.

Christmas was fast approaching. Earlier, Daphne had not planned anything special for the festival. Just a small dinner for Lord David, Mr. Moorhouse, the Bushes, and her in-laws. A bit of decoration of the Hall with mistletoe would be enough to mark the occasion. Now Captain Giles was at home, and she wanted a far more festive occasion. He had no objection.

Daphne made a list of those she knew, discovering that, when put together, it constituted a much longer group than she had expected. The various visits that the nearby ladies had paid to mark her marriage had increased her circle greatly. There were more than twenty families she really must invite, and, in many of them, sons had returned for Christmas, and daughters were present. In all, she would be planning a dinner for one hundred people. Could they accommodate them all? The answer involved the furnishing of Dipton Hall by Mr. Edwards about which she had paid no attention, for it was unthinkable at that time that she should ever have any responsibility for the running of Dipton Hall. Steves assured her that the large dining room could take that number though they would be hard-pressed if more still were invited. In the end, not everyone who was could attend, but some houses had more people who would have to come than Daphne had counted on. She was horrified to realize that, as a result of her enthusiasm for a festive occasion, she would spend dinner seated far away from her husband. He would be at one end of the very long table, and she would be at the other. Steves resolved that problem by pointing out that, in his experience, with a very large table, it was not unusual for the host and hostess to sit in the middle of the table, the only remaining question of importance being who should sit opposite them.

That problem solved itself for Daphne when she received a note stating that her mother-in-law, Lady Clara, the Countess of Camshire, would be spending Christmas with them. Lydia had mentioned in a letter to her grandmother that there would be a huge dinner and that her Aunt Daphne had given her permission to invite Lieutenant Charles. The Earl had accepted an invitation to spend Christmas with one of his political cronies in Norfolk, and had seen no need for the Countess to join him. She shared that view completely. However, the prospect of a large gathering at Dipton, with both her sons there, made her wish to participate. In addition, also present would be several people whose company she had come to enjoy, despite their distinctly inferior rank. These considerations had led the Countess to decide to grace Dipton Hall with her presence.

Daphne realized immediately that the only possible person to sit next to the Countess must be her father. They had got along surprisingly well on previous occasions when they had met, and he seemed to have the diplomacy to keep her ladyship from going off on her high horse over some perceived slight. Having decided on the central part of the seating plan, Daphne turned the whole issue of precedence over to Catherine, who seemed to be interested in such things.

Steves was in his element. He added all the staff members of Dipton Manor to those of Dipton Hall and added a few other people from the village to help in the event. He also thought ahead to what would happen after the dinner, something that Daphne had, surprisingly, not thought about. He hired a few musicians and had the ballroom both decorated and heated so that dancing could occur when dinner was finished. On learning of this, Daphne made sure that Giles was aware that dancing would follow the dinner and strongly hinted that she would not be pleased if the gentlemen lingered long over their port.

Mrs. Darling, the cook at Dipton Hall, was absolutely delighted that there would be a large Christmas feast. She had been a bit disappointed that the dinners at Dipton Hall were so modest when Captain Giles was away, giving her little chance to demonstrate the width of her knowledge and her ability to deal efficiently with huge groups. She planned remove* after remove for the dinner and badgered Steves to be sure that they were each served with the right sauce. She was able to persuade Mrs. Hancock, Mr. Moorhouse's cook, to join her in the cooking, and indeed to do some of it at Dipton Manor, and she was able to call on the kitchen staff at Dipton Manor as well on the many wives of farmers and tradesmen in and around Dipton who had had earlier experience in service. If Mrs. Darling had her way, Dipton would never have seen such a festive feast before.

Christmas dawned bright, clear, and cold. Giles and Daphne avoided much of the hubbub involved in the servants getting everything ready for the evening's events by taking a walk after luncheon to the location where the drainage project at which they first had met was now completed. But all too soon, their ears started to freeze, and they retreated to the warmth of Dipton Hall. There Elsie and Ralph, the footman who was acting as Giles's valet, impatiently waited to dress the host couple before the guests arrived.

The first coach came about three in the afternoon; the short days, cold weather and possibly treacherous roads made people eager to get to Dipton Hall early. Soon there was a steady stream of arrivals. Steves and Tisdale had arranged for the coachmen to be entertained in the servants' hall at Dipton Manor, where much food and very thin beer had been laid on so that they could stay warm while waiting to be called for the return trips.

No one seemed to mind that the time designated for the evening to start was more like tea-time than dinner-time. The guests mingled in the large drawing-room, each one supplied with a chalice of mulled wine. As the numbers increased, the gathering spilled over into the small drawing-room and then into other rooms where cheerful fires were blazing. Most people knew each other and many of the young people made a beeline to one of the smaller rooms where the men could compare the situations they had encountered since they left home, and the women could express admiration and surprise at these adventures.

Steves, his chest arched forward like a rooster's, announced dinner. Giles led Daphne into the dining room, followed by the Countess and Mr. Moorhouse. The other guests followed along, two by two, and if the order of precedence was not always what the participants thought it should be, Daphne could not be bothered about such details. The feast was indeed a feast and went on, remove after remove, for over three hours. Talk was lively. It started out in the proper way of speaking to the person on one side of the diner then switching to the person on the other. However, before long, conversations became more general, and the dining room became very noisy as voices were raised competitively so that the speakers could be heard.

As the time approached for Daphne to lead the ladies out, Major Stoner, who was seated next to Lady Marianne a third of the way down the table, started banging on his glass with his knife, this apparently being the approved way of getting attention in the mess in India.

"My Lords, ladies and gentlemen," the Major declared. "A great many can recall their disappointment that Dipton Hall did not take its proper place of leadership in our community under the former owner. We suspected that it might change when Captain Giles allowed a ball to be held here. It became even more evident when he was able to win the hand of one of our own. It is now confirmed by this gathering. I would like to thank our host and hostess and recognize how splendid it is to have them take their proper place among us. I give you Lady and Captain Sir Richard Giles." The major raised his glass, and the other guests rose to their feet and murmured, "Lady and Captain Giles."

Daphne was not sure what the proper etiquette should be in a feast like this one, but she could tell, rather with amusement than with distress, that, by the look on the Countess's face, Major Stoner's performance was not the correct one. The Countess looked only a little less displeased when Giles rose to reply.

"I thank you for your kind words, Major Stoner. I do not know many of you as well as I would like, and it may be some time before I do. Bonaparte, unfortunately, does intervene in what I would most like to do and will continue to do so until we defeat him." Murmurs of agreement from the military men present interrupted Giles at this point, but he pressed on. "I assure you that Lady Giles and I intend to play our proper part in this community."

Giles sat down, and Daphne rose to indicate that it was time for the ladies to withdraw. This they did, as the men rose from their chairs to assemble around Giles. The port was poured once and then again. The conversation was going well, but Giles remembered Daphne's warning. He would certainly prefer talking to her than listening to these people.

"I think, gentlemen, that we should join the ladies. I understand that there is to be dancing, and I am sure you all know how the ladies enjoy that."

Giles and Daphne led the way onto the dance floor, followed by Mr. Moorhouse and the Countess of Camshire. Others joined them in short order. After the initial dance with Daphne, Giles did his "duty" dances with his mother, half-sister, and nieces. After that, he refused to dance with anyone other than Daphne. Everyone seemed to have a good time, and, despite the early hour of the dinner, supper was served very late in the evening.

St. Stephen's Day* dawned cold and clear. It was, of course, the day on which most of the servants were allowed to go home or otherwise entertain themselves, with only a skeleton staff to deal with the needs of the gentry. Daphne had already made sure that all her servants would be rewarded for their service in the past year with extra payments and gifts of food or other items that would be most valued. As the houses of the gentry went, Dipton Hall experienced a minimum of inconvenience since many of their staff had come from London when the Earl of Camshire had closed his London House and were quite content to have their time off on some other occasion. Almost everyone remained indoors, but Giles and Daphne were restless and got a stable boy to saddle their hunters so that they could have a brisk ride over the frozen fields. Giles once again was forced to show Dark Paul who was in charge when the horse took the opportunity of a loose rein to swerve violently on landing from a jump, an attempt that was easily frustrated by his rider since Giles had planned the maneuver to see if the stallion would still try to establish his dominance.

The weather remained cold and clear for the next few days. Daphne and Giles spent much of the time working on Mozart sonatas, interrupted by short walks and longer rides. After the third expedition on their hunters, in which Daphne had taken the lead somewhat to Dark Paul's distress, Giles remarked. "Serene has a lovely smooth gait and jumping style. I would truly like to see the estate where you bought her. I have always been curious about where trained horses come from, even as a boy at Ashbury Abbey. I would enjoy going over to – what is it called?"

"Salton Masham Grange. I would enjoy seeing the stables again. Let's do it."

"Tomorrow?"

"Yes, tomorrow, and we might as well ride the hunters to get more used to them."

It was a pleasant journey to Salton Masham. Giles had never been on the road past Ameschester and had never paid much attention to what lay between Dipton and Ameschester. Even in the depth of winter with snow on the ground, he found any number of pleasing vistas and was constantly remarking on the estates they were passing. He pointed out many things that Daphne, who had known the area since she was a child, had long since ceased to notice. She found much more to admire and enjoy than she anticipated when they left Dipton Hall to go to Salton Masham.

Salton Masham Grange lay in a valley and presented a pretty picture as the two riders topped a ridge to see it lying before them. Giles paused and pointed out the features of the landscape to Daphne, such as the way the house was positioned with gardens to one side and the stables to the other, with vistas stretching to the stream that flowed through the valley, and the horse paddocks giving way to fields that in turn gave way to the woodland that climbed to the next ridge. Daphne was enthralled, as much by the enthusiasm with which Giles pointed out the features as with the view itself. On her previous visits, she had simply ridden past the viewpoint, hastening to get to her destination. Plumes of white smoke rose from several of the many chimneys of the house, but their location suggested that they came from the kitchens rather than from the family's rooms. Smoke also rose from the corner of the stables, which was occupied by Mr. Griffiths's office. Based on their guess that the master of the estate was not in residence, Giles and Daphne proceeded directly to the stables.

Mr. Griffiths came out of the stable block to greet them, "Lady Giles, how do you find Serene? I heard that you were in at the kill in the last hunt."

"Yes, indeed. She is a marvelous horse, Mr. Griffiths. This is my husband, Captain Giles."

"An honor, sir. An honor. That must be Dark Paul you are riding. You are, I am told, the first rider to keep your seat on him throughout a hunt."

"What do you mean?"

"You probably haven't heard, but he has succeeded in ridding himself of anyone who tried to take him over the jumps before you. Not just Lady Giles – and that hardly counts since she was trying to ride him side-saddle – and Lord David, but everyone who tried to ride him, even his former owner. I am afraid that your man who bought him for you knew good horseflesh but was not aware of the stories about how horses perform which circulates among those of us who follow hunting closely."

"Dark Paul certainly has tried several times to unseat me. So far, I have been able to show him who is in charge, and he is starting to accept me. Now, Mr. Griffiths, Lady Giles tells me that you are willing to let us look over the stud farm."

"With pleasure, sir. It is, I believe, an excellent operation, though the present owner has no real use for it."

Giles showed a keen interest in all aspects of the farm as Mr. Griffiths showed the various features to them and detailed his methods for breeding and training horses. Daphne was surprised. She hadn't known that this was an interest of her husband's. She realized that there were still many things about him that she had yet to discover. She hoped that they would prove to be as pleasant as those she already knew.

When the tour of the stables had been completed, Giles turned to Mr. Griffiths and said, "I understand from Lady Giles that the stud farm here will be closing."

"Yes, sir. The new owner has no interest in horses, I am afraid. Everything is for sale except the stables and, of course, the land. I do not know how much he wants for it. Lady Giles can tell you more than I can about the business side of the farm. She looked at the accounts and got far more understanding from them than I ever have."

This statement produced a red face from Daphne, who had not told her husband about how she studied the monetary aspects of the venture. Giles only gave a glance at Daphne before pushing ahead.

"I understand that the owner is away at present."

"Yes, sir, Mr. Audley has been away for Christmas, but I expect him back by New Year's Day. Certainly before Twelfth Night*."

"Do you have a big celebration on Twelfth Night, Mr. Griffiths?" asked Daphne.

"Oh, no, my lady. Quite the opposite. Mr. Daniel would stand for no frivolity in the servants' hall, *ever*. Mr. Charles feels much the same. He will be returning so that he doesn't have to endure Twelfth Night festivities wherever he may be spending Christmas."

Daphne and Giles then took their leave. By mutual agreement, they stopped for tea in Ameschester.

"I didn't know that you knew so much about horses, Richard," Daphne opened the conversation.

"Yes. My father was very keen on racehorses, especially for the jump races, to own them and, even more, to bet on the results. He was equally unsuccessful at each endeavor, just as in most of his ventures. But when I was growing up, there were always hunters and racehorses in the stables, and our stableman was quite knowledgeable. I will have to tease Edwards when I see him about getting fooled over Dark Paul, but the way the horse is shaping up, the laugh may be on those horse traders who thought they had pulled one over his eyes. I was surprised to learn that you had examined the accounts."

"Didn't I tell you? You know that I am interested in the financial details of well-run farms, and I had never seen the accounts of a stud farm. I seem to be able to learn a great deal from financial records. Many of the considerations for a stud farm are the same as for our dairy farm, but others are quite different. The basic structure of that stud farm seems to be very solid, though I did see some aspects that could be improved."

"I wonder what will happen to Mr. Griffiths when they sell it."

"He will have to look for employment elsewhere. A new owner should take him on if he can persuade Mr. Griffiths to leave Salton Masham."

"I don't suppose that you would consider adding the stud farm to Dipton Hall if we could afford it."

"It is up to you, of course, Richard. You certainly could afford it. As you know, Mr. Edwards sends me copies of his reports, and you are indeed very well off."

"The decision about whether to buy the stud farm may be up to me in principle, but with me at sea, the burden of overseeing it would fall on you, I know. If you do not want it, then I don't either. I know that legally it is all mine, but I think of it as our wealth. You already have undertaken more than I could even imagine that you would do or that I could undertake myself if I weren't at sea."

"Oh, managing a horse farm would not be a problem if we had someone like Mr. Griffiths to do the real work. I enjoy all that I am now doing and would enjoy the extra interest. Yes, I think we could easily include a stud farm in our other activities at Dipton Hall. To make it successful, I think the trick would be to make sure that one's reputation for first-class mounts for gentlemen is maintained. Running the racing side at a profit is much less certain. I am not sure that one can make money off the racing stable directly. Too many people are prepared to put too much money into that aspect of horse breeding for one to count on its being profitable. But if the other half of the business is well run, a good reputation for racing horses may help to keep the whole operation profitable. If overseeing it becomes too much, we could always hire a steward for Dipton Hall who would only need some overseeing."

"You know far more about all this than I do, my love. However, I would like to know that Dipton Hall is breeding good horses."

"Well, let's study the details about how it would affect Dipton Hall before plunging into it. We would need much larger stables, to begin with, of course, and if we move the stables, we really will have to think about how it will affect the vistas and another shaping of the grounds that may be needed to show our home at maximum advantage. I don't think your seat should be overshadowed by our business. I imagine that we can find a solution to that problem if we put our heads together, so, yes, we can certainly undertake having a stud farm at Dipton Hall."

"Good."

They left the tea shop, well pleased with their conversation. After they had mounted, Daphne raised another subject.

"Richard, what do you think about Twelfth Night?"

"What about Twelfth Night?"

"We have never had much of a celebration at Dipton Manor. It is not my father's sort of thing. He did allow the servants to have a bit of a feast and some music in the hall that night, but we didn't take part in it."

"When I was growing up," replied Giles, "at least when I was little, there was quite a celebration, or so I remember. But as my father's affairs deteriorated and he became more irritable, I think it rather was phased out. You would have to ask my mother whether and how they celebrate Twelfth Night at Ashbury Abbey now. Why do you ask?"

"I think, maybe, we should encourage some sort of celebration. It might mean a lot to the servants. Did you notice how wistful Mr. Griffiths seemed when he mentioned how it isn't celebrated at Salton Masham Grange?"

"I did. You are right. I do not have to leave until after Twelfth Night, so I can participate in the festivities."

Daphne laughed, "then so can Carstairs. Elsie for sure will want us to permit something for Twelfth Night."

224

Chapter XV

Daphne and Giles spent the next few days forming more detailed plans for how Dipton Hall could fit a stud farm among its other activities. They sketched plans for the stables and layouts for the necessary paddocks. Daphne insisted that when they considered one part of the estate for the stud, they should also consider where the uses to which it was presently allocated would be accommodated elsewhere. Dipton Hall, with its extensive home fields, was a successful, ongoing operation, and she did not want to compromise that accomplishment by taking on the new activity.

The planning was well advanced by New Year's Day. The following day, Daphne and Giles again rode over to Salton Masham. When they topped the rise leading to the valley in which it lay, the view of Salton Masham Grange revealed smoke coming from most of the chimneys, indicating that the owners were at home. They proceeded to the main house and told the butler that they had come to see Mr. Audley.

The master of the house rose to greet them from a comfortable-looking chair. He was a tall, slim man, appearing to be about forty years of age, with mutton-chop whiskers. They hardly went with his long nose and austere face. Its lines suggested that displeasure was his habitual expression.

"Sir Richard, Griffiths told me that you had been looking at the stables. What can I do for you?" Mr. Audley ignored Daphne, except for a minimal initial bow.

"We understand that your stud farm is for sale."

"No, it isn't. I did indicate to Griffiths that I would be closing the enterprise and was thinking of selling it completely, but I have reconsidered. With this war, the army will require a great many horses. Especially draught horses to pull carts and guns. And they will not be too fussy about quality as long as the creatures look strong. I am going to switch to raising such animals immediately."

"What will happen to your existing stock and training equipment?"

"Oh, I am sending all the horses and foals to auction. I expect to make a much better profit than if I have them properly trained and sold afterwards. Many have already been sold or have been spoken for, and the rest will go soon."

"Then I am sorry to have troubled you, sir. Good luck in your new venture."

"It is not a matter of luck, but of seeing where the demand is. I am surprised that you, a naval captain, have the time to consider breeding horses and training them. If you spent your time at sea, as you are supposed to, honest men would not lose ventures to the enemy."

Giles tried to maintain his calm. "Have you suffered misfortune, Mr. Audley?"

"I have, sir! I have. A very promising venture to Spain, bringing in sherry. Disappeared. Probably taken by privateers or pirates. What is the Navy doing, sir, to protect our trade? Nothing! And I laid out good money to get the wine cheap by bribing the tax people in Cadiz."

"Where was this cargo destined to go?"

"To Cornwall, sir, to Cornwall."

"And to which port?"

"No port, of course. To be landed in a secluded bay, away from the excise."

"So you complain about the Navy but want to escape taxes to help pay for it?"

"Of course not. I pay more than my share of taxes. Far more."

"Well, good day to you, sir. I trust that your horse-breeding will be as successful as your smuggling and bribery. Come along, Lady Giles."

Giles turned and marched out of the house, with Daphne trailing along behind him, pausing only as they accepted their coats from the butler.

"Wretched man! Breaks the law, cheats the government, and complains about the Navy. I wouldn't buy an old pan from that tinker!" Giles fumed. "Certainly not his breeding and training facilities. Pity the poor army sergeants who are stuck with his horses."

Daphne had never seen Giles so angry. She hesitated to confirm with him what seemed obvious – that this was the end of their plans to raise and train hunting or riding horses. She was disappointed, but Giles seemed to be more than disappointed. As they approached the fork in the drive, where one branch led to the stables and the other to the house, Mr. Griffiths was waiting for them.

"I'm sorry, Lady Giles, Sir Richard, that you have made a trip for no purpose. Mr. Audley only told me this morning about his new plans, and especially about how he would be disposing of the hunting aspect of the stables. I feel badly for having misled you."

To Daphne's surprise, Giles immediately resumed his usual air of affability. "No reason to feel badly, Mr. Griffiths.

You weren't to know. Are you going to stay on to manage this new venture?"

"I am not! If Mr. Audley were seriously intending to raise good working-horses and develop excellent bloodlines for them, I would be happy to stay. But that is not his intention. He intends to breed any old cart horses to each other, no selection, no training, just foist them off on the army. He claims he knows jobbers who will be taking any sort of animal at fixed prices, quality be damned. I can't have any part of that, sir."

"Then what will you do?"

"I do not know. I will have to find another position, hopefully, one where my real skills are needed. I don't want to stay near Salton Masham, not now, not to see the reputation that Old Mr. Audley built up for Salton Masham Grange dragged through the mud."

"I cannot guarantee anything, of course, but there may be a position at Dipton Hall for you. Lady Giles and I will have to do some calculations and see how horse breeding or training might fit in with what we are doing. If it is convenient, come over to Dipton in the next few days, and we can talk more about it."

Giles and Daphne rode off to Ameschester.

"Richard, what is going on? Why did you invite Mr. Griffiths to come to Dipton Hall? Surely our horse plans are dead after what Mr. Audley said, aren't they? Isn't that why you got so angry?"

"No, Daphne. I was angry at that sanctimonious hypocrite complaining about Navy protection for his illegal smuggling venture. I have every hope that his breeding venture will fail, though it probably won't. But I see no reason to abandon our plans, though we may have to change them.

Develop our own bloodlines rather than take over Salton Masham's. Griffiths has a great reputation and may be invaluable in setting up a breeding operation. Of course, it is up to you as well as to me, in fact mostly up to you since I shall be at sea. But I don't want to abandon the idea."

They rode on, talking animatedly about what would and would not be possible and where Griffiths might fit into the plans. The reason for Giles's enthusiasm for Griffiths also became evident.

"Daphne, I hope you won't misunderstand me. I believe that you already have your hands full with running Dipton Hall and all its agricultural affairs as well as those of your father. In fact, I think you should think of getting some sort of manager to help you and take over some of the load. When we first talked of it, I had hoped that I could play a bigger part, especially with the proposed raising of horses, but realistically that will not happen until Boney is beaten. And I hope that soon you will have additional matters to occupy you."

"What are you thinking of?"

"Ugh…well…you know…ugh…children." Giles was blushing so furiously that Daphne could see it even on his weather-beaten face.

"Oh!" was her response, and it was her turn to feel a rush of blood to her face. She had hoped to have children, though the timing of her brief honeymoon had made it impossible that she would be with child. She had every hope that this visit by her husband would produce the desired result, but she had never even considered mentioning this to her husband. Neither of them knew how to discuss the subject together. However, she did hope that his concern would have a genuine basis in fact before long.

"Griffiths has much more experience in raising first-rate mounts than we have," Giles firmly changed the subject. "In fact, he is very well known for being the guiding hand behind Ashton Masham Grange in the horse world, and it has been one of the top places. I was thinking that we should snap him up if we can, even if his real use to us may be somewhat speculative at this point."

"You have a very good point. I like Griffiths, and he probably knows more about raising animals in general than I do, quite apart from horses. I wonder what we should offer him. We should be able to provide him a very nice cottage to live in. The one that became vacant when Mr. Gramley's steward was dismissed is still available, and it is really quite a superior residence. I know that Mr. Griffith's wife doesn't really want to leave Salton Masham, but having a nice place ready to move into might make the transition easier."

They rode on talking animatedly about the possibilities that having an expert on breeding and training horses would bring to Dipton Hall.

When Griffiths appeared at Dipton Hall a couple of days later, they quickly reached agreement about employing him, and he suggested other ways he might help them in addition to those for which they had already planned. In particular, he looked over the rough plans they had drawn up for placing the new stable block and suggested several improvements. Daphne, in particular, realized that he would be more of a help than she had expected. He had a good feel for the possibilities of the countryside and how it could be exploited in a way that would keep, or even increase, its charm. He would be an excellent addition to the staff of Dipton Hall.

The twelfth day of Christmas saw all the servants at Dipton Hall extra busy. They wanted no failures in service to endanger the treat promised for the evening. All the servants from all the residences closest to Dipton Hall -- Dipton Manor, Dipton Dower Cottage, and Dipton Vicarage would join together for the celebration, and so it could be arranged with minimal inconvenience to their employers. The gentry would all have luncheon at their own homes and then would gather at Dipton Hall for dinner. That meal would be served at five, and the festivities in the servant's hall would commence at eight o'clock. Though the servants didn't discuss it for fear that doing so would somehow reduce the possibility of its occurring, each one hoped that, if their masters and mistresses were not inconvenienced, they might continue the celebration in years to come.

Daphne noted that, at tea, all the servants seemed to be nervous, trying extra hard to please and not be intrusive. Even Elsie seemed to be on edge as she helped Daphne to dress. The atmosphere seemed to be even worse as they filed in for dinner.

"What is going on?" Daphne whispered to Giles as they entered the dining room, and she noted that the footmen seemed to be as stiff as metal soldiers.

"They are afraid that they will make a mistake, and then we will be angry and cancel the festivities."

"Surely not. No one would do that, would they?"

"We wouldn't. But I am sure my father might or even my mother. Most of the servants don't know us all that well, particularly me. It is most unfortunate. If Ralph doesn't unbend a bit, he will spill the soup onto my mother's lap."

Daphne couldn't help giggling at the thought of that event and then realized that her hilarity would make the servants even more nervous. Luckily, no such disaster occurred. The meal proceeded as usual, and no untoward event occurred before Daphne led the ladies into the drawing-room. A bowl of nuts was knocked over at the sideboard while the three men gathered at one end of the table. They all studiously avoided taking any notice of the mishap.

Surprisingly, the nervousness of the servants spread to the drawing-room. Catherine Crocker stumbled worse than ever when she attempted to play the pianoforte, and Daphne's performance was far from her best. Things only improved when she and Giles tried a movement of the piano and violin sonata on which they had been working. Giles seemed to be totally unaffected by the prospect of visiting the servant's hall later in the evening, and his confidence transferred to Daphne. His sangfroid spread to the others so that when eight chimed on the clock in the drawing-room, they all descended to the servant's hall in an orderly parade.

The servants had completed all the arrangements to receive them but were all nervous at what they could only consider a bit of a reversal of roles. The trestle tables on which the dinner for all the servants from the different houses, both indoor and outdoor, had been served had been cleared away, and a table with an enormous punch bowl, cups, and ladle had been set out.

Daphne had warned Giles about what his role was to be. He stepped confidently behind the table, picked up the ladle and a cup which he filled before handing it to Daphne. She, in turn, passed it to the first servant in a line that had quickly formed on the appearance of their master and mistress. When all the servants had been served, Giles and Daphne prepared cups for all the gentry who had dined with them. Giles then poured cups for himself and Daphne, raised his own cup high, and said, "Here is to all who have served us in the past year. We thank you all."

Everyone took a sip from their cup before Steves replied, "Here is to our masters and mistresses. May they and their houses prosper!"

This time all cups were drained. Daphne, who had invented the ceremony herself when no one else seemed sure as to what should be done, nodded to Giles, who in turn announced, "Let the dancing begin."

Steves nodded to the musicians, who were in a corner of the Hall, to play. Giles asked Mrs. Wilson, the housekeeper at Dipton Hall, to dance while Steves invited Daphne. Pairings of the other quality persons with their senior servants followed while the footmen asked the ladies, who were in the majority, to dance. The exception was Mr. Griffiths, whom Steves had asked to come for the night when he learned that the horse expert would be joining the staff at Dipton Hall. The new stable master, greatly daring, asked the Countess of Camshire to dance and did a very serviceable job guiding her onto the dance floor. A vigorous country dance ensued, following which the upstairs party retreated to their proper quarters. Daphne suggested to all of them that they retire early so that the servants who attended them at bedtime would be freed to take part in the rest of the revelry in the servant's hall.

Elsie drew the curtains in Daphne's bedroom at exactly the usual time the next morning even though, as Daphne knew, the music had gone on late into the night. The fire in her room had been lit even earlier. Daphne still basked in the slightly guilty pleasure she felt when she had indulged herself by having the fire lit well before she rose each morning. It was now a pleasure to wash and get dressed without shivering as she used to. When Elsie had finished helping Daphne to dress, the lady's maid nervously blurted out a request.

"M'lady, Carstairs and I need to get married before he leaves. May we?"

"Captain Giles said he would have to leave on Tuesday. He already has somewhat overstayed his time here and needs to get back to his ship. Now, it is already Saturday morning. You will hardly have time to get ready, will you? What is the rush?"

"Ugh...well, you see, m'lady...I don't know how to say this."

"Oh, just blurt it out, Elsie."

"Yes, m'lady...well...ugh... last night... Carstairs and I...ugh...the punch was rather strong...."

"Elsie, are you trying to tell me that you and Carstairs got too intimate with each other?"

'Yes, m'lady...and...well...I...I might become with child. And if I am not married, you would have to dismiss me...and I don't know what would happen to me then. So, can we get married?"

"Certainly. You are right; Mr. Steves and Mrs. Wilson would be horrified if you were pregnant and would be terribly unhappy if I didn't dismiss you. Yes, if Carstairs is willing, marrying him right away would get rid of any embarrassment. You still do want to marry him, don't you?"

"Oh, yes, m'lady. We just didn't think there would be time, what with Christmas and Twelfth Night and you and Captain Giles being so busy."

"Let's see. The banns have already been published, haven't they, and for both you and Carstairs in this parish?"

"Yes, m'lady. Lord David suggested he read them for both of us since Carstairs really doesn't have a parish, so his residence can be considered to be Dipton Hall when he is ashore."

"Then there is no reason that you shouldn't get married on Monday. I expect you don't have your wedding dress ready yet, or the other things you need. In fact, do you actually have a special dress?"

"Not really, my lady. I have never needed anything special."

"Then you had better use one of mine. Maybe the blue silk. It would go nicely with your coloring."

"Oh, my lady, I couldn't."

"Of course you could. You've been with me a long time and have served me very, very well. You had better take today and tomorrow off, and the wedding and wedding breakfast can be on Monday. Betsy can look after me. I will tell Mrs. Wilson. You will not want to sleep here on your wedding night, I expect. The Dipton Arms should have a very nice room. Here is a guinea to help pay for what you will need."

"Oh, thank you, m'lady."

"Speaking of the Dipton Arms, has Carstairs made any progress in acquiring it?"

"I think so, m'lady, but it is still a bit uncertain."

At that point, Giles entered the room. "Elsie, I hear that Carstairs has persuaded you to marry him right away."

"Yes, sir."

"Very good. You will have to be quick about it. We leave on Tuesday."

"Elsie has already told me about it, Richard. They are to be married on Monday."

"Are they? Good. We will have the wedding breakfast here, I presume."

"Oh, sir, thank you."

"I was going to suggest it," said Daphne, rather huffily.

"Then we are in agreement, my love."

Despite the rush, the wedding went off without any problems. Elsie looked marvelous in the blue dress, which she had altered with the addition of some white lace. Steves supported Carstairs, and her own father gave Elsie away. The ring appeared at the right time, which made Daphne wonder where and when it had been acquired. The happy couple was pelted with rice as they left the church, and the wedding breakfast continued long after the wedded couple had left the celebration so that only necessary work was carried out at Dipton Hall that day.

Giles departed in the coach just after daybreak. Daphne felt strangely listless. She knew that it resulted from the ending of the hectic and intense time she had been having with Giles. It seemed that every time he went away, his absence left a larger and larger hole in her life. There weren't even many tasks of any urgency to occupy her attention. After Giles's coach had disappeared from sight, she wandered into the library to find a book to read but discovered that Mr. Edwards's minion had apparently bought books based on how attractive their bindings were and not according to the likely interest of their content. For that diversion, she would have to await her recent order of novels to be delivered. She played the piano-forte for a while, but her fingers showed no inspiration in finding the keys. At luncheon, the attendance was again reduced to just four women, with no topics of conversation that seemed to interest any of them, not even when the girls tried to revive the subject of the Hunt Ball because it was still months away.

After lunch, Daphne decided that she must get some fresh air. She would choose Moonbeam as her steed, for she would ride to some of the tenants' homes whom she had not seen since before Christmas. She had Steves arrange for a hamper that she had meant to take to one farmer whose mother was poorly and then went upstairs to change.

Elsie was back at the Hall and immediately appeared to help with the change of clothes. She was bubbling with delight at her wedding night though she was quite unable to say what had been so pleasant. Daphne did realize that Elsie's delight at being married to Carstairs was tinged with sadness that he was away again. That was a feeling Daphne could share, but she also realized that she could share Elsie's joy at a very successful wedding night.

The third of Daphne's visits was to one of Dipton Hall's tenants, who had let the thatch on his barn deteriorate to the extent that it no longer kept the winter rains out. Daphne was adopting the same direct interest in the Dipton Hall tenancies that she had taken in those of Dipton Manor. Those tenants had found that Daphne was not just interfering but had good, modern ideas that led to better yields. They had also discovered that, unlike some landlords who did everything in their power to recapture any increases in income coming from improvements, Daphne made sure that the lion's share remained with the tenants. The word had spread about the nature of the landlord of the tenants of Dipton Manor, but that information had not always been taken to heart by the tenants of Dipton Hall. That was the case here. Daphne had to make it quite clear that there would be dire consequences if the thatch was not renewed immediately and other changes whose need she had observed were not made by Lady Day, which was the next quarter day*. Daphne rode away somewhat perturbed. She suspected that drink was as much to blame as sloth for the condition of the farm and feared for what would happen to the man's wife and their already threadbare children if he lost his tenancy. But lose it he would if he did not make the required changes.

Daphne's other visits went more happily, with tenants reporting problems they were encountering and wanting to discuss their plans for the spring. She arrived home in a much less gloomy mood than she had started the day. Yes, Giles had returned to his ship, and that would leave a large hole in her life until he returned, but she would continue to make her life full of other interests. And she much preferred her existence now to what she had experienced before Giles had entered her life.

Chapter XVI

Giles and Carstairs boarded *Impetuous* just as the sun was sinking from sight in the west. Giles found a perturbed Mr. Milton when the ceremony for boarding his ship had concluded.

"What is the trouble, Mr. Milton?" he inquired when they were alone.

"Sir, progress on the repairs has slowed completely in the past week."

"Why is that?"

"I am not sure, sir. Sometimes the Dockyard makes the excuse that needed supplies, especially timbers, are not available. Other times, I just get a shrug and no excuse even. Mr. Cornwall also seems embarrassed by the delay since he had promised more prompt attention, as had the Superintendent. Mr. Cornwall let slip that the information that other, very senior, captains are using their influence to take men away from us, even though there is less urgency to get their ships back on station."

"I was afraid of this. I will see what I can do when I go ashore tomorrow. Otherwise, how are things, Mr. Milton?"

"Very well, sir. The larboard watch was given leave first, despite some objections from the port captain. They all returned on time except for one able seaman, Rathers. He turned up the next day, still drunk as could be. He claimed he had mixed up the port where *Impetuous* was anchored."

"How did you deal with it?"

"Threw him in the brig until he sobered up, sir. Then stopped his rum ration for a month. That I thought was punishment enough. Mr. Dunsmuir was afraid that I would have him flogged when you returned, but I pointed out to him that the important thing was that he had rejoined before we needed to sail."

"Quite right, Mr. Milton. It is what I would have done."

"I am afraid we were not really ready for you, sir, tonight, and your servant is in the starboard watch which is gone now. The wardroom servants can probably find something for your supper, sir. Or dinner, if you have missed that meal."

"Thank you, Mr. Milton. It is more than I could expect. Carry on."

Giles got no satisfaction when he visited the Superintendent's office the next day. The good effect of the Admiral's letter seemed to have worn off, and the other names Giles had cited no longer seemed to carry weight. As he contemplated this sad state of affairs when he returned to his cabin, Giles wondered if gold had changed hands to account for why the needs of other captains had suddenly jumped ahead of his. He also wondered how he could broach the subject to suggest that he might well contribute to the Superintendent's needs. He was pondering this question when he heard a voice hailing *Impetuous*, "Ahoy, *Impetuous*, Sir David McDougall wishes to come aboard."

"Welcome him aboard, Mr. Milton," Giles bellowed in a voice that he knew would be heard clearly on the quarterdeck. Sir David was the special friend of the Warden of the Cinque Ports, had held a major position in the previous government, and probably would hold such a position again if the present government fell.

Giles went on deck immediately to welcome his guest.

"May we speak somewhere privately, Captain Giles," said the visitor in his low Scottish burr.

They retreated to Giles's cabin, where the guest gladly accepted a glass of Madeira.

"You made quite an impression on the Warden and myself, Captain Giles. He thought I should come and see you."

"Oh, why? I don't see how I could make much of an impression; I only saw you for a few minutes and just to bring the Comte de Fourcoup to you."

"Not quite, Captain. The way you captured the Comte, the way you had captured that pirate and recognized the importance of what you saw when you searched his ship, the way you performed the raid on Boulogne, successfully extracting an important document from the French, even the way you conveniently got rid of that Hoxley creature. All these actions speak most highly of you."

"But, sir, the end of Captain Hoxley was pure chance. It could just as well have been me whose head was blown off."

"But it wasn't. I would rather have someone who is lucky rather than intelligent, any day. Not that you are not intelligent. I find luck seems to come to people who prepare and think out the alternatives first. However, I didn't really come to tell you how highly we think of you, but with a proposition, for you to consider."

"Yes?"

"You may know that things are not completely smooth in the House right now. The Prime Minister is on shaky ground over the war and finances, and other matters. He is likely to fall before too long, and pressure will be put on the Warden to form the next government. We need stable chaps, right-thinking chaps, in the House, ones who think about more than feathering their own nests. You are such a man, we feel."

"I don't know about that. But I don't see the relevance. It is not much more than a year since the last general election."

"Ah, true, but there are by-elections. And there is a vacancy at Dipton."

"Is there?"

"Yes, Mr. Gramley, who owned Dipton Hall before you, was one of the two members from Dipton Borough. He was elected just before he died, and his seat still is not filled. He was not much of a member. He used the position mainly to pedal influence, but he couldn't be counted on. For sale to the highest bidder. No great loss, I can assure you. No one has got around to moving the writ* for the by-election, so the seat is still vacant. We were thinking that you would be a very suitable replacement. Most of the electors are either your tenants or those of your father-in-law, so you should have no trouble winning. A barrel of ale to celebrate, announced ahead of time, of course, should be all it will take."

"I don't know anything about politics, and I am away at sea much of the time."

"That hasn't stopped many other naval captains from being members of parliament. They are either assigned to home waters or get jobbing captains*. Anyway, there is no hurry; things are not likely to come to a head for some time. Now, is there anything I can do for you?"

"Not that I can think of. I am rather trapped here because the Dockyard thinks it has more important things to do. I was expecting them to be finished in two more weeks, as they promised, but now the Superintendent claims he has other priorities."

"Does he? I may be able to help there."

Sir David, his business finished, left without further pleasantries. Giles hardly considered the approach that Sir David had made to him about becoming a member of parliament. He was not the sort to take on a position to which he had no intention of devoting himself, and he had no desire to spend much time in London for the Season. He did wonder whether Daphne would like to take part in the London Season. He would ask her in his next letter. He also wondered if he did not have a responsibility for selecting the second member from Dipton. For that matter, he didn't even know who the first member might be. Daphne would know, of course.

Giles's musings were interrupted by the arrival of Mr. Cornwell with a large gang of shipwrights and laborers. "I am afraid that the Superintendent placed your schedule in the wrong month, Captain Giles," Mr. Cornwell lied with a straight face. "We are here to see that the work progresses as quickly as possible."

Giles made no remark except to express satisfaction that the work should be executed as quickly as possible. That was the case. Indeed, it was only nine days later that Mr. Cornwell declared the work completed, and it all received the approval of the relevant petty officers. The basic quality of *Impetuous* had not been improved, however, a point made clear when Mr. Cornwell expressed the hope that the carpenter would have large quantities of tar and oakum* on hand for caulking the leaks that were likely to develop.

The starboard watch had reported for duty a couple of days before the repairs were complete. Almost everyone had returned on time, the one exception being an able seaman named Baten. His absence was all the more surprising since he was from Chatham and was said to have been intending to spend his leave close at hand. The consequences for Baten could be very serious if he missed their sailing, for he would be presumed to have deserted. Giles sent Lieutenant Macauley with a file of marines to see if they could find the missing seaman. They returned empty-handed with the news that Baten had been taken by a press gang while he was too drunk to explain coherently that he was one of *Impetuous*'s crew. The fact that someone in the press-gang had hit him over the head with a belaying pin when he started to protest his seizure may have played a role in his not clearly expressing why he should be exempt from being pressed. The press-gang had been from *Medusa*, a seventy-four, which was said to have sailed from the Nore to join Admiral Gardner.

Impetuous weighed anchor the following day and found the North Sea Fleet just where Mr. Brooks had expected it to be, off the Goodwin Sands. Giles saw that *Medusa* was sailing immediately behind *Penelope*. Giles did not care how lofty or influential *Medusa*'s captain might be; he wasn't going to let him get away with stealing one of *Impetuous*'s crew members. Following orders signaled from the flagship, Giles brought *Impetuous* into position off *Penelope*'s quarter and had himself rowed across to the flagship immediately.

The flag captain greeted Giles warmly, but when the flag lieutenant observed Giles's angry expression, he ushered him quickly into the Admiral's cabin.

"Captain Giles, welcome back. What is the trouble?" asked Admiral Gardner.

"*Medusa* pressed one of my men."

"Oh, dear. We cannot have that, can we? I've had trouble with Captain Brown before this. Mr. Arbuckle, signal to *Medusa*: 'Captain to repair on board. Oh, and add, 'Bring muster roll*.'"

"I expect to get him back immediately," Giles said.

"So you will if *Medusa* actually has him. Now tell me, how did the repairs go? I am surprised to see you back so soon."

"The repairs were completed on time, though the Dockyard did warn me that *Impetuous* is not the best-built ship in the fleet. Your letter did wonders, and when its influence waned, Sir David McDougall lit a fire under them again."

"How was he involved?"

Giles explained how he had been visited and the effect of remarking to Sir David the delays he was encountering.

"You are obviously becoming a man of influence, Captain Giles. I would be delighted to have more men in the Commons reliably in favor of the Navy. We in the Lords may believe that we run the country, but the Commons still controls the purse strings. Now, while we await Captain Brown, let's talk about your next cruise."

"Yes, sir?"

"The Baltic trade. Naval supplies. Stockholm Tar, timber, and so on. Very important even though much of our tar comes from America and some from tar-pits. Much of it carried in neutral bottoms.* Can't interfere with that, though, with the French coast under blockade, we have turned a blind eye to privateers seizing those ships near the ports. But much of it is also carried by our own vessels, and recently they have been disappearing. Pirates or privateers, we don't know which, but certainly more have vanished than can be accounted for by storms and shipwrecks. I am shifting two of the frigates away from the Flemish coast to farther east. *Impetuous* is one of them. You'll be patrolling off the mouth of the Skagerrak along the Danish coast. *Mithradates*, Captain Blenkensop, will be patrolling between the Skagerrak and the Thames. You are senior to Blenkensop. Since he will be coming here regularly, he will be reporting to me. He will meet you at a rendezvous you will determine. He has gone ahead and will meet you off the Skagerrak in two weeks' time. Remember that most of the shipping will be neutral, but you will have to check them to make sure that they also have not been taken, whether they are neutral or captured British ships."

At this point, a hail was heard from outside, answered by a cry of '*Medusa.*'

"Ah," said the Admiral, "Captain Brown must be arriving."

In a few moments, Captain Brown was ushered into the Admiral's cabin. He was a thin man who looked to be in his forties, with graying hair and a face that said its habitual expression was discontent.

Admiral Gardiner introduced Giles to him and continued, "Captain Brown, you have just joined the Fleet coming from the Nore, have you not."

"Yes, sir," was the reply, though Captain Brown's expression expressed annoyance at being asked a question whose answer the Admiral should have known already.

"Did you happen to send a press-gang ashore while you were at the Nore?"

"Yes, sir. I was short of men as a result of several being injured or dying on my previous cruise."

"Captain Brown, did you obtain a warrant for the gang?"

"No, sir. There wasn't time, and the office was closed."

"The pressing took place in Chatham?"

"Aye, sir."

"Did it succeed?"

"Only partially, sir. We only got three men."

"I see. Let's see your muster roll ... Yes, here we are ... Coswell, Harrison, and ... I am having trouble reading the third name ... looks like Caten ... but it could be Baten? First name is clear enough – Timothy, but it rather looks as if the first letter of his surname has been written over. Do you know him, Captain Brown?"

"Yes, sir. He was about to be flogged when your summons arrived. The sentence will be carried out when I return."

"What was his offense?"

"Talking back to an officer and refusing a valid order."

"Oh, dear. And I see that he is listed here as able. What was he saying?"

"He claimed that he was already on a Navy frigate and shouldn't be pressed. My lieutenant, who was in charge of the press-gang, says that he was passed out drunk when they took him."

"Was he? What was the name of your man, Captain Giles?"

"Timothy Baten, sir."

"Then we had better get the man in question over here, shouldn't we? And your lieutenant, Captain Brown. What is his name?"

"Drew, sir."

"Send the signals, Mr. Arbuckle. Now gentlemen, while we are waiting, would you join me in a glass of Madeira?"

A very uncomfortable interlude for the two captains ensued. Admiral Gardiner seemed to be unaware of the tensions in the room, as he talked of the grouse shooting he had enjoyed recently, the scandals involving other admirals or senior captains, the prospects of the French coming out, rumors that the King's madness might be returning, and so on. Before too long, however, the boat from *Medusa* arrived, and Lieutenant Drew and a rather scruffy-looking seaman were shown into the cabin. The seaman was notable for a black eye and a large bruise on his cheek.

"Mr. Drew, I gather that you were in charge of the press-gang that descended on Chatham," the Admiral began.

"Aye, sir."

"Did you press this man?"

"Aye, sir, we found him in a tavern, and he put up a bit of a struggle, yelling that we had no right – well, those weren't exactly his words, sir."

"And then?"

"He was subdued, sir, by being hit on the head with a cudgel. We then carried him to the boat and took him and the other two we had caught out to *Medusa*. In the morning, we had to pour a bucket of water over him, but he still seemed confused. I got his name for the muster roll, but he objected to being enrolled, saying he was already in the Navy. He spoke pretty rough to me, sir, and refused to be silent, so I had him put on remand. Captain Brown sentenced him to three dozen lashes. They have yet to be administered, sir."

"I see. There seems to be some confusion about his name. Is it Baten or Caten?"

"He told me Baten, sir, or, at least, that is what I thought he said, but Captain Brown said it must surely be 'Caten' and had me change the muster roll accordingly."

"Captain Giles, I suggest you return to your ship with Baten here. Do not leave the fleet until you get my written orders."

"Aye, aye, sir."

As he was leaving, Giles heard the Admiral resume, "Captain Brown, this is a very serious…." The door closed behind them before he could hear more, but, clearly, Brown was in for some sort of tongue-lashing.

The Flag Captain was on hand to bid Giles farewell. "This is your man?"

"Indeed he is."

"Admiral Gardiner has not been pleased with Brown and must be delighted that you caught him out. I wouldn't worry about any enemy you may have made. Brown's influence has been on the wane."

As the ceremony greeting Giles on *Impetuous* ended, Baten shyly approached Giles.

"Thank you, Captain. I didn't expect that you would look out for me."

"You're welcome, Baten. Better see the doctor about your wounds, especially your head. And I'll tell your officer that you should only have light duties for a day or two."

"Aye, aye, sir. Thank you, sir."

"What was that about, sir?" inquired Mr. Milton.

Giles explained. He was surprised by the lieutenant's next remark, "I wonder if Captain Brown is about to be relieved of his command." Giles hadn't seriously thought of the possibility, and, certainly, Milton wasn't about to be made captain of a seventy-four or likely to be affected by whatever changes occurred. However, Milton's remark proved prescient. At two bells of the afternoon watch, a signal was flown from the flagship ordering Mr. Milton to report to the Admiral.

Giles restrained his curiosity with difficulty. It was highly unusual for a first lieutenant to be summoned by an admiral of a fleet without his captain also being required. What did the Admiral think that Milton might know about the taking of Baten? Giles's puzzlement was only increased when Carstairs reported that Milton was returning with another lieutenant in the boat. Curiosity got the better of him so that he went on deck even as the boat was hooking onto the side of *Impetuous*. Milton ascended the ladder first, so he must be the senior of the lieutenants. If Milton was surprised to see his captain on deck awaiting him, he did not show it.

"Captain Giles, may I introduce Lieutenant Hendricks? May we see you in your cabin, sir?"

Giles led the way below and slipped behind his desk.

"What is it, Mr. Milton?"

"Sir, I have been appointed master and commander into *Swan*."

"What wonderful news, Mr. Milton! I confess that I shall be very sorry to see you go. You certainly deserve to get your step. What has happened to Captain Duncan?"

"He has been made post-captain, subject to confirmation, and appointed to *Midas*."

"That is more good news. She is a frigate, is she not, captained by Captain Blenkensop?"

"Yes, sir, a thirty-two. Captain Blenkensop is named to *Medusa*, sir."

"And Captain Brown?"

"I am told that he will be going ashore for health reasons, sir. His first lieutenant, Lieutenant Drew, seems to have caught the same malady and will also be going ashore."

"I see. Well, again, congratulations, Mr. Milton. I have been very happy to serve with you. It does, of course, leave me without a first lieutenant again. Mr. Miller is still very junior."

"Thank, you sir. I agree about Mr. Miller, though in time he will make a splendid premier. That is where Lieutenant Hendricks comes in."

"Mr. Hendriks? Yes. I did wonder what you were doing here."

"Yes, sir. Admiral Gardiner appointed me to you. I was third on *Medusa*."

"I am very glad to have you. I am sure Mr. Milton will be happy to introduce you to the wardroom while his things are being gathered. I hope you will sup with me later in the day so that we can get to know each other better."

Lieutenant Hendricks appeared to be a rather nervous man, about twenty-five years old. He was the son of a doctor in Hull. The nervousness might be put down to being suddenly placed in a new position with a bit of a cloud over his head with the sudden changes in the officers of *Medusa*. It might also come from being appointed first lieutenant on a crack frigate. More disturbing to Giles than the nervousness was the revelation that all of Mr. Hendricks's service had been in ships of the line and that he had never seen combat. There was, of course, nothing that Giles could do about that. However, he would have to be careful to give Mr. Hendricks more explicit instructions than he usually would need in orders to his First Lieutenant. The interview was pleasant enough, and when Mr. Hendricks settled in and became used to *Impetuous*'s ways, he might well become a good shipmate.

Impetuous received her written orders just after dawn the next day. There was a fresh breeze from the northwest, and Giles, even without reading the orders, told Mr. Hendricks to make sail, all plain sail to the royals. In the usual fashion, Mr. Hendricks bellowed the orders to accomplish this, hoping that the other lieutenants and the petty officers would know what to do in detail. A minute later, after consulting the master, Giles gave the course to the helmsman. He turned to Mr. Hendricks, "We usually let the petty officers trim the sails on this ship unless there is something unusual, though the first lieutenant has to make sure that they are, in fact, doing the right thing."

The first lieutenant was surprised. On *Medusa,* the lieutenant of the watch used to fuss over the petty officers, even though the petty officers certainly knew what had to be done. Hendricks watched in astonishment as the top men raced up the masts while the landsmen prepared to trim the sails. They seemed happy to be performing the tasks, and there was none of the low-level grumbling that had accompanied any general order on *Medusa*. It took Hendricks a few moments to spot what struck him as really unusual: the bosun's mates were not "starting" anyone with their rope ends. In fact, they did not even seem to have rope ends. Instead, they were participating themselves where an extra hand might speed up some operation. He would have to get used to Captain Giles's ways, but they seemed to be effective. What was clear to Mr. Hendricks was that the Captain expected to have the ship running in top-notch condition, and it would be up to him to make sure that this occurred, even though Mr. Milton had told him that the Captain did not think flogging improved performance or morale.

Chapter XVII

Daphne's lassitude kept returning during the first few weeks of January. It certainly wasn't like her, but she had to make a conscious effort to feel a real interest in the two estates. She started to think that possibly she should get a steward for Dipton Hall to lighten her load. Not that she wanted to abandon her interests, planning, and management of the agricultural activities, but some of the routine work was getting to be less satisfying as she became more familiar with the needs and cycles of farming the new estate. She also wanted more time for planning with Mr. Griffiths.

Daphne's usual enthusiasm started to return as the days lengthened, and the first hints of the coming spring became evident when she was going around the farms. The urgency which she felt to get the facilities for horse breeding and training was mitigated when Mr. Griffiths pointed out firmly that nature's schedule did not correspond to an eager young woman's. Producing a colt took eleven months from start to finish, and then it would take time before the offspring would be ready for training. Had Salton Masham Grange's broodmares been available, the endeavor could have got off to a major start that very spring, and the plans would have to be developed and be implemented quickly. Things could be more relaxed now that that possibility was closed.

"Unfortunately, we don't have much to start with right now," Mr. Griffiths remarked regretfully. "There are two mares that would be excellent. Stallions are not the problem. You can always arrange for a good stallion, for a fee. A single stallion can service upwards of two hundred mares in a year, though, usually, they do not have such a heavy schedule, partly because mares are not always fertile and there are good and bad times of the year to have foals."

"Which are the two mares?" Daphne asked.

"Serene Masham, of course, and Moonbeam."

"Yes, I wouldn't want to be without either, though I won't be using Serene often in the summer when there is no hunting."

"You told me that Moonbeam was bred on your father's estate, did you not, Lady Giles?"

"Yes, she was, but I don't know which horse was the sire. It was an unintentional breeding, and the male could have been any of four stallions. Moonbeam's dam is Moonshine."

"Does your father still own the horses?"

"Yes, he doesn't like selling them."

"Do you think he would allow me to examine them to see if I can determine which one is Moonbeam's sire?"

"I'm sure he will. I'll ask him next time I see him. He probably would allow you to breed them again if you wanted. I can see that is what you have in mind. Very likely, he would let me have Moonshine. He doesn't need her now that I am married, but I suppose that we should get some mares of our own as soon as possible. I never realized how long it takes to produce a foal."

"That would be a good idea, my lady. There are several auctions in the winter that might have promising mares."

"Then I will suggest that Captain Giles think about it in my next letter. I really want his approval at each step of the way."

The next meeting of the Hunt came along, and Daphne rode in it while Lady Marianne and her daughters demurely followed from afar. For them, the prime attraction wasn't the hunting but the mingling with the other riders that took place before the hunt started. Lydia and Lieutenant Charles seemed to zero in on each other and act as if no one else were there. By contrast, Catherine seemed to be very distant with Captain Hicks and more welcoming to some other officers from Lord Moresby's Regiment. Daphne was finding Major Stoner less objectionable. That may have been the result of his remark, "You have a very good bottom, Lady Giles, very good! As good as any man in the Hunt." She had been about to take offense when she realized that the Major was referring to how well she could ride.

Even the failure to be invited to the Hunt dinners had ceased to bother her. Lord David's enthusiastic description of the gatherings had quite convinced her that she would not have enjoyed them, and her presence would simply have put a damper on the enjoyment of others. It seemed that these dinners were simply a longer version of what happened at other dinners when the ladies had withdrawn, with the men consuming more alcohol in proportion to the lengthier time. Mr. Summers kept fussing over the details of the ball, even after Daphne had assured him that all was in hand.

A marked change for Daphne came one day in the middle of February. She awoke feeling poorly even before Elsie pulled the drapes. Almost immediately after getting out of bed, just as she was handing her nightgown to Elsie, she was overcome with a wave of nausea. She only just had time to grab the chamber pot before she vomited into it. As the heaving ended, she realized that that was not the most pleasant receptacle in which to put her nose.

"Elsie, we had better have another chamber pot here," she announced, remembering that she had not felt well the previous morning though she had not had to throw up. "I don't know what is the matter with me. I'm never sick."

"Oh, m'lady. I wonder if we have caught something. I was sick first thing in the morning, too, and I am not feeling very well right now. Should we call Dr. Vardour?

"No, not that quack. Let's see how we feel later. I am feeling quite a bit better already."

The next day brought the same problem, and for Elsie too. Elsie also complained that she had felt sick in the middle of the day. On the third day, Daphne finally became worried. "Send for Mr. Jackson, Steves," she ordered when she came downstairs for breakfast.

The apothecary arrived soon after Daphne completed her breakfast. He examined her, asked some questions about her time of the month, and then stood back. "Daphne, you have the only woman's problem that I am happy to diagnose."

"What? Am I sick?"

"Not really sick. No, I wouldn't say that."

"What is it? Stop teasing me."

"You are with child."

"I am? But I've been throwing up every morning."

"Yes, that is one of the symptoms. It is called 'morning sickness.' Didn't you know?"

"No. No one told me."

Jackson realized that having been brought up without a mother by a father who might be supremely ignorant about any of the details of human reproduction, Daphne might well have no idea of what she was going to encounter as a result of being pregnant.

"Yes," he told her. "For most women, it is the clearest early sign that they are pregnant."

"How long does it last?"

"There is no fixed rule. In most cases, it doesn't last longer than six weeks."

"I am going to throw up every day for the next six weeks?"

"Yes. Quite possibly for eight weeks or even longer, but it should start getting better in six weeks."

"When will the baby come, do you think?"

"Probably at the beginning of October, but it could be many days on either side of that. But I have to warn you that there is a chance that you may lose it before that; in fact, you may miscarry quite soon."

"Oh, no. why?"

"I don't know, just that it happens quite often."

"Oh. How can I prevent it?"

"I don't know. The best approach seems to be to just keep doing what you would normally do until the baby is about to be born. When your water breaks, you can go to your room and summon some help. A midwife or me – I am what is called a male midwife."

"What do you mean by my 'water breaks'?"

Jackson spent the next several minutes trying to rectify Daphne's almost total lack of understanding of what it meant to be with child. He ended with some admonitions.

"First, keep on doing everything you normally would until it becomes too uncomfortable. Second, call on me if anything seems to be wrong, except what I have told you is normal. Don't wear stays. Luckily they are not in fashion now, thank heavens, but some ladies try to hide their condition by tight lacing."

"Can I still go for walks and rides?"

"Of course. That would probably be good for you and the baby. Just don't try to ride Dark Paul side-saddle. That would not hurt the baby, but you might fall off again and break your neck, which would not be good for you or your baby."

Elsie had been listening to everything that was said with full attention. Much of what Mr. Jackson was saying was new to her since she had lost her own mother when she was ten, had no older sisters, and had entered service when she was thirteen. The maid was now worried about how long she could keep working and how she would look after herself until Carstairs could make provision. Her mind was somewhat set at ease after Mr. Jackson had examined her as well and confirmed that she also was pregnant.

"How long can I keep working? I know that ladies don't want servants when their condition shows."

"I suppose they don't. I hope that doesn't apply to you, Daphne. No, Elsie, if Lady Giles will let you, you should keep working until it becomes too much for you. For some, that would be after about six months; others wouldn't need to stop until the baby decided it was time to arrive. Just as I want Daphne to stay as active as possible until the end of the period, I want the same for you, but whether or not you can keep on working is, of course, up to Lady Giles here."

Mr. Jackson left, but Daphne remained seated for many minutes, reflecting on what she had learned. He had long been Daphne's mentor and the repository of her secrets when she was growing up. She couldn't very well go against what he suggested, though she knew most ladies might. Thank heavens that Elsie and Carstairs had got married when it was possible that they would have a child! With Carstairs as devoted to Richard as Elsie was to Daphne, Elsie could keep working until it was impossible. If that meant that others would have to take up some of her duties when Elsie's time approached, well, so be it. The servants all had good positions. The housekeeper, Mrs. Wilson, might not be happy. She would probably want Elsie to be dismissed immediately. Well, Mrs. Wilson was getting uppity, and it would do no harm to put her in her place.

Daphne was glad that Mr. Jackson had said that she should remain active until the baby came. She had never liked sitting around the house engaged in needlework, which she hated, or other activities that involved little movement. But what about when the baby came? How long would she have to stay in bed? How long before she could resume her normal life? What about breastfeeding? She had seen how her tenants' wives often nursed their offspring for a long time after they were born. Would she have to and for how long? The new mothers she had visited among the gentry seemed to stay inactive for some time after being delivered of a child, but she had never known them to nurse their babies. They had mentioned something about wet nurses, but Daphne didn't really know what was meant by the term. She didn't know anyone to ask about nursing since she didn't really like talking to Mr. Jackson about distinctly women's matters, but she supposed that she would have to ask him anyway.

Then there was Richard. They had always presumed that there would be children, but they had not made any plans about when it would come about. Somehow, children had always been something to think about later. Would he be happy? She thought he would be. Would he be interested in the child? She knew that many, maybe most, aristocratic fathers did not seem to be really interested in their offspring. She hoped that wouldn't be true of Richard. She would, of course, write to him at once to tell him about the news. But then there was the chance that she might not carry the baby to term; indeed, Mr. Jackson had indicated that she might not carry it very much longer. Should she wait to tell him until she was more certain that her condition would continue? Probably not. If the baby did disappear – and what did that involve? – he would find out and would be just as hurt by her losing the baby, and he would be disappointed that she had not told him.

The baby wasn't due for a long time – more than seven months. There was lots of time to plan for it, and, for now, she should just keep on with what she was doing. Would she be able to hunt next season? Now she was being silly. That wasn't important. But it did suggest to her that she might not be able to do as much supervising of the building of the new stables as she intended. The latest letter from Richard had approved the plans, though with some suggestions and the thought that she should consult Mr. Edwards about an architect. He had couched it as a thought for her to consider. However, Daphne knew an order when she saw it. Even so, it was a good idea. And his letter had enthusiastically suggested that Mr. Griffiths try to buy at least four mares at the upcoming auctions. He had named several sales that he knew were coming up, which usually had good stock, and wondered if Mr. Griffiths was thinking of attending them. Daphne was aware that if Mr. Griffiths had not been intending to go to those events, he was now bound to be present at each of them.

Daphne snapped out of her reverie to descend to her room to write letters. First, a long one gave Richard the news. She also suggested that he tell Carstairs the news about Elsie. Her maid, she knew, could hardly write and would find it a chore to get the news of her child to Carstairs by herself.

Next, she wrote a letter to Mr. Edwards about an architect and to see what his advice might be on someone to help plan the expanded grounds of Dipton Hall. That done, she still had time to seek out Mr. Griffiths and convey to him not only the good news about building the stables but also Giles's instructions about the auctions. He, in return, reported that he had determined which horse he thought was Moonbeam's sire, saying it was easy since three of the horses were geldings. He suggested that, if Mr. Moorhouse agreed, they should have Moonshine serviced by that stallion in May with the expectation of getting a foal in April.

Things returned to normal after the flurry of activity resulting from the news that Daphne was with child. February slipped into March and March into April. The big event was the Hunt Ball, but the fact that it was not the first ball at Dipton Hall that Daphne and her servants had put on made it almost a routine part of the life of the house.

The three women with whom she shared the house were not nearly as nonchalant about the event. They seemed to spend endless hours discussing what would be the best way to enhance their gowns and how their hair could be best arranged. They would be far too busy on the day itself to even contemplate joining the hunt itself, even for a short period.

Daphne was so relaxed about holding the celebration marking the end of hunting season that there was never any question that she would participate in the hunt itself. Serene Masham surpassed herself on this occasion, keeping up with the dogs seemingly without effort. Daphne had learned that giving the mare a minimum of guidance produced the best result, and Daphne was again in at the kill. So, for once, was Major Stoner.

"You have a magnificent bottom, Lady Giles," he roared at Daphne. "And a splendid horse. Got her at Salton Masham Grange, didn't you? Pity they closed."

"It is. However, Captain Giles is going to start a stud farm at Dipton Hall. We have hired Mr. Griffiths to run it. He was the stable master at Salton Masham when they were breeding hunters."

"Have you, by George! Put my name down for one of your first horses, what. Free to Ride, here, my horse, is not a patch on yours, and he is getting a bit old."

Major Stoner seemed to have forgotten his earlier opinion of women in the hunt. If it were not that, on this occasion, the activities would be capped by the Ball, she thought he would invite her to the Hunt Dinner. Not that she would want to go anymore: Lord David's description had quite removed her fascination with the event.

Daphne had made sure that her ball would be superior to the usual balls held by other Hunts. That would really establish her position in the community! The minuets she had included in her previous ball had provided elegance, but few people had danced them and none of the younger people. She was intending to surprise them all on this occasion by including several waltzes among the more usual country dances. This dance was considered very daring among the more staid members of Dipton society. Daphne had read that the waltz was very popular in London. Many of the younger ladies in the Dipton area had found out how to perform the dance from their older brothers, and they had then imparted that skill to the less fortunate of their peers. Daphne would drag Dipton's conservative ways into the nineteenth century.

Everything went smoothly on the day of the Ball itself. The weather was mild, with no rain to make the transition from coach to Hall awkward. Everyone was prepared to have a good time, Greetings were exchanged enthusiastically, and various groups formed depending on their interests, be it talking, playing cards, watching, or dancing. All went well with the dancing until the second waltz was coming to an end. The final notes were overshadowed by a ringing slap delivered by Lydia Crocker on Lieutenant Charles's face. All the dancing stopped as Lydia glared at her partner, still so annoyed that she did not realize the magnitude of her offense, while he looked more angry than embarrassed. Everyone on the dance floor was horrified at this turn of events and extremely curious about the reason for it. Whether or not they found out, they all knew that here was the prime topic of gossip in Dipton and Ameschester for weeks to come.

Lydia was turning away, presumably to rush from the ballroom in tears, when Thomas Dimster, the elder son of Sir Thomas Dimster, stepped forward. "I say, Charles, old man, I think that you had better leave since you have so distressed Miss Lydia."

"It's none of your business, Dimster. You were a prig at Cambridge, and you are a prig now."

That produced a horrified gasp among the onlookers. Would this lead to a duel? Everyone had heard of duels, but none of them had witnessed one or even the cause of one.

"Nonsense, Charles. It just won't do, causing a scene like this."

Lieutenant Charles seemed about to explode when Lord David stepped in. "That's enough, Charles, old boy. As Dimster here said, we are not at Cambridge anymore, and you have distressed my niece. Now come along."

Lord David rather forcibly linked his arm in Lieutenant Charles's and guided him from the ballroom.

Apparently, Lord David had known each of them at Cambridge and could serve as a peace-maker.

Mr. Dimster presented his arm to Lydia Crocker and guided her towards a corner of the room. She seemed to have quite recovered from the incident, even though she clung very tightly to Mr. Dimster's arm. Before they reached the corner, Major Stoner came up to them. "Well done, young man, well done! Couldn't have handled it better myself. I can tell you, if he had been in my regiment, there would be consequences. It is all right, Lady Marianne," he continued addressing Lydia's mother, who had come over to see what was amiss with her daughter, "all seems well, thanks to this young man."

"But what was the fuss all about, Lydia?" Lady Marianne asked.

"Mother, he made a most improper suggestion to me and, when I objected, he made one that was even more rude."

"How awful for you," interjected Mr. Dimster, "I am afraid that Charles was very wild at Cambridge. Sent down for much more serious offenses than I was. You did absolutely the right thing, Miss Lydia. He had it coming."

The little group broke up, with Mr. Dimster taking Lydia to a corner where they would not be bothered about other people. Major Stoner accompanied Lady Marianne to the sidelines. It was notable that for the rest of the evening, Mr. Dimster quite monopolized Lydia, apparently completely to her delight, while Major Stoner appeared to find it necessary to smooth Lady Marianne's ruffled feathers repeatedly.

Daphne was quite relieved at this turn of events. She had encouraged the match between Lieutenant Charles and her step-niece, but she had become steadily more concerned about how many glaring weaknesses he had exhibited as a potential husband. Much as she would like to see Lydia married, she did not want her step-niece to be miserable in her choice.

There were no more serious incidents at the Ball, and everyone seemed to have a good time, except possibly some young ladies whose dance cards had not filled up at with either the speed or the names they had hoped for. Daphne's own card was full, and she discovered that two of Lord Mosley's officers knew how to waltz in a very proper manner while still providing her with the excitement of whirling about the ballroom floor. Her father had taken her in to dinner; no crises had arisen about the musicians, the food and drink, or the adequacy of the service. Mr. Summers thanked her most fulsomely for hosting the Ball, hinted that he hoped she would do it again, and then, at the last minute, remembered to add how very much he hoped that Captain Giles would be present on the next occasion. That was a sentiment that Daphne fully endorsed. For her, the whole evening had been tinged with sadness that her husband was not present.

Major Stoner's thanks were more direct. "Good show, Lady Giles, good show! Pukka Ball! Pukka Ball! I told Summers that you wouldn't be able to have the ball, not with Captain Giles absent. No one to organize it properly, what? But you proved me wrong! Yes, indeed! Indeed! When I am wrong, I admit it! Very good evening! Excellent!"

Since the lead-up to the ball had been so easy, Daphne felt very little let down when it was over and found her nieces' constant rehashing of it grew tiresome quickly. Lydia clearly was in no way distressed with having Lieutenant Charles removed from the picture. Mr. Dimster had ridden over to Dipton Hall every day since the ball, and it seemed that Lady Marianne had taken up reading so that she could fulfill her chaperone duties while not dying of boredom. Daphne was more concerned about Catherine. Captain Hicks seemed to be losing interest. That was just as well in Daphne's opinion since Catherine seemed to be dreading a future filled with nothing but discussion of horses and banking. However, while several quite eligible young men had shown interest in her during the ball, and two of them had even accompanied their mothers to Dipton Hall for the calls to rehash the Ball, nothing had really developed from these encounters.

A few days later, when Daphne returned from giving Serene a run. Steves met her to announce that Mr. Dimster was in the drawing-room and would like to see her. The butler's manner indicated that very serious matters were at hand and that Daphne might be happier if she changed out of her riding clothes first. Since she had to change anyway, Daphne took Steves's unspoken hint and immediately went up to her dressing room. Elsie also indicated by her manner that she regarded the forthcoming interview as being of the greatest importance, though Daphne could not extract from her the reason for her strange attitude. It did not matter. Daphne guessed that, like her, they wondered if this had something to do with Lydia's hand. She had already heard that young Mr. Dimster had spent a great deal of time at Dipton Hall while her attention had been on other matters over Christmas.

Daphne decided that, for an interview of this importance, she should use her own room. It was not nearly as Spartan as it had been when first she started using it to go over the accounts of the estates. But a place of business it still clearly was. Daphne had also learned from Richard's tales of how he was greeted by the Admiral that there was an unquestioned advantage to having her back to the light during an interview involving business.

At Daphne's request, Steves showed in a very nervous young man. Daphne directed him to sit in a comfortable chair in front of her working table.

"Steves tells me you want to see me."

"Yes, my lady."

Mr. Dimster lapsed into silence.

Dear me, thought Daphne. Am I going to have to pry this out of him?

"About what, Mr. Dimster?" she inquired.

"Well... Miss Lydia and I ..."

"Yes?"

"We have been seeing quite a good deal of each other, especially since the Ball, but also before that...."

"I've noticed." Daphne could have bitten her tongue. Sarcasm was not likely to speed up this interview.

"And ... and ... and... we want to get married."

"Do you? And so?"

"I understand that Captain Giles is Lydia's guardian."

"He is."

"And we would need his permission to get married."

"Yes, you would."

"He's away, and, Lydia says, you don't know when he will return."

Daphne had to bite off another utterance of, "I've noticed." Instead, she contented herself with saying, "that is correct. Captain Giles is serving with the North Sea Fleet."

"I … that is, we … well, we wondered if you could write to him to get his permission."

"I suppose I could, but I would have to know quite a bit more about you before I could do that. All the things that Captain Giles would need to understand before he would even contemplate giving you his permission."

"What would you like to know?"

"First, do you love Miss Lydia?"

"Oh, yes. Didn't I make that clear?"

"It is always wise to check." Daphne was beginning to feel a complete fraud. She was probably the same age as Mr. Dimster, and she had no real knowledge of the income needed by a young gentleman to marry. She wasn't sure that Richard did either.

"Does Lady Marianne approve?"

"Yes. She was the one who told me that I should ask you to write to Captain Giles. She said that if I wrote to Captain Giles, he would just ask your opinion and that that would slow everything down."

"Did she, indeed? What is your income?"

"I have an allowance from my father that I live on. I have lodgings in London. We have quite a lively group of Cambridge men there. If I got married, my father would want me to live in a cottage on our land, so I could learn something about the estate. Maybe become his steward. But he has indicated that he will not raise my allowance if I marry. I am his heir."

"Is the estate entailed*?"

"Yes, it is."

"How big is the allowance?"

"Four hundred and fifty pounds a year."

"I see," said Daphne in a rather frosty tone.

"My father wants me to run for Parliament. If I am elected, he will increase my allowance to at least one thousand pounds a year."

"Would he! Does he have a riding in mind?"

"He did rather suggest that I might be able to obtain the second seat for Dipton."

"I see." Daphne had heard from Giles that the seat was virtually in his gift. Was that the reason for this young man wanting to marry Lydia? This influence and patronage business was quite beyond her understanding. "Is that what you want?"

"Not really. I wouldn't like the late nights, and I am told that it is hard to have a good marriage if you are an MP."

That made Daphne pause. She knew that Giles had been approached to be an MP, and she had expressed to him the information that she would support anything he wanted to do.

"I am not sure that that would be a good idea. Do you know you might be able to find a position learning to manage an estate if you wanted to and so not be so beholden to your father? There are such positions available." Daphne carefully did not say that the position she was thinking of was at Dipton Hall.

"If I could get such a place, I think that would be better. I do not like being under my father's thumb."

Daphne thought for several moments. She decided that she liked young Mr. Dimster, though she was most dubious about his father. If it came down to it, she might even suggest to Captain Giles and her father that young Mr. Dipton not be elected MP for Dipton. But as a husband for Lydia, he certainly seemed preferable to Lieutenant Charles or his ilk.

"Have you talked about this to Lydia?"

"Oh, yes. And she has agreed. She said Captain Giles would be providing a dowry."

"Yes. I believe that he was thinking of at least £10,000, in consols*. Valued at four percent per annum, so that would yield £400 per year. I imagine with that amount, together with your £450, you should have enough to allow you to marry."

"That is very generous of Captain Giles. Oh, yes, that would certainly allow us to marry, and without my becoming an MP first. Thank you very much, Lady Giles."

"I will, of course, have to confirm the amount of the dowry with Captain Giles, as well as whether he will grant permission at all. I will write to him immediately. We had better postpone publishing the banns until he replies. Now, you will want to convey what I have stated to Lydia. I hope you will stay for dinner."

Daphne took out a sheet of paper as the young man hastened from the room. She detailed all that she had learned from Mr. Dimster and gave Richard her recommendation that he would be an acceptable husband for Lydia. She also told him that she had said the dowry would probably be £10,000, but she thought that £12,500 might be better. She mentioned, in very negative terms, his father's wanting his son to be the MP from Dipton. After some reflection, she added the young man's comment about members of the House and marriage. She did not want to influence Richard very much, but a little mild guidance might be in order.

As Daphne sealed the letter, she realized that the last little bit had been her first deliberate attempt to influence a choice that was entirely his own. She hoped that she wasn't about to become one of those women who spent much of their time thinking about how to "manage" their husbands. It was one of the most tedious topics raised frequently when the ladies came to call or were in the drawing room waiting for the men to join them after dinner. Of course, she did want to have her own say in how their child would be raised.

Before going to join the others, Daphne rubbed her stomach fondly. She knew that it was too early to feel the baby kicking, but she was sure that she was more rounded than she had been. How she wished that Richard were at Dipton!

Chapter XVIII

A strong westerly breeze hastened *Impetuous*'s departure from the fleet. She sped eastward under a bright, pale blue sky, seeming as eager as her crew to demonstrate her abilities after her long lay-up. But avid as they were, little of interest came their way for many days. They did see a good deal of shipping, heading to the English Channel, staying far enough away from land to be out of sight of the coast. Some were Swedish ships and some Danish, and many flew the Union Jack. *Impetuous* spoke to all of them and inspected most.

Giles suspected that many of the Scandinavian vessels might really be on their way to France, but, with papers listing English ports as their destination, Giles could not proceed to investigate further. It would invite an international incident that Bonaparte could exploit if Giles were to break open the desk of some Swedish captain to see if it contained a different bill of lading, one which showed that the cargo was destined for a French rather than an English port.

The only respite from the routine and unrewarding stopping of trading ships and the constant practicing came from the bi-weekly meetings with *Mithradates*. Giles dined with Captain Blenkinsop every time they met up. The captain of *Mithradates* had been having no more luck than Giles. He was getting restless and despondent, for he had been counting on getting some prize money. There was very little prospect of that with the way their search had been unfolding. Captain Blenkinsop was not the most entertaining of dinner companions, but these occasions were a relief from Giles's having to eat alone or guard his words when he entertained his own officers or dined in the wardroom.

The more important aspect of the meeting with *Mithradates* was that she brought mail. The news was, of course, not entirely up-to-date. The gap between the writing and the receiving of Daphne's letters could be anything from one week to a month. But it was far better than if Giles had been assigned to the West Indies or even to the Mediterranean. He adopted the practice of skimming over all her letters as soon as he received them so that he could provide replies to any questions needing an immediate answer. Then he would go over them at leisure, savoring every word.

In the first weeks, the most momentous of these matters to be dealt with quickly had to do with the plans for the stables and the grounds and with Mr. Griffiths's desire to start breeding in the spring. Later packages contained the plans for the works to be done, first in rough form and then in more detailed drawings. They, of course, had to be studied, and his comments would have to wait for the next meeting with *Mithradates* in order to be conveyed to Daphne.

Giles was touched that his wife sought his approval for major decisions and took his suggestions very seriously. She didn't always adopt them, but she always expressed in detail very good reasons for ignoring or modifying them. Knowing her impatient and decisive nature, he had earlier presumed that she would forge ahead with any projects she wanted to undertake and only inform him after her decisions were made. That would not have been the usual pattern in a marriage, but Daphne was anything but usual.

The most important of the letters that he received arrived in a third batch. Daphne was with child! Giles sat back in his chair for several moments as he absorbed the news. He hadn't expected to learn that he was to be a father, though now he realized that he should not be surprised by this development. Was he pleased? Most decidedly! His mind rushed ahead to wonder whether the child would be a boy or a girl and how he would interact with them and guide them. He shook his head. This was getting far ahead of himself. Right now, he needed to assure Daphne that this was exactly the development he most wanted. Without even going on to read her next letter, he took up his pen to write immediately. Only after he had filled both sides of two pages, containing his own feelings about becoming a father, but mainly consisting of advice and admonitions about how Daphne must act now that she was pregnant for her own and the child's good, did he pause. He realized that he really had no idea of what was best for his wife or their child on the latter subjects, while he had every faith both in the knowledge and sagacity of Mr. Jackson. He tore up what he had already written and instead only wrote of his own delight and his confidence in Mr. Jackson's and Daphne's own knowledge and judgment. He then sealed the letter and indicated on the package containing his other letters that this one should be read first. Even though he knew that it would make no difference to when it would arrive, he was then in a rush to have the package delivered to *Mithradates* for forwarding to the post office, even though he knew that it did not matter just when it was sent to *Mithradates* since she would not leave any quicker if *Impetuous*'s mail was received a bit earlier.

It was Captain Blenkinsop's turn to entertain. As Giles went on deck to take his barge to the other frigate, he saw that Carstairs was, of course, in the boat. After he boarded it, he told his coxswain the news about Elsie in a voice low enough that it could not be heard by others. His discretion was hardly needed. After taking a minute to absorb the news, Carstairs bellowed, "Blow me down, mates, I am going to be a father!" The effect that this announcement had on the crew of the barge would, on any other ship, have resulted in floggings. Giles, however, was not at all perturbed by the loud, good-natured, and vulgar remarks that were directed at Carstairs. He realized that he would have to order an extra tot of rum for everyone when he returned to *Impetuous*. He was not even much put out when he, himself, had to answer *Mithradates'* hail or even that at the last minute had to give the order, so his boat did not ram the frigate.

After this excitement, life on the frigate resumed the pattern they had established. There was no sign of privateers or of their victims. Giles started to think that maybe they operated on the other side of the Jutland Peninsula, taking their victims in Danish waters and conveying their prizes to some Baltic port, possibly Lubeck or Rostock. They would be violating Danish neutrality possibly. However, with the fear that Bonaparte put into most European hearts, the Danes or the Germans might not make any serious objections to privateer activities. He wrote to Admiral Gardiner seeking permission to investigate this possibility and awaited *Mithradates'* return impatiently.

One day, *Impetuous* overtook a ship flying the Swedish flag. She was reluctant to heave to* in order to talk with the British frigate, and Giles ordered a shot across her bows to warn her to heave to. When she had backed her sail, Giles brought *Impetuous* close enough to allow easy communication over the narrow strip of water separating the two vessels.

"What ship is that?" Giles bellowed.

"*Linnea*, out of Stockholm, with a cargo of Stockholm tar, bound for Portsmouth."

The Danish coast was in clear sight, and they were possibly in Danish waters. The Danes might take exception if he stopped a Swedish ship in their waters. Giles was about to wish the other captain a good voyage onwards, when Mr. Hendricks caught his attention.

"Captain, that man's accent is not Scandinavian. He is pretending to talk like a Swede, but he is from somewhere else, maybe France."

"Why do you think that, Mr. Hendricks?"

"Sir, in Hull, where I grew up, we saw a lot of Scandinavians. That man's accent does not fit at all. He sounds like someone from France trying to sound like a Swede."

"*Linnea*," Giles called. "Stand by to receive an inspection party."

"I protest! We are neutrals. You have no right."

"We most certainly do," Giles retorted in another bellow.

"Mr. Hendricks. Take the launch and inspect her papers. If you smell a rat, search her. You are right about that accent. Thank you for pointing it out to me."

At that moment, *Linnea* swung her backed topsail in an attempt to get away, possibly hoping that the nuisance of giving chase would allow her to escape. Giles's reaction was immediate.

"Mr. Miller. Another shot across her bows, and I don't care if you take out her bowsprit. Mr. Hendricks, man the sheets to get us underway."

The shot crashed out, and while it did not hit the bowsprit, it did sever a jib-sheet so that Linnea's jib lost the wind as it flapped uselessly, and the vessel headed into the wind and lost way.

"Belay the sheet order," Giles reacted. "Mr. Hendricks, Mr. Macauley, take the launch with a file of Marines and some extra armed seamen and inspect her very carefully."

Two bells later, the launch returned with a couple of well-dressed men.

"What have we here, Mr. Hendricks?" Giles asked.

"Sir, this is Captain Jensen of the *Linnea,* and that is the rogue who was pretending to be the captain. He won't give his name. *Linnea* was bound for Portsmouth from Stockholm when she was taken by a brig of war under French colors. A French privateer, supposedly. Captain Jensen thinks that their intention was to take *Linnea* almost to Dover and then cross the Channel at night to Calais or Boulogne."

"Captain Jensen, I am happy to restore your ship to you. Could you take the prisoners to Portsmouth for me? They will probably be judged to be pirates since you are a neutral ship, but that is out of my hands."

"Yes, indeed, sir. And thank you for investigating and freeing us."

"Thank Mr. Hendricks, here. He is the one who realized something was wrong. Now, Captain, I hope you will join me for a drink."

Giles had no right to interrogate Captain Jensen since *Linnea* sailed as a neutral ship well away from any blockaded port, but he could certainly listen to the captain's tales and prompt the other captain to give more information. *Linnea* had been captured about seven leagues south of the Skagen* Peninsula near the entrance to the Skagerrak*. The captor had been a large, heavily armed brig of war. She had been flying Danish colors, and *Linnea* could not have avoided her even if she had wanted to. In addition to the Danish Flag, the ship had a Danish-looking name board, declaring her to be the *Dannebrog* from Copenhagen. The brig had had a very large crew, mostly Frenchmen. The officers were also French. They had imprisoned *Linnea*'s crew on board the captured vessel rather than on the capturing brig, but Captain Jensen could still hear discussions among their captors. In listening to them, he had gained a wide knowledge of the pirates and their plans.

The raiders were from a pair of very large brigs, armed with eighteen pounders, apparently so that they could match anything less powerful than a frigate. They had some sort of base near the mouth of the Skagerrak but had not been operating there for several months while they were refitted and repaired in Rostock. The two brigs had returned to their Norwegian base with large crews so that they could capture and send into port many ships without having to return to get more men or to recover those who had been sent away.

When Giles had extracted as full a description of the pirate brigs as he could, he guided Captain Jensen, who had been drinking brandy rather than wine, on deck, and saw him to the launch with many expressions of mutual respect. His orders then snapped out. "Make sail, Mr. Hendricks, all plain sail to the top gallants. Mr. Brooks, what would be the course to take us to the Skagen? It has been a good morning's work after all the disappointments we have had. I hope that all officers will dine with me so we can celebrate, even though this is a very minor triumph."

It was a convivial and congenial party that gathered in the Captain's cabin. Even the small action involved in rescuing *Linnea* had relieved the boredom of their fruitless search. It was Mr. Stewart who broached the subject uppermost in all the officers' minds. "Will we get prize money for *Linnea*, Captain Giles?"

"I don't think so. But I think we should get some salvage*. I don't know how much, but don't expect a lot. It might be enough to buy a couple of cases of good wine for the wardroom."

This gibe was met with laughter. They all knew that the wardroom wine was hardly drinkable. Indeed, when Giles was invited to dine in the wardroom, he arranged with Carstairs that a few bottles of his own wine would mysteriously be conveyed to the steward in charge of the needs of the officers so that a more pleasant evening could be enjoyed, but no one would have to acknowledge the source of the wine.

Impetuous raced northward. She should be meeting *Mithradates* near the Skagen anyway. Giles wondered if the Admiral would give permission to chase the privateers down the Skagerrak if that was the direction they chose to take. That, of course, was getting ahead of himself. He first had to find the brigs or, at least, get more reliable word as to where they might be.

There was no sign of *Mithradates* when *Impetuous* arrived at the rendezvous. She kept her position, reaching back and forth through the night and all the next day. Giles was becoming anxious, but there was any number of inconsequential reasons why the other frigate should be late. He would stay where he was for a few more days. Night fell, a moonless night with a heavy cloud cover, so the lookouts could hardly see. *Impetuous* was on a starboard reach, with the Danish coast reckoned to be four miles distant, heading towards the passage between Norway and Denmark. As dawn approached, a keen-eyed lookout in the starboard bow hailed the quarter-deck, "Ship in sight, distance four cables, approaching us, two points off the starboard bow."

A few moments later, the larboard lookout hailed to say that he had spotted a brig on the larboard bow also coming towards them. As the light slowly strengthened, there was a hail from the foretopmast that the brigs had their guns run out.

"Hold your course," Giles told the helmsman. Giles was sure that this must be the enemy brigs. He would engage them, even before verifying who they might be. Withstanding a surprise broadside when he was situated between the two approaching warships would undoubtedly put him at serious risk. They were likely sailing under false colors anyway. The two ships were now steering as if to intercept *Impetuous*, one on each side probably with the intention to board. If it was true that each had extra-large crews, they might easily outnumber *Impetuous*'s crew.

Giles was glad that he had maintained the custom of clearing for action before dawn each night. Many captains, he knew, including Blenkinsop, had ceased or limited the practice when they felt no imminent danger because of the inconvenience of having the captain's cabin, as well as the wardroom, struck below*. He could immediately order, "Fire the bow-chasers as soon as they bear, Mr. Stewart. Aim for the rigging. Larboard your helm, quartermaster, until the starboard bow chasers point at the enemy. When they have fired, reverse your helm. Mr. Miller, prepare to fight both sides. Double-shotted round shot for the first two salvos. Then prepare to load with grape* if possible. We are going to cross the bow of the brig to larboard and then come alongside her, starboard side to starboard side, and grapple."

The bow chasers roared out at that moment. Giles could see that they had done no major damage, but they had severed enough rigging that the brig's maneuverability would be compromised until repairs were made. *Impetuous*'s bow swung to larboard. To the credit of the gun crews, who had reloaded very quickly, the bow chasers fired on the new target as they bore. This time there was noticeable damage as one of the chain slings holding up the foresail yard was severed.

Impetuous continued to turn. The leading gun of the starboard battery had the oncoming brig in its sights and roared out. To Giles's surprise, the opposing brig did not turn to swing alongside his ship. Maybe the damage had made her unmaneuverable; maybe she was counting on accepting the fire to respond by raking *Impetuous*'s even more vulnerable stern. If the latter was his intent, Giles was already foiling it. "Hard a-starboard," he instructed. "Lay alongside the enemy."

Impetuous reversed her turn to try to swing alongside her opponent. The guns continued to fire even as *Impetuous* continued to turn. This time, the shots did more noticeable damage, and the brig's foremast collapsed. The brig lost way. Unfortunately, *Impetuous* had not been able to turn sharply enough to come alongside her. Hendricks backed her sail with one hundred feet still separating her from the brig. The two ships lay side-by-side, exchanging broadsides, but there were many guns on the brig that could no longer fire because of *Impetuous*'s original shots. More of the enemy's guns were being overturned by the minute. The wind was slowly carrying the brig down on *Impetuous*. Giles ordered the change from round shot to grapeshot. Even the carronades* were using grapeshot to try to clear the opponent's deck. Mr. Macauley's marines picked off men on the brig's deck, causing more confusion and slaughter. Giles had heard that the scuppers could run with blood in a fight, but he had never actually seen it before. He glanced around his own deck and saw that there were heavy losses.

Grapnels were thrown by both sides, and, soon, the ships were pulled together. Giles wanted to board his opponent and not to have the fighting on his own deck in case the other brig was able to enter the fray. "Larboard guns, remain at your station," he ordered. "All others prepare to board." The topmen swarmed down rigging and grabbed cutlasses and pistols. The starboard gun crews secured their weapons after a final broadside and prepared to join the boarding party. The ships came together, and Giles roared, "Mr. Hendricks, boarders away!" He remained on *Impetuous*. Indeed, he even turned away from the ensuing melee to see what had happened to the other brig.

It was as well that he did. Despite the damage to her rigging, the other brig had succeeded in tacking around the fighting frigates and was now closing in on *Impetuous*'s larboard side with the clear intention of grappling. Giles would have to hold off the crew of this vessel until Mr. Hendricks had subdued the opposition on the other brig. Numbers were now the big question. Did he have enough men to withstand the joint attack of the brigs?

"Larboard battery, load with grape. Fire as you bear," Giles ordered. "Fighting top*, fire on the enemy to larboard. To larboard." He bellowed to the marines who were still in the fighting-top picking off pirates on the first brig.

The other brig glided into position, her broadside sending salvo after salvo of round shot thudding into *Impetuous*'s hull. Grapnels were thrown, and swarms of men lined up to board, even though some were mowed down by the continuing swathes of grapeshot ripping through them. Giles realized that the confusion caused by the salvos gave him an advantage. "Leave your guns," he bellowed. "Boarders away! Follow me."

Drawing his sword, Giles leapt over the bulwarks. His left foot came down on some rounded object, and he felt a sharp pain in his knee. Regaining his balance and ignoring the continuing pain in his knee, he charged at the nearest defenders, cutting them down. Time seemed to slow while his sight became crystal clear. He slashed at a man to his right, severing his arm in a fountain of blood, and the recovery from that blow led the handguard of his sword right onto the chin of another opponent knocking the man immediately unconscious. He used the lull that these actions provided him to slide to the left and slice at the neck of a man attacking one of his sailors. The sudden blockage as this victim fell halted the advance of his opponents and gave room for him to leap forward, ignoring a sharp pain in his knee again as he slipped over his previous opponent. His men surged after him, and their momentum carried them forward, putting the defenders further off balance so that they could be killed with cutlass or rendered unconscious with belaying pins. Giles attacked like a berserker, almost unstoppable in his fury, and his battle madness seemed to protect him from being wounded. However, the wave of men from Impetuous slowed, and it might have stopped and been forced back by the press of pirates had not a loud, unintelligible battle-cry resounded from their left. Lieutenant Hendricks, his business finished on the first brig, had come to Giles's aid. Soon their opponents started to throw down their weapons and plead for mercy, apparently realizing that they might be better off to accept the possibility of hanging at a later date, even a very strong probability, to being slaughtered on the spot.

Giles leant on his sword for several moments, regaining his breath. Apparently, the captain and officers of the brig had been killed, for no one offered the surrender formally though it was clearly taking place. He gave orders to secure the brig and was pleased to learn that Mr. Hendricks had already given the equivalent orders for the other ship. He reflected that his last doubt about Mr. Hendricks had been laid to rest. His first lieutenant had already shown himself capable of becoming an excellent first lieutenant as far as running a frigate was concerned. Now he had proved his mettle in combat.

Giles ordered that the dead pirates be thrown overboard unceremoniously and their wounded gathered at the mast to be looked at by the surgeon when that officer had finished with the wounded from *Impetuous*. The damage to the brig had to be evaluated as quickly as possible. Orders given, he turned away to reboard *Impetuous* to discover how she had fared and the state of the other brig. He slipped in a half-congealed pool of blood, and the pain in his knee reasserted itself in almost blinding agony. Using his sword as a crutch, Giles hobbled towards the bulwarks to cross to his own ship. He arrived there and realized that it would be impossible for him to climb over to the frigate; his knee would not permit it. Giles was so drained that he was tempted to just sit down. But he knew that others would need to work actively despite the fatigue that always followed fierce fighting. He must set an example.

Carstairs saw Giles's difficulty in crossing between the ships, though he could only guess at what the problem might be. He picked his captain up, carried him across to *Impetuous*, and gently set him down on his feet. He snatched up a cudgel and handed it to Giles to lean on, the club providing a much better support than the sword. The coxswain had blood running down the side of his face from a cut at his hairline. Giles ordered him to have his cut attended to and somehow joked that he hoped that Elsie would like the scar. He leaned on his cudgel as several of his officers and petty officers reported to him. *Impetuous* was leaking badly as a result of taking cannon balls close to the waterline and also from the general weakening of the ship from the prolonged firing of her guns. The pumps were just holding their own, and Mr. Evans, the carpenter, hoped to make headway on reducing the leaks soon. However, the carpenter thought it would be best to fodder* a sail over the worst of the leaks. Giles ordered that two sails be prepared with oakum so that the relief could be provided as quickly as possible.

Impetuous's rigging had been scarcely affected by the fighting and would be repaired much sooner.

The brigs were a different story, having suffered great damage, and one of them had lost a mast. The carpenter would have to find a spar to replace it after clearing up the downed spars and rigging. Luckily, the privateers had not succeeded in clearing away the mess, and much of the rigging and many of the associated spars could be rescued.

A rough reckoning suggested that the brigs had lost half their men, and another quarter was wounded badly enough to be incapacitated. The remaining ones had been safely locked away, with the marines and some of the seaman keeping careful watch over them. Only one of the officers seemed to have survived, though he was among the seriously wounded. He was still unconscious and might not survive the night. Lieutenant Miller, who reported this, suspected that other officers might be hiding among the prisoners since the privateers had no uniforms or badges of rank.

Giles refused to leave the deck but did arrange for a chair to be placed on the quarter-deck so that he could take the weight off his injured leg. Dr. Maclean, the surgeon, had wanted to look at the leg, but Giles told him, rather testily, that the doctor should deal with the seriously wounded before looking at his own injury. The ships remained grappled together throughout the day except when they were parted to allow the two sails to be foddered under Impetuous. That action did stifle the leaks enough that the pumps were clearly gaining on the water in the bilge, and there was some hope that Impetuous could withstand a bit of a blow. Giles ordered the three ships to be joined together again for the night. As much as possible, he wanted his crew to rest, for they were exhausted from having no respite after the intense fighting. Luckily the current was carrying the raft of ships to the north, well away from the land.

Morning found no other vessels in sight, and the repair work resumed with a well-rested crew. By noon they were ready to proceed, and the little convoy set off. Since *Impetuous* was in the most precarious state and it was doubtful that even the most unskilled midshipman could get lost when he was accompanied by a competent master's mate on the coming journey, Giles kept his lieutenants with him, and he ordered Mr. Stewart and Mr. Dunsmuir to command the brigs.

Giles was sure that their recent triumph would not be enough to justify Mr. Hendricks' getting his step. The brigs had brought a heavier weight of metal than *Impetuous* to the battle since they had twenty-two eighteen-pounders apiece while the frigate only totaled thirty-six, and the combined crews of the brigs had been significantly larger than *Impetuous*'s. But brigs were not frigates, no matter how powerful they might be, and even taking two of them would not be regarded by the Admiralty, or even by the Admiral who should have known better, as a major victory. Mr. Evans reported that being under sail had increased the leaks, and *Impetuous* sailed along to the constant clank of the pumps and the thump of caulking mallets striking oakum. They were headed directly to the Thames and Chatham without even trying to find the fleet. They hoped they would not founder before reaching their destination.

Giles realized that *Impetuous* would again have to spend long weeks at the Chatham Dockyard. He was not sorry about that. It would mean a long stay at Dipton Hall, and he was more than ready to be with Daphne for an extended period.

288

Chapter XIX

Daphne told Lydia that they couldn't expect to hear from Captain Giles for at least three weeks, and it could even be as long as seven weeks before a reply was received. No amount of impatience would make the mails move any more quickly. Daphne's letter would have to get to Chatham, then be taken to the North Sea Fleet. Next, it would have to await the arrival of *Mithradates* at the Fleet. *Mithradates* would then require at least a week before she could meet *Impetuous*, after which the whole process would have to be reversed. This information did not stop Lydia from hovering near Daphne any time mail was received.

The end of the hunting season meant that spring was bursting out. Daphne was being woken as dawn was breaking, and, from her window, she would see all the myriad shades of green as life returned. The display of color became more and more striking as the days lengthened. Lambing season was well advanced, and calving was starting. Daphne had many a pleasant ride through the countryside, stopping to talk with her tenants and workers about how they were proceeding and discussing how damp it had been and when plowing could start. The plans were all completed for the new stables, and it was time to start building. They would all be moved to a place to the side of the Hall, about three hundred yards distant, while the existing stables would be used for an expanded coach house and stables for visiting horses. The new stables would be screened from the house by shrubbery, which could soon be planted. Daphne had liked the work of the architect that Edwards had recommended, and both she and Giles were very pleased with the sketches he had drawn of the new building while Mr. Griffiths had suggested only the most utilitarian modifications.

The grounds were a different matter. Neither of the experts whom Mr. Edwards recommended had, in Daphne's view, a proper appreciation of the landscape and its possibilities. She became very annoyed with each of them when they began to suggest that they knew much better than she did what the latest trends were and how to accomplish a truly striking view from the house and the associated parterre that was required. She dismissed the first one in a huff and was even more annoyed with the second one when he came up with completely different ideas. Each authority claimed that his was the only possible way to treat the area in a satisfactory and modern way, though the second expert's ideas were totally at variance with those of the first one. Both were, in Daphne's view, equally senseless. The only thing they could agree on was that Daphne's suggestions and tentative sketch plans were totally unacceptable.

Daphne had, in fact, for several years, been keeping up with the changing fashions in the best-regarded estate layouts. Unfortunately, Dipton Manor, her father's home, did not lend itself to much improvement, so her ideas had lain dormant, waiting for the right moment. Dipton Hall was quite a different matter. Its grounds had never been groomed for any harmonious effect and were ripe for improvement. Daphne lost her temper at the second expert when he was extremely condescending about her "amateurish and ignorant" ideas of the proper layout for a Gentleman's grounds. She told him in no uncertain terms what she thought both of his manners and his plans. She ended by stating that if this was the best that he could come up with, then she could easily do much better herself and without the expense for his services. Having said that, Daphne felt obliged to at least try to do the design herself.

The plans for the new layout using Daphne's creativity went forward very quickly. In the course of the attempts by the experts, Daphne had determined all of the relevant measurements and, while rejecting the others' ideas, she had already formed strong notions of what was both feasible and attractive. Her design consisted of a gently falling lawn ending in a stone-edged pond, though she had yet to determine how feasible this feature would be, and she might have to settle for bordering the stream itself with stone banks. The avenue so created would be defined by woodland and dotted with flower beds, especially rose beds. There would be wide perennial borders and ornamental shrubs to mark the border between the woods and the lawn. Behind the pond, another grass alley would rise, without flower beds, to an ornamental, circular temple beyond which a hedge would separate the gardens from the fields.

Daphne knew that she would need her husband's approval before proceeding. She could send him the plans, of course, and a description of what she intended, but it would be better if she could also include enticing but realistic sketches of what it would all look like when completed. Here she faced a dilemma. Though she had been given lessons in drawing and watercolors, as had all young ladies, she turned out to be quite hopeless at rendering what she imagined into a drawing. Even her doting father had suggested that possibly her talents lay elsewhere. The sketch, in which she tried to show how the grounds would appear, looked nothing like what she intended: the perspective was all wrong, the flower beds looked more like a disaster of tall weeds than of attractive plants, the pond tilted in a way that was quite impossible and the temple looked more like a smoke-stack transported from some industrial city than an attractive addition to the landscape.

Daphne had been creating her sketch in the large drawing room because that room would have the central view of the completed grounds. She was about to tear it up in disgust when her step-niece, Catherine, came into the room and saw what she was doing.

"What are you drawing?" Catherine asked.

"Oh, just some ideas I had. Nothing realistic," Daphne replied in a voice that clearly indicated that what she had been doing was none of Catherine's business and that her comments would not be welcome,

"It looks like your drawing starts with what we can see from the window, and then…I don't know… it looks like some strange new landscape. Rather scary…not very realistic." Daphne was even more annoyed. The unsolicited comments were all too true.

"Are these the plans you have been talking about?" Catherine continued. Daphne had the plans laid out on the table where she had been trying to sketch what the finished grounds would look like, and Catherine was examining them. Daphne had been talking incessantly about the grounds at dinner; she railed about the stupidity of experts and made it clear, in very dismissive terms, that she didn't welcome the ideas of the relatives she had acquired through marriage. She was about to order Catherine to stop looking at the plans when her niece spoke again, rather shyly.

"These are very exciting. I love the way you have placed the pond. I suppose that the ground is rising on the other side of the stream, but you cannot really show that on the plans. Oh, you are certainly creating what will be an outstanding vista when it is finished, especially with the placement of the flower beds and the climax marked by the temple."

Daphne was stunned. Catherine was able to read the flat plans and could imagine what it would look like, not as a bird's-eye view but as it would really appear to someone standing on the ground.

"Have you been trying to draw how it will appear from here?" Catherine asked.

"Yes, but I don't seem to be able to do it."

"Can I try?" Catherine asked, rather tentatively.

"If you like. My drawing is quite hopeless. You cannot do worse."

Catherine did not seem to be put off either by Daphne's ungracious reply or by her aunt's tearing up her own drawing and stomping out of the room. Instead, the young lady spent the whole afternoon working on her own picture. When she was satisfied with it, she went to Daphne's workroom.

"I've finished my drawing, Aunt Daphne."

Daphne went back to the drawing-room expecting to see something little better than her own attempt. Instead, she discovered that Catherine's sketch corresponded closely to what she had intended. In places where the drawing did not match what she wanted, she found, in checking the plans, that Catherine was right and it was her own plans that failed to incorporate her intentions. All she had to do was revise the plans, and Catherine would rub out the offending part of her drawing and then insert the new detail. Before long, the two ladies had their heads together as they discussed the best placement of the various features and how to get the most harmonious whole. Even when the plans corresponded with her intention, the drawing revealed that improvements could still be made. Their work was only interrupted by Steves's pointing out that tea had been laid.

"Could you do this sketch again with all our changes in it?" Daphne asked before they broke off.

"Certainly. And I could try to picture how the Hall will look from the bridge over the stream before it widens into the pond and of the whole layout from the temple."

"Oh, please do! I want to send them to Captain Giles with the plans for his suggestions and, hopefully, his approval."

Tea and dinner became much less painful occasions than had been the norm earlier when the ladies dined by themselves. Daphne and Catherine discussed the possibilities for the grounds, and the others were drawn into the discussion. Lydia had little to contribute, but Lady Marianne did have some sensible suggestions for Daphne to consider.

When she came down to breakfast the following morning, Daphne realized that Catherine had risen extra early in order to work on her drawings. By noon she had produced all three. They did indeed bring to life Daphne's ideas, and for the first time, Daphne felt really confident that her intentions could be successfully carried out. The drawings showed the flower beds in full bloom with a blend of colors in the rose beds and the perennial borders, just as they might appear in June. Daphne realized that she had not really visualized how the beds might be planted or how they would blend with the rest of the garden. Catherine had even drawn in two swans swimming in the pond. Further changes were agreed upon. Even some of Lady Marianne's thoughts were included, and Catherine again committed to redoing her drawings to correspond to the new designs.

Daphne had always regarded Catherine as a rather withdrawn and boring young lady. She had known that her niece made drawings, as so many young ladies did, but had never examined them. Catherine could play the piano adequately, and she worked diligently at practicing it while her needlework was exemplary. These were skills that were supposed to appeal to eligible young men though Daphne had never understood the reason for this supposition in respect to needlework. In her view, the skills were provided in anticipation of the long hours that married ladies seemed to spend with little to occupy them. Much more important, in Daphne's mind, as a skill of use in courting, was the ability to converse. Catherine had none of her sister's ability to chatter charmingly and emptily. Her best hope for a suitor seemed to be someone as boring as Captain Hicks, but that would leave poor Catherine bored and disgruntled if she had to listen to the likes of that banker constantly.

Catherine's sure sense of landscape and of art made Daphne see her in a new light. If Catherine's conversation lacked sparkle, maybe giving it substance might help. Catherine had never shown much inclination to read, partly Daphne suspected, because the appropriate tomes that were supposed to benefit young ladies were serious works by the likes of David Hume or John Locke. She had, indeed, discovered that the best way to rid herself of a bore after dinner, when the men joined the ladies, was to ask the man what he thought of the ideas of John Locke. Daphne herself had never got very far into such works, but she had found that she enjoyed reading novels. In addition, the insights she gained from such books could be used to enliven her conversation. Maybe the same would hold for Catherine. She would have to introduce her to the novelists whose volumes were not in the library. They were kept, inconspicuously, in Daphne's room. Fanny Burney might be a good place for Catherine to start.

Daphne's next letter to Giles outlined, again in detail, the ideas for the grounds of Dipton Hall, but now they were accompanied by the detailed plans that Daphne had drawn up and the drawings that Catherine had produced. As a result, now there was something concrete to ask him. Did he approve of the general ideas? Did he have suggestions to make as to how they could be improved? Could she proceed with the initial work?

Now it was Daphne who was waiting as impatiently as Lydia for an answer to her questions about Lydia and about the grounds. However, when the next letter arrived, she at least had the consolation of hearing about his thoughts and his doings, even if the latter seemed to be very dull. She, of course, kept busy with all her other activities and was not bored even though she and Richard were apart.

One afternoon, a few weeks after the sending of the plans, Daphne turned into the drive leading to Dipton Hall riding on Moonbeam with the groom trailing along behind her. She spied a coach at the portico and urged the mare into a canter so that she could discover what was happening. This was no hour for a neighbor to be making a call, so something else must be afoot. While still some distance away, she saw that a man was being helped from the carriage, someone with an injured leg who needed to have crutches given to him before he could walk. It was Richard! She urged Moonbeam on, then halted her without any preparatory slowing and was out of the saddle even as the mare skidded to a stop. Daphne only realized at the last moment that throwing herself into Giles's arms would not be the best idea if he had an injured leg.

"Richard!" she cried. "Daphne," he responded and cast his crutches aside as he leapt one-legged towards her. Without the crutches and with his painful knee, he lost his balance, and instead of gathering Daphne into his arms, they fell in a tangle of garments to the ground. Both were unphased by their collapse. Elsie, who had come to the front door when Steves cried that he thought the master was arriving, and

Carstairs, who had been accompanying Giles, rushed to untangle the two and get them on their feet and into the house. Giles was very good-humored about the incident, teasing Daphne, "You really don't have to sweep me off my feet every time I return to Dipton, you know. I would be quite happy to greet you standing up."

It was almost tea time, and both Giles and Daphne needed to change. Giles could not climb the stairs easily, a problem that Carstairs solved by picking him up and carrying him upstairs to his dressing room. Daphne climbed the stairs behind them with Elsie trailing along after, but she did not go to her own room but instead went to Giles's dressing room. They had far too many things that had to be said right away to go through the usual rituals of getting ready for tea, and neither felt the need to be reticent in front of either Carstairs or Elsie. Hardly had Daphne and Giles started to express their delight at being together than Daphne started to question Giles as to how he had been injured and how serious the damage to his knee might be. He tried, at first, to make light of it, to which Daphne replied that, if it were nothing, he would not have to use crutches. The story emerged that he didn't actually know what was wrong, just that it seemed to be related to stumbling on a dead body in boarding a brig and slipping in a pool of blood. These facts did not emerge immediately. It took repeated questions from Daphne to establish that this was not just some normal, if unusual, shipboard accident, but instead was one picked up in the course of a desperate melee.

Once the circumstances that led to the injury were established, including that there was no visible wound to be treated, Daphne summoned Steves to send for Mr. Jackson to come as quickly as possible and to explain to the apothecary that the problem was a serious knee injury. That, of course, was not the end of Daphne's questioning of Giles. She wanted the full details of the taking of the brigs. Giles complied, successfully minimizing what a desperate personal fight he had been in.

Before turning to other matters, Daphne took mercy on Elsie, who had been staring anxiously at the bandage on Carstairs's head. The lady's maid was somewhat relieved to learn that it covered a deep cut that had been stitched by the surgeon after he had poured rum onto it. Carstairs did admit that the treatment had hurt far worse than getting the wound. However, the wound seemed to be healing without any putrification.

Mr. Jackson arrived at that point and shooed Elsie out of the room because he would need Giles to remove his trousers. He knew it would be futile to ask Daphne to leave, even if most people would have considered her staying somewhat improper.

When it was uncovered, the knee proved to have swollen to the size of a small squash. Mr. Jackson ran his fingers over it and then had Giles relax his muscles as he very gently moved the joint forward and back. This did not cause much, if any pain, but the minute the apothecary twisted the leg just a little, Giles emitted an unguarded yelp.

Mr. Jenkins leaned back. "You have obviously injured your knee. I suspect something may be torn in it that will not heal quickly, if at all. I will know better when the swelling goes down. To get that to happen, use that knee as little as possible. I know that it is undignified, but have someone carry you up and down stairs and between rooms. Do your best not to put any weight on your leg. Have someone help you out of your chairs and make sure that they steady you until your crutches are in place. I will be back in three days unless there is an emergency."

Daphne and Giles continued to talk all through tea time and were only persuaded to stop when it was pointed out that they must change because the dinner gong was soon going to be sounded. Before this break, Daphne questioned Giles about her letter concerning Lydia's marriage. Giles had not received it, probably because sorters in the post office or aboard *Penelope* had put it in the wrong mailbag. Daphne quickly outlined what she had found out and what her recommendation had been.

"I imagine that you will want to interrogate the young man before you make any decision, Richard," she concluded.

"I don't think that is necessary, my dear. Your judgment on this subject is undoubtedly better than mine. The one thing I am dubious about is the dowry."

"Do you think my recommendation is too high? What about the original ten thousand?" Daphne replied huffily.

"No, my dear. I was just wondering if I shouldn't make it fifteen thousand. I take your point about not wanting him to be an MP. Even though your father and I can make sure that he will not be the member for Dipton, we cannot prevent him from getting another seat in a pocket borough* which will lead him into even more dubious obligations. I think the higher sum should mean that he doesn't have to try to sell his vote to maintain his family."

"I agree, of course. I just did not want to appear too extravagant. I imagine that we will have to provide the same dowry to Catherine if she ever finds a suitor."

"I imagine," Daphne continued, "that if you did not get my letter about Lydia, you also didn't get my one about changing the grounds."

"I did receive that one. It found me when I met the Fleet on my way to Chatham. It was among the letters waiting for *Mithradates* to take to us."

"So what do you think about it?"

"I think the plans are marvelous. We can go over them after dinner or tomorrow if you like. Incidentally, did you do the drawings? They are superb!"

"No, they are Catherine's. I did do the plans myself."

"Well. Let's talk about it later."

Dinner was a lively affair with Giles pressed again to tell the story of his battle with the brigs. Lydia was overjoyed to hear about the approval of her wedding. Giles left the news about the higher dowry until he could meet with her Mr. Dimster. Catherine was duly praised for her drawings. That led to conversation about her paintings, and Giles even drew out of her some of her other interests. Daphne was delighted with Catherine's responses. Previously, Catherine had tended to give some unintelligible mumble when her uncle asked her opinion. Maybe there was hope that she could land someone better than Captain Hicks.

It wasn't until they had retired for the night that Daphne finally broached the subject that had been highest in her mind after she had got over the surprise of seeing Richard at all, "How long can you stay?"

"It depends on the Admiralty, of course, but several weeks at least. *Impetuous* was badly damaged in our fight and needs a lot of repairs, not only because of the battle but also because she seems to have always had some serious defects. We barely made it back to Chatham. I don't expect to hear about her state for several weeks. I can be here for the next part of the year. Maybe help with getting the stables underway and the improvements to the grounds and just get to know the area better. It is what I most want. If only this war would end, I would resign my commission so that I could spend full time here."

Daphne was overjoyed. She was all too aware of how little time they had spent together. There was so much to do and so much to talk about. From her point of view, even Mr. Jackson had good news when he examined Richard's knee after the swelling had subsided almost completely.

"Your knee is not as bad as I feared. Nothing is cracked in it, nor are there any little bits of bone fragment that could lead to your leg being virtually useless. Your knee won't recover completely. It will also hurt when it is over-used or used in strange ways. You should be able to walk with just a cane soon and be able to dispense even with that if you are lucky and do not become sedentary. But I would not recommend any more hand-to-hand fighting on shipboard!

"Now, it will help if you use a knee brace. I have found that they work wonders in some cases like this. It is my own invention. It allows the knee to flex but not to twist, which is where most of your pain comes from. I have brought my assistant with me today. He will be the person making the device. He only needs to measure your leg, and the brace will be ready soon.

The brace did seem to work. Giles had tried riding before he received it and had found that the pain in his knee prevented the activity, and trying to ride had made the swelling return. After his knee returned to normal, he found that he could mount and ride with only minor pain when using the brace. He also could walk some distance before his leg forced him to call a halt to that activity.

Giles was more than contented. He would have a good, long break from *Impetuous* and the duties of being a naval captain; there were exciting projects underway at

Dipton Hall, and he could see them developing first hand rather than having to rely on Daphne's descriptions in her letters; every day he realized more and more how fortunate he had been when she agreed to marry him. The child, which was on the way, fulfilled one of his unconscious dreams. In fact, one of his greatest pleasures occurred when she allowed him to feel the baby inside her kicking vigorously. Being at Dipton, he could help plan the nursery and make sure that everyone knew how important it was to guarantee Daphne's comfort in the difficult time when the birth occurred. He would have to sail again, of course: there was no question about it as long as Bonaparte threatened the independence of Britain and its way of life. However, he did not need to leave very soon, and, in the interim, he would enjoy his riches.

Author's Note

This novel is a work of pure historical fiction. The events included in it did not happen, though similar ones may have. In particular, the attack on Boulogne under Richard Giles should not be confused with the very real (and rather farcical) attacks under Admirals Nelson and Keith. Otherwise, harassment of French preparations for invasion of the type in which Giles was involved was common.

Some of the major appointments mentioned were real, but they are occupied here by different people. For example, the admiral in charge of the North Sea Fleet was Admiral Keith. Admiral Gardner is fictional. The reason is to avoid controversy over the portrayal of the character and opinions of the real office-holders, which are not without dispute among historians.

Some readers have mentioned that Daphne seems to be far too 'liberated' for the time. I do not suggest that she is typical of ladies of the period, but they were much less restricted than in the usual portrayal of ladies in the later, Victorian, period just as society was much less tight-laced than it would later become, both literally and figuratively. This is not to say that the legal position of women was not appalling, just that it was not as bad as it might seem. For example, Jane Austen rather overdid the extent to which widows were automatically impoverished unless a relative took mercy on them. It was quite true, however, that unmarried single women had few financial rights, and their opportunities for sustaining themselves independently were often bleak. Daphne could have existed, though she is not patterned on any particular lady.

Readers who are interested in reaching me can email me at jgcragg@telus.net. I always enjoy hearing from readers, both those who liked the yarn – they are always very encouraging and from those who do not – whose criticism suggests ways to improve the next attempt. I might add that reviews given on Amazon are appreciated. Incidentally, reviews on one Amazon site are not usually transferred to another. For instance, Amazon.com often has different reviews from Amazon.uk. It is a point worth considering not only when buying books but also when considering other things that Amazon sells.

Glossary

Blue light: A type of firework that could be fired into the area giving quite strong, blue light over a considerable area.

Belay   Tie down. Regularly used by mariners to mean stop.

Belaying Pin   A substantial rounded piece of wood, with a shaft that would go through a hole on a railing or other horizontal fixed piece of wood and a bulbous knob on the other end, used to provide a place to secure lines. They made very useful cudgels.

Beating (to windward or into the wind)   Proceeding to windward in a series of alternating tacks.

Between wind and water   That part of a ship's hull that can be above or below water depending on how the vessel heels.

Bollard   A short, thick post on a wharf or jetty to which a ship's mooring lines may be fastened.

Boney   Nickname for Napoleon Bonaparte

Bottom   (1) A synonym for a cargo ship

    (2) In relation to riding a horse – someone with excellent ability to ride easily and elegantly was said to have a "good bottom."

Brig   (1) A two-masted square rigged ship.

    (2) Slang for the prison onboard a ship.

Carronade	A short gun, frequently mounted on a slider rather than a wheeled gun carriage, only used for close-in work. They were not usually counted in the number of guns by which a ship was rated.
Churching	A church service to bless a woman after successfully giving birth.
Clear for action	When a warship was preparing to fight another, all moveable items used for everyday living were stowed in the hold so that the decks would be unobstructed. This included the partitions which made "rooms" such as the captain's cabin or the wardroom.
Come out	Young ladies "came out" when they were allowed to participate in adult gatherings, dinners and so on. At that time, they would be regarded as eligible for marriage and, in higher echelons of society, to be presented to the King at court.
Consol	A bond issued by the British Government with no stated redemption date, paying to the holder a specified amount per annum.
Entail	A provision that the inheritance of real property would go to specified members of a family (or other specified group) usually to the closest male relatives. Usually implied that the present owner could not leave it to someone else and was usually put on a property to prevent the immediate heir from dissipating the inheritance but would pass it intact (more or less) to the next generation.

Fighting top	A Platform on the mast where the main part met the top mast from which marines could fire their muskets on to the deck of an opposing ship.
Fodder (a sail)	Draw a sail treated with oakum under the bottom of a ship to slow leaks.
Grape(shot)	Musket balls, or sometimes small scrap metal, used to fill bags which were them inserted in cannot as if they were cannot balls.
Grapnel	A metal hook or set of hooks attached to a line that could be thrown and hook on to the edge of another ship or a wall or other object.
Gunwale	The side of a boat.
Heave to	stopping the forward motion of a ship by turning one sail to work in opposition of the others.
Jobbing captain	A post captain who has not been appointed to a ship and who is employed to captain another captain's ship temporarily.
Jolly boat	A small boat, usually the smallest on a ship.
Larboard	the left-hand side of the ship looking forward. Opposite of starboard. Now usually called "port".
Larboard watch	Crews were usually divided into two watches, who alternated the times when they were on duty with each other. The other one was called the starboard watch.
Lady Day	see quarter day
Lead line	A line in which knots have been tied at fixed distances, with a large piece of lead at the end

	which was used for measuring the depth of water.
League	Three nautical miles
Leeway	The speed with which a boat is blown strait downwind when it is drying to sail
Miss stays	When tacking, failing to have a turn that switches the direction from which the wind is coming so that the ship is stuck and unable to complete the turn.
Muster Roll	List of all men serving on a ship.
The Nore	Anchorage in the Thames estuary off the mouth of the Medway River. A major anchorage for the Royal Navy in the Age of Sail.
Oakum	Fibrous material got from unravelling old ropes used with tar to caulk wooden ships.
Painter	the mooring line at the bow of a small boat.
Pocket Borough	(later usually called a rotten borough) A formerly well-populated town that still returned two members to parliament even though population had fallen so low that one or a few landowners could select the next MP certain that they could control the election.
Press (ed) (gang)	The Navy was enabled to seize men to serve on warships, without any form of due process. Exempt were gentlemen and certain others who had "protections." While the process was supposed to require authorization from appropriate officials, it was standard for captains in need of men to send out parties to

seize any one they could find who did not appear to be a gentleman.

Quarter day	the days on which traditionally rents were due, tenancies expired or began and other matters settled. They were Lady Day (March 25), Midsummer Day (June 24), Michaelmas (Sept. 29) and Christmas (Dec. 25)
Quarter deck	The outside deck of a ship at the stern.
Read (himself) in.	A Captain was not formally in charge of a ship until he had read out loud his commission to command the vessel in the presence of the crew. This action was referred to by the captain reading himself in.
Rafted	Ships or boats are rafted together when they are tied to each other while at anchor
Redoubt:	A minor or subsidiary fort. Here referring to a gun platform made level with guns firing over a parapet.
Remove(s)	(Applied to dinners) Separate dishes at a dinner. There usually weren't courses as we know them, at least not after the soup, and instead a variety of different dishes would be served in turn.
Salvage	Fee paid by a boat's owner to rescuers of a ship in danger but not abandoned.
Shrouds	A rope ladder formed by short lengths of rope tied tightly between the stays of a mast.
Sheet in.	A line controlling how much a sail is pulled
Sheeted in	pulled in by a sheet

Skagen	Northern most cape in Denmark
Skagerrak	The passage (strait) between Norway and Denmark.
Slow match	A fuse in the form of a rope which burned at a premeasured speed used to blow up barrels of gunpowder or other bombs while allowing the persons lighting it to escape.
Sounding	Taking the depth of water with a lead line.
Spring line (or just spring)	A rope attached to the anchor cable which by being pulled in or let out could be used to change the direction in which the bow of the ship (or its broadside) was pointing when at anchor.
Spotted-dick	A pudding made with dried fruit, usually served with custard. Lighter than a plum pudding.
St. Stephen's Day	The day after Christmas. The term Boxing Day now used in the United Kingdom and some of the Commonwealth to refer to this day did not come into common use until the middle of the nineteenth century.
Stay(s)	(1) A line used to prevent a mast from falling over or being broken in the wind
	(2) Corsets
	(3) See missed stays
Step	Promotion from lieutenant to commander.
Sternsheets	Seats or planking in the stern (back) part of an open boat.
Stove in	Broken or snapped inwards.

Stow	Put out of the way safely (against a ship's motion)
Strakes	Planks used for the hull of a ship.
Strike (struck) below	Clearing out the partitions and furnishings on the fighting decks of a ship, including especially the captain's cabin, and stowing them out of harms' way.
Tack	Change the direction in which a ship is sailing and the side of the ship from which the wind is blowing by turning towards the direction from which the wind is blowing.
Taffrail	Railing at the stern of the quarter deck
Third rate	Naval ships were rated by the number of guns they carried. A third rate would have somewhere between 64 and 80 guns.
Twelfth Night	The evening of the Twelfth Day of Christmas, January 6, which is twelve evenings after Christmas Eve. Oddly enough this is also the date of "Old Christmas" the date to which the revision of the calendar assigned December 25 according to the unrevised calendar. Traditionally it was the time when roles between servants and master was reversed. By the early nineteenth century it had been much toned down and when celebrated it often was a party for the servants at which their masters would make a short appearance. Often not celebrated at all.
Walmer Castle	A shore defense castle dating from the sixteenth century. The residence of the Warden of the Cinque Ports.

Wardroom   The part of a ship used by the senior officers of a ship other than the captain.

Warden of the Cinque Ports.   A largely ceremonial title by the 19th century, though some holders did take their possible duties of defending the coast seriously.

Watches   (1) The day was divided into seven watches as follows

Afternoon watch: 12:00-16:00

First dog watch: 16:00-18:00

Second dog watch; 18:00 – 20:00

First Watch (sometimes Evening Watch) 20:00-24:00

Middle Watch: 0:00-4:00

Morning Watch: 4:00-8:00

Forenoon Watch 8:00- 12:00

(2) The crew was divided into two watches, arbitrarily called the Starboard and Larboard Watches, who alternated the times they were on duty. The dog watches meant that on alternating days they alternated which watches they stood (were on duty.

Wear (referring to a ship)   The opposite of tack where the maneuver of changing which side of a ship the wind is coming from is accomplished by turning away from the wind.

Wherry   A long, light rowboat used for carrying passengers.

Wedding portion

A dowry, so called because it was regarded as the portion of her father's estate that an unmarried daughter might expect to have.

Writ

The document authorizing the holding of a by election. It's being issued had to be moved and passed in the House of Commons first.

Printed in Great Britain
by Amazon

27596931R00182